The Sugar Skull Ghost Thief

The Sugar Skull Ghost Thief

Dedicated to Babers. May her ghost haunt us all.

1 | Ghost Town

The bus hissed, almost sighed, as it approached my final destination. I let out a sigh as well when I saw what constituted for a bus depot, where I would be left to figure out my next move.

I pressed my forehead against the cool glass of the window to absorb the scene more thoroughly. Imbued in the blue hue of the window's tinting sat a run-down gas station. It looked like it was built in the fifties and left to rot.

The bus wobbled abruptly as it made its way off of the paved road and onto an uneven dirt lot. The jolt swayed me away from the window, then right back at it. BONK! I hit my forehead against the glass. And while it didn't hurt much, I gave the spot a rub while looking around to see if anyone noticed. The few fellow travelers were fixated on gathering their items as they prepared to disembark.

I looked out of the window again. Outside was the unknown, a strange new place. Part of me felt like staying there behind the glass, looking out at the world from my safe little box. But I had a job to do.

I grabbed my duffle bag from under the seat and hiked my backpack onto my shoulder and headed out. As soon as I stepped off of the bus, I was greeted by a gust of wind blasting dirt and dust into my face. I was instantly knocked off kilter, grit filling my eyes and mouth.

I stumbled blindly out of the way of a few passengers exiting from behind. "Welcome to Las Cruces," a man quipped as he brushed past me.

The bus emptied quickly and rumbled off. By the time I cleared my eyes, I was standing entirely alone. The whole place had an air of absence, a void of life. I hiked toward the gas station. Set in front was an old, pathetic wooden bench. A sign on the wall above it that read "BUS/AUTOBÚS." The sign looked as worn and pathetic as the building and the bench.

The entry door was locked. A hand-written sign informed me that the place closed at five PM, one hour earlier than my arrival.

With no plan in place, I decided to simply sit and consider my situation. Maybe something would come to me. The bench creaked and moaned as I sat down. With my luck, it would choose this day to finally crumble to the ground and die.

There was not much to gaze upon there on the outskirts of Las Cruces, New Mexico. Why they declared this desolate spot as a bus depot was beyond me. In the short distance ahead, about a half mile out, was a trailer park. Catty-corner was what looked like a neighborhood. Between me and what could be loosely categorized as *civilization* was a field of dirt; a lonely weed here or there.

I felt like a ghost in a ghost town.

It wasn't exactly the vacation I had in mind but it was the one I had agreed to, sight unseen. It was only twenty-four hours earlier when Chuck, my landlord/roommate, made the offer. I was sitting in my bedroom fretting over a side project for my boss at the café where I work. The project was to create a commercial for the café. He bought me video editing software and gave me a paid week off to create the thing. Apparently it was a lot cheaper than hiring a professional to do it.

Unfortunately, I was unqualified and inexperienced to produce such a thing. Sure I was taking graphic design classes at the local community college but I had only racked up one piddly semester and nothing involving video editing. I didn't know why I had said I would take on the project. It must have been the idea of a week away from the café. I was burnt out big time and when my boss, Mr. Argyle, proposed it to me, I jumped on it. At the time I thought *How hard can it be?* I reveled in the fact that I got what was essentially a paid vacation plus some new video editing software that I would be able to keep for my own use.

The high wore off when I figured out that I had bitten off more than I could chew. I didn't realize that making a commercial — even just a short one — might take a lot of work. What script would I use? Would there be actors? What about music? Add to that my complete and utter inexperience with the software and I was stuck.

In the quiet absence of the Greyhound bus' motor idling, I detected another gust of wind. This time I closed my eyes and mouth in time. The granules of dust, dirt, and dead grass swept over me, leaving a layer of grit in its wake. I pulled out a handkerchief and wiped my face with it. Not too many twenty-something year old guys like me carry around handkerchiefs but they came in handy in situations like that.

I kept my eyes closed and just laid my head back on the wall. The bench complained with my every movement but it was holding up. I thought about the commercial again, where I was in the whole process.

I had been able to figure out a few things with the video editing software. I had imported a picture of the sign on the door that said "Café." There were all these effects I could apply to the scene: lens flares, colored filters, a thing called "vaporize," another thing called "liquify," and some other stuff with names that were foreign to me.

I had until the following Monday morning to finish the commercial, but, even though I had been working on it for four hours straight, I was not getting anywhere. As I sat there in my room back in Three Peaks, Colorado, my stomach sank and panic began to set in. "This isn't going how I thought it would," I had said to myself. "I want to get away from all this. I need a vacation. A *real* vacation, not some *staycation*."

I had never put much stock in the Law of Attraction as it had always seemed kind of weird and a bit too New Age for me. But what happened next was more than a coincidence.

Less than a minute after I uttered my request, Chuck popped his shaved head into my doorway.

"Hey, Perk," he said, "you want to take a vacation and make some extra cash while you do it?" Why, hello, Law of Attraction.

2 | Ride

I opened my eyes in a vain hope to see some form of life around me. I was still alone on that rickety old bench; no vehicles, no people, no kids on bikes. In the distance I could hear cars and trucks whizzing past on the interstate. There was no reason for anyone to get off at this exit, except for a bus to drop off passengers. I was stranded.

The sun had set yet it was still light out. Twilight. I wasn't sure of the time on account of my phone not working. It was worse than dead. What's worse than dead? About an hour into my journey, I decided to use the bathroom at one of the bus stops along the way. I was sitting scrolling through my Facebook feed when my hand slipped up and I dropped my phone. You know how those toilet seats in public bathrooms aren't completely circular but more horseshoe-shaped? Well, that leaves a lot of room for a phone to fall into. I'm not proud of what I did thereafter, but I felt it necessary. I fished my phone out of the dirty toilet and tried to wash it and dry it. But, in spite of my efforts, the thing wouldn't start up. It was shot. That stunk, in more ways that one. I was left with no communication for the duration of the trip. And, what was worse, now that I was at my destination, I had no way of contacting anyone.

I would not have chosen southern New Mexico as a getaway but that is what fate had in mind. The previous night when Chuck gave me the proposition, I was only thinking about one thing: getting away. After I had reached Las Cruces and had the time to ponder, the whole thing seemed less like a vacation and more like a grand errand.

Apparently, Chuck and his girlfriend, Tess, had been wanting to get an old Volkswagen Microbus but hadn't had much luck finding anything affordable back home; not anything affordable that actually ran, that is. He said they found a guy selling one down in a place called Old Mesilla, New Mexico, right outside of Las Cruces, New Mexico.

From what Chuck told me, the guy selling the bus was asking about half what it was worth. Chuck had walked into my room and leaned against the doorway. "The guy's only asking seven thousand for a fifty-nine," he said as he stroked his goatee. "He's put work into it too. Up here, something like that in that condition is worth fourteen, maybe even fifteen. We gotta jump on this."

"How do *I* fit into all this?" I asked.

"I don't have the time to go make the deal. Neither does Tess. I need someone down there to make sure the thing is legit and pay the guy. Then drive it back, of course."

"You want me to travel down to some old New Mexican ghost town with seven grand in my pocket to buy an old beat up VW bus and drive it back here, hoping it makes it?"

Chuck paused for a second, still stroking his goatee. "Pretty much," he said. "But it ain't that beat up. He restored it about sixty percent. He says it runs. Don't worry, you'll be fine. Worst case scenario is it breaks down but that's no big deal. I know a guy who'll tug you back on the cheap."

I was pretty much sold. My only worry was the money. I've never had seven thousand dollars in my pocket. Chuck must have read it on my face. He said, "You won't be carrying the money. You'll take a bus there—like a Greyhound—and I'll wire you the cash. You'll have it when you get there."

Something else popped into my mind. On the outside, Chuck looked just like an average guy in a black tank top and jeans. But, below the surface, he was always thinking, always working an angle. I had been renting a room from him for about a year and a half and, in that time, I had learned to hesitate just a bit. He was smarter than me and, if I jumped too quickly, I ended up with the short end of the stick. "How far is it?" I asked.

"About five hundred and fifty miles."

"That doesn't seem like much of a vacation, riding a bus for five hundred and fifty miles only to pick up a bus and drive it back another five hundred and fifty miles."

"Listen, I'll pay you five hundred bucks to do this."

"Five hundred?" That sparked my interest.

"Yeah, and I'll buy your bus ticket out there plus one night in a hotel. I'll throw in gas money, of course. Two hundred should get that thing back here but I'll want receipts and the remainder, understand?"

I did. "Five hundred and a hotel room for a night sounds good," I said. "Would I have to come back right after—like the next morning—or can I make a longer vacation out of it? Maybe stay a couple of days then drive back?"

"I don't care. I'm only paying for one night though. Any additional nights are on you. All I care about is that you make the deal and secure the bus. And don't wreck it, of course. We're not in any big hurry."

"OK, sure," I said.

"Perfect," Chuck said without any emotion. "When can you go? Like I said, I've only got a week from the time I pull the trigger."

"The sooner the better. I'm off this week, working on a project for my boss."

"OK. Let's plan on tomorrow. I'll book everything. You pack your bags." With that, Chuck turned and swiftly left my room.

A vacation. Wow! And paid for, no less. Sure I didn't know what I would do there, other than pick up the Microbus, but that didn't matter. It was a vacation nonetheless, what I had asked for.

After a brief moment, Chuck returned to my room. "You're all set," he said. "You leave tomorrow at 6:00 AM. I'll print out the rest of the information for you by morning; hotel, where I'll send the money, the guy's name and number, everything. Just be ready by five-thirty. I'll take you to the bus depot."

I felt a tingling in my stomach. It was excitement mixed with fear. Even though I didn't have a car of my own, I still knew how to drive. But it had been a while. The thought of driving made me a bit nervous. Add to that the responsibility of driving someone else's car and my stomach turned. But I told myself that it was going to be an adventure and, after all, it was a vacation and a vacation was exactly what I had asked for.

I woke up early the next morning. It didn't take me long to get ready, never does. I just shower, put some gel in my hair; it's thick and looks tousled no matter how much I comb it so I just throw it back with my fingers, no brush needed. I gave myself a quick look in the mirror. Not impressive but not unimpressive, just regular old me. I wore pretty much the same thing every day. If I wasn't in my work clothes of a turquoise blue polo and jeans, I was in a black T-shirt and jeans. The shoes were always the same: low-rise Doc Martens.

I'm not a big guy but I'm an OK height, a hair over five ten. I'm thinner than I'd like to be. Girls say I'm cute enough but I'd be cuter if I would just bulk up a bit, but I guess I don't have the discipline for all that muscle building. I'm just a regular guy with no real plan, other than the current plan to pick up the Microbus. I grabbed my grey hoodie and my duffle bag and headed out. I was ready for whatever.

After arriving, *whatever* had turned into sitting and waiting for nothing. My best guess on time was around six fifteen or six thirty. The arrival time for the bus was six o'clock and the driver said we were on schedule.

The weather was warm—at least for a guy from up north—so I took off my hoodie. Mid-October was a lot colder in Colorado than in Southern New Mexico. Even so, I kept my hoodie out, just in case I needed to use it as a blanket. I pulled out the paper Chuck had given me with all the information. He put the name and location of the hotel but no phone number. There was a phone number for the guy I was supposed to meet, Jared, but that make-shift bus depot was lacking, among many things, a pay phone. Even if there *was* a phone, I didn't have any quarters. I contemplated which direction to walk. Maybe I could go ask one of those people in the houses in the distance, see if I could use their phone. I sat and sighed in procrastination.

I heard the muffled growl of a car approaching. I looked in the direction of the sound and saw a lone, small, red car heading toward me at break-neck speed on the same road the bus had used to arrive and depart. The car was coming from my left and, when it got close, passed in front of me then made a wide U-turn in the dirt parking lot in front of me. The car skid to a stop emitting clouds of dust which engulfed the car in a brown fog.

From behind the shroud of dust came a girl's voice. "Are you Perk?"

"Yeah," I answered, obviously confused.

"Get in. I'll take you where you need to go."

3 | Maya

The dust began to settle as I gathered up my belongings and made my way to the car. When I got there, I ducked my head to get a look at this mysterious chauffeur through her open window. The driver was a girl, around twenty-two or twenty-three, petite and dark-skinned, wearing black skinny jeans and a white halter top that showed off her boobs. They were big for her size but not huge. I'm a guy. I notice these things and stare if I'm not careful. Even though she was wearing shades, I could tell that she was pretty. Really pretty. Needless to say, I didn't put up a fight. I hopped into her car and she tore off as fast as she tore in.

"My name's Maya," she said, not offering her hand. "You're supposed to buy a VW bus, am I right?"

"Do you have ESP or something?"

"Yes, I have ESP and I'm using my powers to kidnap grown men who are buying VW buses," she said plainly staring straight-faced ahead of her.

I didn't respond. For all I knew, that was the situation. Then she cracked a smile and looked at me. "Oh, yes," she said with a strange accent, drawing out the "yes" low then high again. I guess that was an expression around these parts. "Look at you all freaked out."

"Who are you, exactly?" I asked, even though I knew her name.

"I told you. I'm Maya!" She turned the radio on and flipped through the pre-set stations. All of them seemed to be playing commercials at the same time. "Ugh!" she groaned, "You would think one of them would, I don't know, play music or something!" With that she turned off the radio. The windows were open and warm air was flying in and out of the car as we rushed along. She drove fast, weaving in and out of traffic, the muffler on her car making the distinct *vroom* noise of a street racer. "I'm not some psychic," she finally let out. "I work with Jared, the guy selling you the bus. I guess your friend, the guy that's buying the thing, realized where the bus stop was and how you didn't have any way to get to where you needed to go. He asked Jared if he could pick you up but he's at work. He asked me to pick you up instead."

"Oh," I said. "That makes sense. Nice of you."

"Not really. I owe Jared a favor so…yeah. Here I am." She motioned to her dashboard with her chin. "Stupid AC doesn't work. Busted during the hottest part of the year. It's not bad now, but still. I need air flow. I hate being stagnant." She was small and compact and had an ocean of wavy dark hair that danced and whipped around her face from the air rushing in. Overall, she was cute, if not a bit erratic and seemingly dangerous behind the wheel. Still, a dangerous ride with a pretty girl beats what would have been (according to Google Maps) a twenty-one-mile walk. That's how far the bus depot is from Old Mesilla if you can believe it.

She took the interstate through town and exited on another interstate looping backward a bit. We popped out at an exit with a sign that had an arrow and "Old Mesilla" printed on it. Maya knew exactly where everything was so she just kept on racing through the streets. "This car is modified," she said proudly, sensing my fear. "It's meant to be driven."

"I'm sure it is," I replied looking down at my hands and noticing my white knuckles. "Where are you taking me?"

"Out to the desert and leaving you to die so the coyotes have something to eat." Again, she said this straight-faced. "Not really," she said without a hint of humor, "I'm taking you to go see Jared."

"I don't have the money yet."

"Don't worry. Jared just wants to know you're here, to meet you. I'll take you to get the money and you can make your deal. The bus is there at the restaurant. Once you pay for it, you can drive it." The whole thing felt shady and, at the same time, trustworthy and real.

I didn't get a chance to fully take in my surroundings since I was scared for my life in that car. Next thing I knew, we were in the parking lot in the square of a historic-looking part of town. We had made it to Old Mesilla. I thought it was weird that we basically had to travel from one small town to another small town—both of them connected, by the way—and it was twenty-one miles. I started to feel like I was in some sort of *Twilight Zone* episode.

We got out of her car and I stretched, still recovering from the trip. She took off her sunglasses and threw them carelessly through the open window of her car, onto the driver's seat. She had large, cat-like eyes with thick eyelashes that burst outward.

From what I could see, Old Mesilla was old yet charming. But not old and charming like Savannah, GA (although I've never been there, only seen it in pictures and movies), but old and charming like some sort of ghost town that had been halfway restored. As we got out of her car, I shared my impression of the place with Maya. She snorted. "There's a lot of things around here that are done halfway. New Mexico is

'The Land of *Mañana.*' You familiar with that word? *Mañana?*"

"Yeah. Means tomorrow, right?"

"Yup."

"So the 'Land of Tomorrow' means you're halfway to tomorrow or something?"

"Means 'We'll do it tomorrow.' It's a laid back way of thinking. A lazy way of thinking. Doing things *la moda floja.*"

I didn't say anything since I didn't know what that meant.

"Means 'the lazy way.' Well, actually, it means 'loose fashion.' You know, like wearing sweatpants because you don't want to get dressed up?"

Her comment made me look at her clothes, and I couldn't help looking at her chest again.

"Look at you all checking me out!" she teased.

"No, I…" she had caught me. "I was just admiring the fact that you don't dress in sweats." I could feel my face and ears turning beet red. My ears most of all. They're a dead giveaway that I'm flushed.

She walked up to me and pinched my cheek. *"Ay, que chulo!"* She said it like she was talking to a baby. She let go of me. "It's ok, dude," she said with a confident tone. "I know you can't help it because I'm…" she paused mid-sentence and acted like she licked her finger then pressed it to her butt and made a *Sssss* sound then continued, "red hot!" Then she laughed and pushed me roughly. I couldn't tell if she was being friendly or flirty or messing around with me. All in all, she seemed playful though. And, to her benefit, red hot. I had not encountered a girl like this one before. She seemed confident in who she was, almost cocky, if that makes sense. She turned and walked toward one of the buildings on the square. I made a mental note to look up *"chulo"* with Google Translate. Or ask her about it. One or the other. Should be the same either way.

I enjoyed watching her walk. She bounded up and down

with vigor, her thick, wavy, hair bobbed about her as if it was alive and heaving. I was enthralled with her, greedily consuming her image with my eyes. She had a passion to her that was new to me. I followed her, taking only my backpack which held my laptop. I let my duffle bag of clothes in the car. No one would want my clothes and the place seemed pretty barren anyway.

As we walked, I took in my surroundings. First, the weather was perfect. There was only the slightest chill in the air, yet there was a warmth that emanated from somewhere, probably the ground. The sun must have shone hot that day and the earth was giving back some residual heat. A soft breeze rustled the leaves in the trees that lined the outer perimeter of the square. Everything was pretty quiet so the sound of the leaves gave the impression of a whispered applause. We were walking from the parking lot at one end of the square to the opposite end. The square looked to be the size of a small neighborhood block. In the middle was a large gazebo made of wood and what looked like adobe. It looked old, like it was made in the eighteen hundreds, yet well maintained. Concrete pathways cut through the grass surrounding the gazebo in eight equidistant directions, like sunrays.

Maya walked directly toward the gazebo and stepped up into it. I followed. She stopped and swung around and said, "Dance with me!"

4 | Calavera's

I didn't know what to make of it. She clicked her heels together as she stood straight and held out her arms, waiting with her eyes closed.

"Dance?" I asked confused. "Now?"

She just stood there waiting, straight-faced, breathing out of her nose calmly. I thought it was a joke and gave a quick look around. There was no one in sight, just quiet storefronts. I guess Tuesday nights were dead for business. *I wanted an adventure,* I told myself and resigned to her whims. I gently placed my backpack down and stepped up to her, placed my right hand around her waist, and held her right hand with my left hand and started to dance with her. There was no music so I led it pretty slow. "Faster," she said as she opened her eyes and gave me a sly grin. "Can't you hear it? The music? The beat? It's a waltz!"

My mom put me in a dance camp when I was a kid, middle school age. At the time she said that I would thank her for it, that one day it would come in handy. I never believed her. I had gone to a few school dances and had danced at crowded bars but there was no waltzing going on at either of those places. Now, I was waltzing with a beautiful girl. And I was good at it too. She seemed to waltz just fine and followed my lead. I instinctively pulled her close to me as we danced faster and faster. My mom was right and I was thanking her over and over again in my mind. Maya started singing a tune, nothing I could recognize, just a series of hums and *"la-la-di-da-la-la-la."* Almost like she was making it up. I couldn't see her face, we were dancing so close that we were looking over each other's shoulder. I got lost in the pleasant aroma of her hair.

I could hear the smile in her voice as she sang her little tune. She was enjoying the moment. As was I. I twirled her around away from me, then back to me and dipped her. She let out a "Whoo!" and let herself drop in my arms, head back and hair falling all over the place like a waterfall. I pulled her up fast and held her close to my chest and smiled. She smiled right back at me and looked me deep in the eyes and, with a half-cocked smile said, *"Suavecito."* I winked at her and made a mental note to look up that word as well. The whole dancing on the spot and winking thing is not normally me but, in her presence, I felt more passionate, more masculine. It felt good.

She pushed away from me, turned her back, and sighed heavily. "No! We cannot!" she said in a melodramatic way using a heavy Spanish accent. *"Mi papá…*he will kill you if he ever found out. You being a poor peasant boy and me being the governor's one and only daughter. *¡Ay, dios mio! Mi corazon!"*

She was putting on like we were in some *telenovela*. I had seen them on TV before, and I recognized a few of the words and sayings. But, outside of *corazon* and *dios mio*, most of the words eluded me. I never knew what the actors in those telenovelas said but I liked watching them. The women were always so beautiful and passionate.

She swung around to me and held one hand over her heart and reached her other hand to me. *"Bésame con tu boca loca!"* she cried out dramatically. I didn't know what that meant so I just stood there. *"Ay-yay-yay!"* she said and swung back around and headed out of the gazebo as if nothing had happened.

I quickly picked up my backpack and ran to catch up with her. "What does *Bésame con tu boca loca* mean?"

"It's a shame you don't know. Missed your big chance."

I didn't like the sound of that. I don't like missing out on big chances and especially not with fiery latina girls who like to play-act *telenovelas* and dance in the middle of a public square with no music.

"The restaurant is this way," she said pointing ahead of her to one of the buildings on the square. It was a big building from what I could tell, yet I couldn't see much. There was an adobe wall that surrounded the entire place, like a compound, with an arched entryway in the middle leading into a courtyard dining area filled with trees. The entire wall face was covered in a mural. One side had "Calavera's" scrawled across it. On the other side was painted a skull amid dozens of roses.

I stopped to take in the image in front of me. I'd never seen anything quite like it. "This is your family's restaurant?" I asked confused. What did a skull and roses have to do with food?

"Yes," Maya replied nonchalantly.

"You guys like the Grateful Dead or something?" The sign reminded me of Bertha from the Grateful Dead. I had some of their music. I liked it, kind of folksy but raw.

"Grateful Dead? You mean *Día De Los Muertos?*"

"What's *Día De Los Muertos?*"

She turned around to look at me. There was shock in her eyes. "You don't know *Día De Los Muertos?*"

"No. You don't know the Grateful Dead?"

"No. But the dead are grateful that we have *Día De Los Muertos.*" She said it as a matter of fact. The conversation confused me but, at the same time, intrigued me. She didn't know the Grateful Dead yet there was this skull with roses all around it. She knew about this *Día De Los Muertos* thing and it somehow corresponded with the dead being grateful. Were the two linked in some way? "Come on," she said, leading me through the arched entry way. It had old wooden doors painted teal. Looked like they worked but not for security. Probably just for show.

Inside the gate was a patio filled with round concrete tables accompanied by concrete benches, three per table, with umbrellas set on poles in holes in the center of each table. The flooring was covered in multicolored broken tiles, like a mosaic. There were grown trees sprouting from holes in the flooring at various places, as if the trees had been there before the building and they tiled around them. There were two big arched wooden doors leading into the main restaurant dining area and, between the doors was a fountain with water flowing. All in all, a pleasant place. Yet there were no customers dining outside. I thought that was odd for being so close to dinnertime, especially with the beautiful weather.

Before we walked in, I stopped and touched Maya on her shoulder, signaling for her to look at me. "I'm here for a few days," I said, building up to something.

She stopped and turned to me. "That's nice," she said plainly.

"Maybe you could tell me about this *Día De Los Muertos* thing of yours."

"Maybe you could tell me about this Grateful Dead thing of yours."

"OK." I liked this girl even though she seemed out of my league, her being spicy and all. "It's a date then." As soon as I said it, I instantly felt myself blush.

"A date? Well, aren't you fresh?"

I shrugged. If I was fresh, it was only because she was fresh too. She got me in the mood.

"Fine. It's a date," she said, "but only if you meet *mi Mamita y Poppy* beforehand."

"I'm guessing *Mamita* and *Poppy* are your parents. You serious? I gotta meet them before we go out?" That's not how things normally go for me. If I meet a girl's parents, it isn't until way into a relationship, if at all. Usually the girl and I don't work out long before the meeting-the-parents thing.

"Of course. What kind of girl do you think I am?" I thought *the kind of girl who describes herself as "red hot"* but I didn't vocalize that thought. She continued: "Poppy is very traditional and I respect him for it. Mamita doesn't seem to care about the tradition but she's always curious to see who asks me out. I, myself, may not be traditional, but when I'm home, I abide by my father's wishes. After all, I still live in his house."

"When you're at home? But you live in his house. Where else would you be?"

"I want to go to graduate school up in Albuquerque. UNM. If I go, there's no way a guy can meet my parents before going out with me. What, am I supposed to have some guy Skype my parents or something from Albuquerque?"

"I guess not."

"So, until I go, it's Mamita and Poppy for you!" She turned to go in but stopped abruptly and turned back to face me. "I've got to warn you though, this is not a good time for them," she said. "For any of us."

"Why?"

"I'll tell you in a bit. Let's just go in and get you set up with Jared, OK?" She opened the door and we entered.

5 | Jared

Inside, there was a room to the right with a long bar top in it. I could see the length of it beyond the arched entryway. In fact, all the entryways were arched, trimmed with darkly stained molding. The ceiling of the bar was adorned with metal tiles of gold lamé with low hanging chandeliers equipped with electric lights made to look like candles; they even flickered. Behind the bar were large mirrors set in an alcove with glass shelves where hundreds of bottles of liquor sat.

A tall white guy with a thick beard and a pony tail stood confidently behind the bar. He was wearing a buttoned-up white shirt with a black tie and a black vest, everything fit tightly. Looked hipster, except for the ponytail. One couple sat conversing at a table at the far end of the bar room, across from the bar. They were too young to be Maya's parents, must be customers getting drinks after work. Sitting at the bar half way down was a chubby, middle-aged man hunched over his drink. He didn't look healthy and his threadbare black t-shirt stretched over his rolls. He sat still, heaving a bit as he breathed. Maybe he was asleep. I couldn't tell.

To the left of the entryway of the bar room was a small hostess stand with no hostess. Ahead were two other entryways set at forty-five degree angles. The right led to what looked like a hallway with framed pictures. It was dimly lit. The left led to a dining area. That room wasn't as dark. I could sense natural light, as if there was a skylight transferring the remains of daylight from outside. The soft chattering of conversations mixed with the subtle clatter of eating utensils on plates could be heard from the main dining area. Not too many customers from what I could tell. Instrumental music played softly. Maybe traffic picked up later in the evening. Or earlier in the day, hence the use of natural light. In my experience, places that aren't open for breakfast and/or lunch have no need for natural light.

Maya put her arm in mine, crook to crook, and led me toward the bar. The bartender looked our way. When we were within talking range, he stood erect, pulled down the front of his vest and said with a half smile, "You brought the traveling man." He had a slight southern drawl with an edge to it. If I had to guess, I would have thought he was in a rockabilly band. He looked at me and gave me a winning smile below his styled mustache and garnished the effect with a wink.

"I did," Maya said flatly then signed deeply. "Now we're straight. No more favors." She gave him what amounted to a tight-lipped grin. I felt bad, like I had been an inconvenience to her.

"Almost straight," Jared said as he cocked an eyebrow. "You still gotta run him to get his money. Poor guy just rode a bus for twelve hours. Least we can do is help him run one small errand." He gave me a sympathetic and knowing look. I felt like he was on my side, not that Maya wasn't. I was just happy to have someone pulling for me. He thrust out his hand, reaching for a handshake. "Jared," he said smiling again.

"Perk," I replied, shaking his hand.

"Perk the traveling man. You enjoy your bus ride?"

"It was…long."

"Well, the bus ride back ain't going to be any shorter. But at least you'll be in a veedub." He cracked a half-smile. "Go get the money and head on back here quick. Who knows? it might get busy." That last part he said with a half snort.

Maya held her hand palm up and fingers splayed then snapped her fingertips together, touching her thumb tip. "*¡Cállate!*" she said angrily.

Jared chuckled, as if looking at a pouty child. "The new schedule is up," he said. "You've got a double-double. Can't be helped. No one else to work." He shook his head solemnly.

Maya replied with a grunt, grabbed my hand, spun me around, and we went out the way we came in, only faster. Outside she told me, "I hate that guy! If it wasn't for that stupid favor I owed him, I wouldn't even talk to him!"

"Seems nice enough to me," I said.

"Pfft!" Maya exclaimed. I was no stranger to workplace drama. I figured they must have had some sort of ongoing argument or simply just drove each other crazy. Could've been anything. Maya added nothing to her initial response, only silence as we walked out.

"I know what *cállate* means," I said. "It means *shut up*. My cook, Compa, tells me that all the time. What's the deal with the restaurant getting busy? Why did that piss you off. I mean, doesn't your family own the place? Don't you guys *want* it to get busy?"

"Of course we do. He was being a jerk because he knows it *won't* get busy."

"Why not?"

"Because of the Sugar Skull Ghost Thief. That's what they're calling it." In an instant, she was deflated. Gone was the carefree, confident girl that had greeted me. Her lively spirit was now replaced with exasperation and a hint of sadness.

"The Sugar Skull Ghost Thief?" I asked.

"Jared said that guy Chuck got you a room at the Mariposa Hotel," she replied, disregarding me question. "They have an indoor pool and a hot tub." That was a random statement for her to make.

"What does that have to do with a ghost?"

"I'm sick of it all! I don't want to deal with it. All I want is to get away from the restaurant, get away from my parents, get away from Jared…everything pretty much." She paused, placed her hands on her hips. "Here's the plan: we get your money so you can do your deal. Then we go to your hotel and swim and I can tell you all about it. What do you think?"

"I don't have swim trunks."

"We'll skinny dip." She winked at me. She was regaining her initial demeanor. I blushed again. "Don't worry. You can borrow a pair of my brother's. You look about the same size. He won't care because he won't know. I'll go home, get into my swimsuit, get a pair of trunks for you, and meet you at your hotel." I pondered the idea, not really believing the proposition. She noticed my hesitation and continued, "Come on. I really need to get away from it all. When I tell you, you'll totally understand."

"I thought I was supposed to meet your parents before we went on a date."

"It's not a date, it's just swimming."

It didn't have to make sense. "Sure," I agreed without contest.

"Bueno pues," she said. "Let's do this!"

6 | Legend

I thought that getting almost eight thousand dollars was going to be complicated, but it wasn't. We went to a strange grocery store that was filled with piñatas and Mexican food items and even furniture for rent right in the middle of the place. All I had to do was tell the customer service clerk my name and show my ID, and she handed over the money. The seven thousand was in money orders, the rest was in cash. Maya took me back to Calavera's, and I traded the money orders for the title to the VW bus and keys.

Maya told me she would meet me at the hotel in a while and tore off. Jared took me around the back of the restaurant to where the Microbus was parked. He gently caressed the bus's side paneling. "She's a beauty, Traveling Man," he said proudly. Apparently, his new name for me was "Traveling Man." I kind of liked it. He proceeded to fill me in on some of the finer details; what to do when it acted up this way or that way, little tricks and tips to watch out for. He showed me where everything was and how to get the tire off if I had a flat. He gave me his number and told me to call if I had any questions. I told him my phone was broken. "You'll be fine," he said with the wave of his hand.

I hopped into the bus to head toward the hotel. It was a standard. Great. I had learned to drive a standard years ago when I first learned how to drive, but that was a long time ago. Needless to say, there was a learning curve involved and it wasn't pretty. It took me the better part of twenty minutes to go roughly three miles. By the time I got to the hotel, Maya was already there, waiting out front.

I parked next to her and she came up to my open driver's side window and stuck her head in. "Finally, Slowpoke Rodriguez!" she said with exaggerated exasperation.

I didn't look at her but simply sang *"La cucaracha, la cucaracha,"* real slow in my best Slowpoke Rodriguez voice. She giggled at that. I hadn't met many girls who are well-versed in *Looney Tunes.*

She threw a pair of Speedos in my lap and said, "There's your swimsuit."

"I can't wear these!" I said holding them up.

"Why not?"

"They're... too small!"

"Whoa! Too small? Well, aren't *we* proud of our junk!"

"No, I mean—"

"I know what you mean, Chulo. Here." She grabbed the Speedos and pushed a pair of regular trunks onto my chest as I got out of the bus. "I just wanted to see the look on your face. I also wanted to see if you would wear them just because I gave them to you. My brother was a swimmer in high school but he can't wear these anymore."

"Why not? Did he get fat?"

"No. He died."

"Oh, I'm sorry." I felt horrible. "I had no idea."

"He died about twenty years ago," she explained. "I was little when it happened. He got sick. One of those things." I could see she wasn't kidding about this.

"Why do you still have his swimming trunks?"

"We still have *all* his stuff," Maya said. "My mom keeps his room just the way he had it. Like a memorial."

"For twenty years?"

"I know. Usually people just get a tattoo or a decal on their back windshield. 'In memory of...' This is our way of remembering him." It was odd but different strokes for different folks, I guessed. "Anyway," Maya continued, "we're not here to talk about my dead brother. We're here to swim. Go get naked and put those on. I'll meet you at the pool. *¡Ándale, Chulo!*" It seemed that *Chulo* was now my new name. I reminded myself again to look it up.

I got myself checked in and changed, got a couple of towels from the front desk and made it to the hotel's indoor pool. She was the only one there, lying on a deck chair, dressed in a bikini and looking down at her phone. I walked up beside her, she didn't look up. She had an absolutely beautiful body. It was smooth and toned, uniform in it's dark brown hue. Her bikini was blue with white polka dots. It fit her perfectly, accentuating each and every glorious firm curve. I got a lump in my throat and chills up and down my body just looking at her for that split second. I dropped one of the towels on her stomach. "Thanks," she said not looking up. "Give me a second, I'm letting my mom know I won't be staying home tonight."

Won't be home tonight? I just met this girl. Her straightforwardness unsettled me.

"Don't worry, *Chulo*. I'm not staying here. I'm staying with my friend, Bibi." She tapped her phone a few times then set it down and looked at me and frowned. "Why you no wear Speedo?" she said with a mock frown and goofy eyes. Then she hopped up. "Take that shirt off and put your towel down."

I did so.

"Empty your pockets."

I did so as well.

"That's the shallow end," she said pointing to the other end of the pool. "This is the deep end," she said pointing to the water in front of us. "It's always best to just jump into the deep end, wouldn't you say?"

"Sure." She grabbed my hand and we walked up to the very edge of the pool, our feet half over on the side. "It's cold, just so you know. On three, we jump in together."

"On three then."

She counted, "One," then jumped in and pulled me in with her. Under the surface, I swam about trying to find which way was up. I could see her doing the same. She looked toward me and smiled, her hair floating weightlessly in the water. We found our way to the surface, and I gasped for air. We treaded water and she laughed, spitting out water as it got in her mouth. I laughed too.

We swam around for a while, not talking, just swimming. She was playful, like a dolphin, and she swam well. She would swim underwater from one end of the pool to the other and back again. Sometimes she would swim underneath me and grab my ankles. Once she rammed me in the stomach with her head. I had never had a girl do *that* to me before. I got into it and started playing too. It was fun. We wrestled underwater until we had to come up for air. It wasn't a competition, just playing.

We ended up at the shallow end of the pool and rested against the side. "Let's get in the hot tub for a while," she suggested. "Then, when we're all warm, let's jump back into the pool. Shock our system."

"Sounds good to me."

I let her get out of the pool first. Not because I was a gentleman but completely the opposite. I just wanted to watch her step up out of the pool. She had a nice bottom half. I couldn't tell before, but her legs and butt were muscular. The water and the light reflected off of her muscles. I, myself, have no butt. I was thankful that I didn't have to wear that Speedo. We eased into the jacuzzi opposite each other and melted into the warm, bubbling water.

"So tell me about this ghost of yours. What did you call it?"

"The Sugar Skull Ghost Thief. Also known as the bane of my existence." She gathered her hair and wrung it out. She had a lot of hair and it seemed to have collected a lot of water. "Do you know what a *calavera* is?"

"No."

"It's a skull. It's also my family's last name, hence the name of the restaurant and the mural out front. Well, the restaurant started back in the early nineteen hundreds. Some say parts of the building are as old as nineteen fifteen. No one knows for sure, can't really carbon date adobe. In any case, my great, great grandfather Isidro Calavera bought the place back in nineteen twenty-seven when it was some old closed down saloon. He named it Calavera's and started serving food. His claim to fame, however, was a concoction he called Calavera's Poison. Basically, it was whiskey that he sold as rat poison." She made air quotes with her hands. "Since New Mexico became a state in nineteen twelve, it was still under the laws of prohibition, although I doubt anyone around here really cared or abided by the law. Still, it didn't hurt for him to market it as rat poison. He was the only guy doing this at that time, and he got popular because of it. We still make it, by the way. You can try some. It tastes like crap but packs a punch.

"Well, after prohibition ended, more players got into the game. And outside players too. Isidro didn't think anything of it, always thought he would be raking in the cash. But the market thinned out on him and, in nineteen forty, he was pretty much all but bankrupt. The stress came down hard on him and he got really sick. My great grandfather Lucio Calavera took over the business. Lucio was a cool dude. There are pictures of these guys at the restaurant. You'll have to check them out. The story goes like this: Lucio goes down to Mexico to visit a distant cousin who is some sort of psychic or something, no one really knows. But he comes back with this skull. It's a real life human skull. Lucio said his relative, the psychic, told him the answer to the problems with the restaurant lay with the skull. The skull was from a man they called 'El Mismo.' It means *the same.* He was a conjoined twin with two heads, one body. They didn't have two names for him, just one. Legend has it, the twins got in a fight over a woman. They both wanted her and refused to share. Weird, huh? So things get heated and essentially the twins choke each other to death. They bury the body but, a year later, grave robbers dig it up. When the townspeople find the ransacked gravesite, there is only one skull. For some reason, the grave robbers took the other skull. The psychic was put in charge of keeping the skull safe until the other skull was found. It brought her fortune somehow. They say the skull is longing to seek forgiveness from his brother so he does good deeds to lure him back, to show that he's a good guy. The good deeds are to help failing businesses recover."

Maya poked her foot above the water and sighed. I noticed its diminutive size. "You have little feet," I said and placed the bottom of my foot against the bottom of hers. "They're not so much feet as they are hooves." With that she started pushing my foot with hers. She poked her other foot out of the water.

"I bet I can beat you in a foot wrestling match," she said.

"There's no such thing as a foot wrestling match," I replied as I put my other foot against hers.

"It's an old Mexican tradition. You wouldn't know about it."

"Really?"

"No. But I'll still beat you. My strength is in my glutes."

She giggled and pushed against my feet. She was, in fact, strong. I told her, "If you beat me, it's not because of the strength of your glutes but because you're digging into my feet with your little pointy hooves." She eased off of my feet, stood up and punched me in the arm. She tried to look angry at me.

"Little pointy hooves? You really know how to charm a girl, don't you?" She sat back down.

"Of all the girls in the world, you have the most beautifully dainty pointy hooves."

She gave me a half smile.

"So how does a ghost fit into your whole story?" I asked her, wanting to get back on track.

"Oh, yeah," she said. "So Lucio returns only to find his father had died from the sickness. It doesn't change the fact that the business still needs to recover. Lucio makes this shrine in one of the dining rooms, the Soledad Room, and guess what? Business starts picking up. Mostly because people start coming to hear the story of El Mismo. Business continued to be good for a long time until a new priest came to town and chastised Lucio for his involvement with the relic. The priest said that the skull represented superstition and was evil because it was increasing money supernaturally outside of the faith. Lucio, being a devout Catholic, was torn. The skull had become their claim to fame. Without it, they didn't have a draw. Like his father before him, Lucio fell ill because of the stress, the internal battle within him. His son, my grandfather Gustavo Calavera, had to take over operations. Grandpa Tavo wasn't as devout as his father, and he refused to get rid of El Mismo. Lucio never reconciled his guilt and died, placing his soul at the mercy of God. After his death, Grandpa Tavo found a way around it all. He took the skull and painted flowers and symbols all over the thing and covered it in lacquer. He then put it in a glass case which he claimed couldn't be opened and told the priest that he got rid of the skull—smashed it to dust—but, since their business hinged on the story, he made a replica skull out of clay and painted it. The priest had his doubts but allowed it. Grandpa Tavo was a very charming and convincing guy. They used to call him Guapo. Means *handsome.*

"Business at the restaurant increased dramatically with the painted skull. I'll show it to you when we're at the restaurant. It really does look cool. Anyways, Grandpa Tavo, bless his soul, was a gambling man. The income from the business only fueled the flames of his gambling desires."

"You have a way with words," I said.

"I know," she said, not skipping a beat. "So Grandpa Tavo gets in trouble. In a single card game with strangers from out of town, he loses everything and then some. He now owes some of these guys like two thousand dollars. He doesn't have the cash. The guys were passing through and didn't have the time to wait to get water from a stone. So they do a number on him. They beat him within an inch of his life: broken legs, broken arms and fingers, messed up bleeding inside and everything. He ends up in a coma but never wakes up. He died from his injuries. They never found the guys that did it. Regardless, My father, Lalo Calavera was forced to take over the business and try to bring it back to life."

Maya immersed herself in the hot bubbling water and came back up. She wrung her hair again. "If my feet are hooves, yours are canoes."

"Hooves, canoes…Get to the ghost, will ya?"

"Patience," she said like a school teacher scolding a child. "It is important to know our history, young man." Our legs were touching beneath the surface of the water. I couldn't tell if that was an invite for intimacy or if Maya was simply a person who liked human contact. I put it in the back of my mind. "Poppy is an old-fashioned man," she continued, "a stoic man. A conservative man. He's not swayed by superstition or stories of seers from the homeland. Instead, his take was always that people like a good story and novelty items. The skull provided both. And that was good for business. So he kept the skull and ramped up the marketing and promotion of it. Calavera's became *the* tourist attraction in Old Mesilla. People used to come from all around to look at the skull and hear the story. The locals, from here and Las Cruces, were steady customers. Poppy seemed to avoid any bad juju and got the business on solid footing. That is, until the ghost."

"The ghost," I repeated sincerely.

"The stupid ghost," Maya returned. "It started about three months ago, a rash of break-in's and robberies around our little village of Old Mesilla. And every time it happened, the culprit spray painted 'EL MISMO' at the site of the crime in big letters. People claimed to see a figure scurrying around in the night wearing a black robe and having the skull as its head. It was kind of funny for a while but the crimes continued. People started to talk. Business started to slow down. Poppy told people that this was some joke, that we were being framed for some reason by a prankster. One of our servers, Esteban, set up a camera to film the skull, like surveillance, so that we would have proof that the skull was innocent. Sounds stupid but it's true. As it turned out, when there was a crime, we reviewed the video and, sure enough, on the nights when the crimes occurred, a ghostly figure emerged from the skull and, after the crime had been committed, the ghostly figure returned to the skull. I saw it with my own eyes. Totally weird, dude. Messed up and all. As I said, Poppy is not a superstitious man but, after seeing the video, he kind of went a bit crazy. He didn't know what to believe. Now *he* got sick as business continued to falter. The crimes have slowed down significantly but the damage is done. Our reputation is shot, at least with the locals. We still get some business from tourists, always have, but it's barely enough to keep the lights on. Poppy wants to get rid of the skull but is now afraid that, if he does something to it, the skull's ghost will seek revenge somehow. It's like he's flipped a switch and is all about the supernatural.

"And now he wants me to take over the business. Whenever things got bad in the past, the son came in and made things all better. He has no son, not anymore at least, God rest his soul. So it's on me."

"That's quite a story."

"It sucks!" she said angrily. "I worked at that restaurant all through high school and college. It's not for me. I want out! I want to go to graduate school, like I told you before. I don't want the responsibility of running a restaurant. I've seen what it can do to people. It wears them down, consumes them. As far as I'm concerned, that restaurant is cursed!"

"So you're saying you want to shut it down?"

"That would kill Poppy. It's his livelihood. He's put everything into that place. It's literally his retirement. If I shut it down, there's no money. There's nothing. Nada! They have no retirement and they still have like ten years until Social Security. And he really can't claim disability for not having as much business as he would like, much less for a ghost."

"Do you think business would pick up if you kept the skull but hid it?"

"Poppy thought of that. He put the skull in another room for a spell to see if things changed. They didn't. The ghost still did its thing. Poppy said that simply relocating the skull won't make it stop, and people would know what we were up to. And, like I said, he fears vengeance from El Mismo if he gets rid of it or destroys it."

"Sounds like you're in a pickle."

"A pickle? How can I be in a pickle? Those aren't hollow."

"No they're not. It's just an expression."

"I'm S.O.L. How's *that* for an expression?"

"Pretty accurate, I guess." I paused, contemplating. "Couldn't he hire a manager to do what he wants *you* to do?"

"The money's not there for the job. We're running on fumes now. We're down to only a few employees, a real skeleton crew. How's that for a coincidence? We got rid of the hostess altogether. One of the servers on the floor usually seats people. We hung on to our part-time what do you call it? He's one of those guys who knows a lot about wine?"

"A sommelier?"

"Yeah, that. We hung onto him just because he doubles as a server. Actually, it's Esteban, the guy who set up the camera. We don't pay him much for being a sommelier. Practically nothing at all. He says he's doing it for the experience so that he can land a better gig somewhere else, a bigger city or something. That's his dream. He's kind of metrosexual. If you see him, you'll get what I mean. As for cooks, it's basically just my mom. Since there's not a lot of business she can do it herself. She's good at it, really good." Maya sat there silently for a moment. "I know what you're thinking. Why doesn't my mom just run the show? She's not a manager, not at all. Great cook, horrible manager. She knows it, says it herself. But sometimes I think she harps on it to convince me to take over. I do a little bit of the management now but not much. I don't want to get stuck here."

I dipped myself below the surface of the water. My shoulders and face had gone dry and it felt odd. Coming up, my legs rubbed against Maya's. They felt good. As I wiped the water from my eyes, Maya said, "Just so you know, I'm not going to sleep with you. Not unless we get married."

That comment threw me off kilter. Sleep with me? Was merely rubbing legs construed as sexual advancement? There was no jest in her voice, no emotion either. She simply looked at me plainly.

"I didn't say anything about us sleeping together."

"But you're a guy, right? And can you honestly say that you would stop it if it started?"

The conversation was blunt and straightforward. Honest and raw. There was a beauty to it, as if all pretense was stripped away. "Honestly? No, I wouldn't. In fact, if we're being honest, I would welcome it. I mean, you're gorgeous. But even better than that, you're fun to be around. Even this short time I've been around you has been amazing."

"You're fun too. I don't meet a lot of guys like you—funny, kind…and cute."

I had to smile at that. "I've never met anyone who finished college without losing their virginity. Guy or girl."

"I'm not a virgin," she said. "But I've found that sex just adds a bunch of pressure to a relationship. And guys will act like charming knights up until they get into your pants and then they turn into jerks. But I guess that's my fault for letting them."

"I don't know about that," I countered. "I guess on one hand you can blame yourself. After all, it is in your power what you will or will not allow a guy to do with you. No means no, right? On the other hand, you shouldn't blame yourself for guys acting like jerks." She rubbed her legs on mine after I said that, possibly in a gesture to say *Thanks.*

"I like how you put it: it's in my power. Because that's how I feel, powerful. Not like I'm holding sex as some reward so that I can have guys do my bidding, not at all. Like I said, it's an after-marriage thing. But powerful in that I control who I give myself to. And I didn't feel like that before. It was always just something I did. We did, as a whole it seemed. Me and all my friends."

"It's kind of the way things go now. I haven't really looked at it as a bad thing. I mean, it feels good to have that intimacy with someone."

"Of course it feels good, dude. It's sex!" She smiled at her joke. I chuckled. It was a nice humorous relief to what had become a serious conversation. "But outside of feeling good, it has an effect on people, before and afterward. Before because there's all this pressure leading up to it. Or even worse, no pressure at all which cheapens it. And afterward because there's a connection between those people that complicates things, especially if there's no commitment."

"But it can make things better, right? I mean, it can make two people closer so they know that they're committed to each other."

"Sex by itself doesn't do that. A lot of times, the two people aren't on the same page. One thinks that it's a committed relationship, and the other is just happy to have someone to have sex with, someone at the end of the day to be with." She was speaking passionately. Not angry, but passionately. This meant a lot to her.

"Isn't it hard though?" I asked. "Not being able to show your affection physically?"

"Here's the weird thing," she said as she sat up straight. "It's actually more liberating. I can show my affection even *easier.*" I was confused and she saw it in my face. She explained it to me. "If you know that, no matter what we do together, that sex is off the table as an option—and by *sex* I meant pretty much all the naked, erotic stuff—then there's a freedom to have human contact because it's not leading anywhere. At least not at this point." I was still a bit confused. She sat back and continued, "Look, we're here in this hot tub, pretty much in our underwear, sitting not five feet from each other. Our legs are touching, I'm sure you realized that." I gulped. "But that doesn't mean that it's an invitation for sex. And if you thought it did before, you don't now, right?"

I nodded in agreement.

"Something as innocent as a kiss on the cheek isn't a benchmark leading to the next rung in a ladder leading to sex," she said. "That is, as long as both people know it doesn't. And here's the cool thing: even if I kiss a guy I'm going out with, that's not something that I will regret in the future. And I don't get a reputation as a girl that puts out. Even better, there's no awkwardness if things don't work out. Also, there's no comparing the person to former lovers. People may say they don't do that but, in my experience, they do. It just solves a lot of problems before they even start."

I sat there, absorbing it all. How she was explaining it made sense, yet it seemed so outside of everything I'd seen that it threw me for a loop. Especially the fact that she was so hot. I could understand some of the girls I met in churches who were all about waiting until marriage, but most of them didn't look like Maya.

"Is this a religious thing for you?" I asked her.

"Pff!" she exclaimed, "Hardly! I'm nowhere near a good little Catholic girl. I only go to mass when my parents drag me there, which isn't often because they know I don't buy into any of it. I'm doing this for myself. And for some of the guys who I would have hurt otherwise. I can break hearts, you know. I could break yours if I wanted to."

"I don't doubt that," I said with complete honesty. "But my heart's kind of used to it. It's like breaking a Lego sculpture. It gets knocked into a million pieces and I just put it back together again." She looked at me like I was a hurt puppy. "But don't cry for me, Argentina. I'd rather use my heart and get it broken than to let it sit in my chest and rot." Maya laughed and then smiled broadly at me. God, she was pretty. She didn't wear any makeup, or at least I couldn't tell if she did. Her long locks of dark hair were hanging heavily from being soaked and flowing over her shoulders and chest. I smiled back. "Maya, I can honestly say, I've never met anyone remotely like you. You have a strong sense of self and self-worth. You come across as flirty and flighty, yet your thoughts are deep reservoirs of logic and understanding. Your amazing energy surrounds you and you captured me in your engaging aura. We already covered your hooves so we won't go there." Maya giggled at that as I continued, "I've only known you for a couple of hours and I feel like it would take a lifetime to unpack, unravel, and understand even that little bit. All in all, you're as multifaceted as a diamond..." she looked down in a show of humility. I paused and added, "...and equally brilliant." She looked up at me biting her lip with a look of happy pain upon her face.

She took a deep breath and composed herself. "You're a sweet talker, you know that? You keep talking like that and I'm going to have to make an exception to my rule just for you. Kidding. Just kidding. Don't get your hopes up." She cocked her head to the side and looked at me mischievously, almost as if she wasn't kidding. "Come here," she said gesturing *come hither.* I got up and moved in close. "Closer," she said. I moved in even closer, holding myself up by placing my hands on the the jacuzzi at each side of her head. She and I were face to face, about a foot apart. "Closer," she said as she held my chin. I moved in even closer. She turned my head to the side and whispered in my ear, "Who *are* you? Where did you come from?" My heart jumped in my chest and I had to resist an all-out shiver. "I've got two things for you," she said seductively into my ear. "First..." she said and kissed my cheek. "That's for being such a sweetheart."

"And second?" I asked.

She moved my face by the chin to face her. Our faces were only inches apart and we were looking deep into each other's eyes. "Second is this," she said as she pinched my nipple and twisted it hard. "Tittie twister!" she exclaimed. I howled and retreated back to the relative safety of my end of the jacuzzi.

"Ow, you really got me," I said, rubbing my chest. "What was *that* for?"

"For making me like you so much!"

I looked at one of her boobs and contemplated if payback was a possibility. She followed my gaze and read my mind. "You wouldn't dare," she warned. I stopped looking at her boob.

"If you do that to guys you like, I'd hate to see what you do to guys you hate."

"Oh, you don't want to know. Keep that in the back of your mind." The moment was light again. Both of us sat in happy contentment for a moment. "I'm hungry," she said. "Let's go get some food at the restaurant. I can show you the skull and you can meet my parents. You still have to, remember?"

"Yes, so that I can ask you out on a date."

"Exactly."

"So us hanging out, getting to know each other at a deep level, talking about everything from haunted skulls to sex, dancing, rubbing legs, kisses on the cheek, and you touching my nipple...If this isn't even a date, I'm excited to see what you're like on an actual date."

"Oh, you have no idea."

I gulped again. "I'm going to need to take a dip in the cold water now. Then we'll go."

"*Miraté,*" she said again to me and attempted to pinch my cheek. I shoved her hand away.

"Get away from me with your pincers of death!" I said.

She bounded up out of the jacuzzi. "*Vamanos!*" she said

and dove head first into the pool. I got up, and dove in after her.

7 | El Mismo

We decided that I should drive to the restaurant in the VW since I needed practice. Also, Maya wanted to ride in it. She said it was "groovy." It was, in fact, groovy. Jared had informed me that it was a 1959 standard Volkswagen Microbus. The exterior looked new and shiny, must have been restored recently, certainly later than 1959. The top half was a dark hunter green and the bottom half was a lighter avocado green. The front of the bus came down in a V shape with the VW insignia smack dab in the front. That model had the split windshield too. Pretty cool.

The bus wasn't as far along in the restoration process on the inside as it was on the outside. The seats were all there but were eaten up. Jared said he was going to do those last since new ones would start to get eaten up with the southern New Mexico summer sun. I asked him if he could tint the windows and he chuckled as if it were a joke.

The interior panels were torn and frayed. Jared didn't say anything about those. The console looked original. By that I mean it looked old. There was no radio installed, but Jared said he'd throw in the emergency radio/flashlight that was sitting on the floor by the stick shift. It was one of those that you have to crank by hand to power up. The dash itself housed a single display item: a speedometer that only went up to 70 miles per hour. Jared said it would drive comfortably at fifty-five to sixty miles per hour, a little faster downhill, slower uphill. I would have to travel all the way back to Colorado going about fifty-five miles per hour at best. I did the math in my head and it would take ten hours if I didn't stop for anything. So I estimated it would take me about as long to get back in the Microbus as it did to get here in a Greyhound bus. That's something Chuck didn't mention to me. Maybe he didn't know. I'm on vacation anyway. A longer ride back is just a longer ride. An extended vacation, in a way.

Maya, in spite of her fiery attitude, was a patient tutor as she helped me with my stick shift driving skills. I thought she might make fun of me but she didn't. Instead she simply guided me along through the process. She was such a good teacher that I was chugging along with minimal stall-outs or mishaps. The bus wasn't the easiest thing to drive and definitely not the most comfortable. The seats were beat up and had been patched with a variety of materials: duct tape, beach towels, rope, and such. The steering wheel stuck straight up from the floor so, instead of the wheel being parallel to the dash, it was more parallel to the floor. Took some getting used to.

"This bus fits you," Maya told me as we drove along. "I mean, if it were all restored and purring. I could see you in something like this. It's old fashioned but fun. That's you, right? Old fashioned, but fun?"

"Me to a T. Good ol' fashioned *butt* fun!" I shot her a glance out of the side of my eye. She was chuckling to herself.

"It's all in the glutes," she returned. We both laughed at that.

Calavera's looked good at night. The paintings on the gate were spotlit with small solar lights set in the ground. Smart use of the desert sun. Why weren't there more solar-powered lights around? The patio dining area was lit by way of Christmas lights strewn through the trees. They bathed the area in a soft glow. There were candles on the patio tables as well, which added to the ambience. No customers outside but lit candles nonetheless. It was cooler but not exactly chilly. I was wearing my hoodie which seemed like just enough to take the edge off. Maya wasn't as acclimated to cooler weather, that was for sure.

"I gotta get my coat," she said. "It's frickin' freezing!" Her hair was still wet which probably didn't help, but freezing? I estimated it to be about sixty to sixty-five degrees, warm for late October. At least to me, that is. She must have been accustomed to warmer temperatures in her region of the country.

We went inside and she led me deeper into the restaurant. The natural light from the sun was gone, replaced now by a soft glow that seemed to emanate from everywhere. The main dining area was a large room with a huge rose bush in the middle with roses on it. I thought they were fake but, upon closer inspection, they were in fact real. I wanted to snip one off to give to Maya. Just a thought. But I let it go. It would be weird, like stealing and giving right back to the person I stole from.

All the tables were draped with black tablecloths. There was a single lit candle in a small glass globe on each table. The lighting was soft and intimate. Looked like this place didn't have a value menu.

I looked back at the rose bush. It was huge yet trimmed nicely. I followed it upwards toward the ceiling and saw something absolutely amazing. The ceiling was slightly concave with a round skylight directly in the center, just as I had thought. The entire face of the ceiling was painted in a mural. But not just any mural, there were hundreds, if not thousands, of dancing skeletons dressed like mariachis, Mexican villagers, gunfighters, priests, everything. There were even dog skeletons. They were dancing around an old Mexican village with flags and flowers everywhere. Now I was really confused. If anything said "Grateful Dead," it was dancing skeletons.

Maya saw me standing there staring at the ceiling. "It's fantastic, ain't it?" she said stepping up close to me, shoulder to shoulder, staring up. "A local artist did it for us. This was back when this place was raking in the cash. I think we paid this guy six grand to do it. It took him around three months to complete it. He worked on it before we opened in the mornings. Do you like it?"

"I've never seen anything quite like it in my life. What's with the dancing skeletons?"

"*Día De Los Muertos,* remember?"

"Yeah. Our date."

"Speaking of which, come meet Mamita."

Maya led me to the kitchen located at the back of the restaurant. Beyond the swinging doors was a small foyer with a cabinet and a shelf. The shelf had napkins, aprons, silverware, to-go boxes, and such. There was another set of swinging doors leading into the kitchen. To my surprise, it was a standard restaurant kitchen. I had thought it would be like a kitchen in some old house but it was fitted with all the normal equipment. There was no soft instrumental music in there, just loud mariachi music. It reminded me of the café, where Compa listened to some of the same stuff while cooking. I have to say, I didn't mind it. I actually liked it. It was a lot better than the stuff I'd heard being played in other kitchens. The aroma was better than other kitchens as well. The savory smells hit me strongly and my hunger was amplified dramatically.

There was a round middle-aged woman in the kitchen rolling out dough. She was sweating yet she seemed quite content, singing happily and boisterously along with the music.

She was a handsome woman, even at her age and weight. She held herself well and bounced about as she worked. I could tell she liked to dance.

"Mamita!" Maya yelled over the music as we looped around the end of the counter and into the guts of the kitchen.

"Mija!" replied Maya's mother. "Where have you been? We were going to make tortillas and listen to Juan Gabriel!" She had a heavy Mexican accent. "And who is this?" she said looking at me with expectation.

"Mamita, this is Perk," Maya said hooking her arm in mine and pulling me closer to her. "He's the guy picking up the bus Jared was selling."

"*Y el es su novio ya?*" Whatever Maya's mother just said didn't seem too positive from the look on her face.

"Ay, Mamita," Maya pleaded, "he's a good guy. *Un noble de nobles,* as you always tell me to look for." Maya faced me with an exaggerated grin that shut her eyes, as if she was proud.

I held out my hand to Maya's mother. "Hello, Mrs. Calavera. Nice to meet you."

She wiped her flour-covered hands on a dishtowel she had over her shoulder, stood up straight (which wasn't very much as she was short, probably only five feet tall) and replied, "*Mucho gusto.*" She gave a slight smile and looked toward Maya and said, "*El guero es muy guapo, ¿que no?*"

"*Si, Mamita,*" Maya said and held my arm tighter. "*El guapo del norte.*" At that both Maya and her mother giggled like little school girls. I had no idea what they were saying.

Maya poked me in the side. "Well, ask her," she demanded. I was confused for a half second, just long enough for Maya to shoot me a glance that said, *You know what I'm talking about!* I figured it out.

"Mrs. Calavera," I began, "I like your daughter and I'd like to take her out on a date. May I have your..." What do I ask for? Permission? I remembered Maya mentioning that her parents dragged her to mass every so often. "Blessing?"

Mrs. Calavera put her hands on her hips and looked sternly at me. "I am not sure," she said, "maybe I want you all for myself!" She winked at me and gave me a wry smile. Then she grabbed my hands and pulled me into a bear hug. She let me go and looked to Maya and said, *"Su alma es puro, Mija. Pura y puro todo."*

Maya pulled me back close to her. "We don't know if his soul is pure. Maybe he's a wildman. Maybe he wants to ravage me and take me to his cave in the mountains."

"Eso es mucho mejor," Mrs. Calavera said with a devilish grin. Then, in one elegant movement, she pulled the dish towel from her shoulder, snapped my butt with it, and returned it to its original resting place. She was standing in front of me, slightly to the left and, for the life of me, I don't know how she was able to wrap that thing around me so that it hit my butt. The towel stung but not much. Mrs. Calavera pulled Maya away from me and hugged her tightly. I could hear the air going out of Maya's lungs, but she didn't fight it. "Go see your father, *mijita. Y Piquito tambien."*

At that, both Maya and her mother acted like they were going to cry and sobbed, "Ohhh!" Then they broke out into a song together, doing a little dance. *"Piquito, Piquito! Que lindo, Piquito!"* Then they giggled and hugged each other. "I love you, Mamita!" Maya said.

"Te adoro, mi amor!" Mrs. Calavera replied.

Maya turned her attention back to me and grabbed my arm again. She liked holding onto me in that manner. "Poppy isn't here," she said to me. "He's at home. I forgot that he wasn't feeling good. We'll need to go to my house to see him. And to pick up Piquito. *Pobrecito Piquito."* That last part she said as if she were about to cry. Whoever this Piquito guy was, he sure was pitied by Maya and her mother.

"How far is it?" I asked. Even though I had to drive the bus over five hundred miles back home, part of me didn't want to drive around town too much before leaving. I guess I was afraid.

"Not far," Maya assured me, possibly sensing my hesitation. "Just around the corner, down the road a bit. But I want you to see El Mismo before we go."

Mrs. Calavera gave a *harumph!* "El Mismo!" she said curtly. She didn't add anything to that, just stewed for a moment in the thought. The three of us stood there in awkward silence in spite of the music from the radio.

"Well, it was nice meeting you, Mrs. Calavera," I said signaling our departure.

"Mucho gusto, Señor Perk," she said with a smile and pulled me in and gave me a hug as forceful as the one she gave Maya. She had strong arms yet her hug was cozy and warm. I thought she was a wonderful person. And, in the back of my mind, I imagined Maya at that age with as much vigor and love. They say a woman turns into her mother. In Maya's case, she could do a whole lot worse.

We exited the kitchen the way we came in. In the foyer between the kitchen and the dining room was a stout, pudgy white guy with long, wavy, strawberry blond hair flowing over half his face. He was looking at his phone and shut it off quickly when we entered. He didn't look at me, only at Maya.

Maya stopped our progress to greet him, although she didn't seem happy about it. "Rocky," she said emotionlessly.

"Did you get my text?" Rocky asked her without acknowledging me.

Maya seemed exasperated with this Rocky guy. I could sense that there was some history there. So far Maya was zero for two in positive relationships with her coworkers (except for her mother, of course). I automatically thought that the guys must be at fault but that was simply because I was crushing on Maya. Was it a red flag? Should I tread carefully around her?

She turned to me and said, "Perk, this is Rocky. Rocky, Perk." She presented Rocky like a wooden game show model. Rocky gave me a look of masked disgust and looked back at Maya.

"You didn't answer my question, Maya," Rocky said to her a bit perturbed.

"I haven't checked," Maya replied with a sigh. "What did you need?"

"I can cover for one of your doubles," Rocky said to her with a strange politeness. "I know how much you don't like working doubles. And I don't mind."

"I'm fine, Rocky. I need the money. And my dad needs me here as much as possible."

"Did you think about what I asked you the other night?" Rocky was sounding desperate.

"I told you before, Rocky," Maya said sternly. "I'm not interested in you like that."

Rocky stared at her obstinately. Then he looked at me and gave me a sneer. Jealousy.

Maya turned her back to Rocky, faced me, and said, "Come on, Perk." Rocky held up his phone and stared at it intently, licking his teeth. Then he poked it and put it in his pocket. I couldn't say for certain, but I was ninety-nine percent sure that he took a picture of Maya's butt while she was facing me.

We left Rocky to whatever he was doing before we interrupted him, and headed out into the dining room. Business had picked up a bit but not much. Just enough to stay afloat. Maybe. Maya pulled herself close to me and whispered in my ear, "I don't like Rocky."

"Really?" I replied facetiously. "I couldn't tell."

"But he likes me."

I didn't tell her about Rocky's butt photo capture.

"He won't leave me alone," she said. "And he's kind of creepy. He does weird things and no one believes me when I tell them."

"Like what?"

"We have a room that has footlockers in it for us. It's like a co-ed locker room with a bathroom off to the side. Anyways, we can go in there and change, get ready for work. There's a lock so it's pretty private. Well, I'll go in and get done up and, if Rocky's here at the restaurant, he'll wait to go in after me. Just wait there at the door. And when I leave, he goes and locks himself in there forever. And he's not getting ready. You get where I'm going with this?"

I nodded. Classic perv behavior. Part of me felt sorry for him, as sick as that sounds. He didn't seem too socially conscious and Maya was a highly attractive girl. Put those two together and the perv comes out like a lion. "Why do you guys keep him around then?"

"He does some janitorial work for cheap. Landscaping and cleaning and stuff. He likes being around here. Around me, actually. He's always staring at me. He thinks I don't notice but I do. He wants us to go out but no way is that happening!"

"Maybe he's just lonely."

"Maybe he's a psychopath." Maya was not kidding.

She led me out of the dining room and into the adjoining hallway. In a hushed tone she said, "When Rocky's around, just pretend you're my boyfriend. He won't be happy about it, but he'll leave us alone."

"I thought I *was* your boyfriend," I said with a half smile. Maya winked at me.

We were in the hall. The walls were lined with pictures packed together as close as possible. She then pointed to one in particular. It was old, black and white, and had lines across it from being folded and flattened out several times before reaching its home on the wall. In the photo, a thin, dark man with a big mustache stood next to a horse. The man was dressed in what looked like an all-white mariachi suit. He was wearing a large brimmed white hat with roses on the brim. "That's Lucio," Maya said. "I told you he was a cool dude. Just look at him. Original hipster. He made his own clothes. Can you believe it. He looks like some old school Mexican pimp."

"I'd like to pull off that look."

"I'd like to see you try, Chulo." She squeezed my arm again. She pointed out all the characters from her story. At times, she fell into tour-guide mode then caught herself and relaxed back into normal mode. In addition to the pictures of the people in her story, there were pictures of the restaurant in various stages in history, at various stages of renovation. It started out small and dumpy but, over time, more rooms were added as well as the patio area. The place did have a rich history and the story of the skull only added to its charm.

"So when do we get to the skull on this tour?" I asked Maya.

"What did I say about knowing your history?" she stated more than asked. "We'll get to El Mismo in a moment. Haven't you ever heard that anticipation increases response? It's no fun to just walk in and see the skull. You have to build up to it. That way you'll appreciate it more." She then described more pictures to me. I wanted to see the skull but there was another reason for my desperation: I was starving and the sublime smells of the restaurant were a special kind of beautiful torture.

There were two rooms down the hall, one near the middle and one at the end. Both doors were on the right-hand side. The middle room housed a large circular table surrounded by chairs. In the middle of the table was a vase with roses. The room, like the hall, was dark, warm, and elegant in an old world way. It could have been a room in a house. There were more pictures on the wall. Maya noticed my disappointment with the lack of El Mismo in that room. "We don't have to go in there," she said. "That's the Coronado room. It's for private dining parties. The pictures in there are just old pictures of the city and stuff."

Maya led me slowly by the arm to the second room at the end of the hall. Nothing prepared me for what I was about to witness. In the middle of the room was a draped object, undoubtedly El Mismo. The covering was deep red tone, and I could tell that, whatever was underneath it was round; only it was much bigger than a skull. While the draped object had no direct light upon it, the room itself was illuminated by dozens, if not hundreds, of red candles along the walls. There were three levels of them along each wall midway up. The walls had been built out at three intervals allowing for tiered shelves. The hardened red wax from thousands of melted candles over time cascaded down the steps of the encroaching walls at each level. It gave the effect that the walls were bleeding.

On the walls above the candles was a mural in a sequential fashion, starting and ending at the entryway door. I gathered that the mural was the story of El Mismo. It depicted a two-headed newborn child, El Mismo, being handed to startled parents. Then it showed El Mismo as a young child being laughed at by bullies only to be followed by an image of him fighting those same bullies and, in the next image, him standing triumphantly over them as though he had beaten them up. Next was him as a young man. Apparently, he had become something of a town hero. He was dressed nicely and his two heads were strangely odd in their features, with thick brow lines, high cheekbones, large teeth, and strong square jawlines. The townspeople and pretty young girls were fawning over him. Then it showed a beautiful woman in a red dress with roses in her hair dancing in front of El Mismo. Several images followed of the woman either on the left arm or the right arm of El Mismo. The brother whose head was nearest to her smiled while the other head frowned angrily. Then when the girl was on the other side, the expressions switched accordingly. This set of images was followed by one of El Mismo's two heads yelling at each other then, rather gruesomely, an image of him choking himself to death, right arm on the left head's neck and vice versa. That was followed by El Mismo's funeral. All the townspeople were there along with a depiction of his love interest weeping and wailing. Then the grave robbers digging up his grave. The graverobbers looked like zombies. The next image was a woman who looked like a gypsy peering down into the open grave. In it a skeleton lay dressed in a suit built for a body with two heads, and only one skull laying there. The last image showed the skull, large and prominent. The features pronounced in a subtly exaggerated manner, like the images of him when he was alive. A banner encircled the skull with the name "El Mismo" written on it with elegant script. The mural itself was breathtaking, even more so than the one on the ceiling in the dining room.

Maya had patiently waited for me to finish my walk from the beginning of the mural to the end which, of course, placed me at the beginning, right back at Maya. I looked at her and she was smiling gleefully at me. "I love the look on people's faces as they see the mural for the first time," she said.

"This is incredible!" I exclaimed. "It's like the weirdest and coolest comic book I've ever read."

"Then you're going to love this!" She grabbed the red cloth and dramatically yanked it off. As she did, a spotlight instantly came on, shining on the object in the middle of the room. I thought I was prepared for him, after the mural and everything, but, when I saw him, I shook my head in disbelief and, if I'm honest, terror and astonishment. Under the drapery was a solid glass globe sitting in a bed of roses atop a pillar. Set inside the globe was the skull of El Mismo. It was permanently encased in the glass, which gave the illusion that it was floating in midair inside the globe. It was tilted back at a slight angle with the mouth slightly open, as if it were looking up at the light. What I thought were exaggerated features were actually toned down in the mural. The skull had drastically pronounced features at all ends, just like the mural's depiction. The sides were painted with a symmetrical pattern of roses entangled in thorns. On the top of the skull was painted a sun with curvy light rays extending outward. Ravens circled the sun. The face of the skull was painted as though it was cracked, each crack acting as a border to a colored *panel.* The teeth were silver and faceted. They glinted, reflecting the light from the spotlight. The jawline below the teeth had a scene of skeletons dancing in the black night. The detail was unbelievable. There must have been at least fifty of the dancing skeletons, in full detail. The whole skull, with the exception of the teeth, was covered with a shiny seal which made it shine inside the glass.

I stared at the skull, my mouth agape. "That is, by far, the coolest thing I have ever seen in my entire life!" I said. "I can't believe my eyes."

"I told you," Maya said proudly. "You can see why Poppy doesn't want to get rid of it."

"Aren't you afraid someone will knock it over?" The podium looked wooden and light.

"El Mismo won't let you. Go ahead and try."

I thought she was kidding until she stepped up and kicked the podium with her foot, like how cops kick in doors. The podium didn't move, not even a fraction of an inch. I walked up and tried it myself. I gave it a shove. Nothing.

"You better stop or you'll make him angry," Maya said to me. I instantly halted. She chuckled and said, "Just kidding. It's something I tell tourists when they try like you just did. The podium is half-inch-thick steel tubing set in a three-foot-cubed block of concrete with rebar woven through the tubing for extra support. Plus it's filled with concrete to the brim. The skull is secured to the top of the podium with a huge bolt extending from the bottom of the glass, embedded in it, which screws into a nut welded into the surface of the podium. And the globe is a special thick plexiglass, bulletproof even. So even if it falls, it doesn't break, only bounces a bit." She moved some of the roses (which happened to be fake) and exposed the nut and bolt on the bottom. "The exterior is wood laminate, like you would put on your floor. Very durable. If this place was hit by a tornado, God forbid, El Mismo would be the only thing still standing. Poppy spent a lot of money getting it all secured like this."

"When did he do it?"

"Not long ago. Kind of sad, actually. Or maybe ironic. He spent all this money to protect El Mismo and then, right afterward, the whole ghost thing started."

"Why is that ironic?"

"Because of how much he spent to have it done. Then business dropped like crazy and there were no reserves. He never thought it would happen. In fact, he thought that getting El Mismo all done up in the glass globe and everything would be an investment, would bring in more tourists."

I couldn't stop staring at the skull. "Can I take a picture of it?" I asked.

"Well, we don't let customers take pics of it, never have. That's why you don't see any pictures of it in the hall, or anywhere for that matter. And the painting on the wall looks like an artist's rendering of a skull. Grandpa Tavo realized that, after the skull was painted and treated and on display, he could create a buzz with a show of sorts, starting in the hall with the pictures then to the mural as he told the story of El Mismo, all leading up to the reveal of El Mismo himself in all his glory."

"So is that a *yes* or a *no?*" I asked regarding the picture.

"Do you swear not to show anyone?"

"I swear."

"Pinky swear?" She held up her pinky.

"Pinky swear," I said and grabbed her pinky with mine.

"Bueno pues. Have at it."

I pulled my phone out of my pocket and clicked the button to get it going. I stared at it for a few moments before remembering that it was broken. Then I remembered *why* it was broken and I slowly returned it to my pocket.

"What's the matter? You afraid El Mismo will haunt your phone?"

"No. I forgot that my phone is broken. Broke on the way here, won't turn on."

"What did you do? Drop it in the toilet?"

I didn't answer.

"You did, didn't you?" This amused Maya to no end. "And you're carrying that toilet phone in your pocket? *Cochino marrano!*"

I stayed silent.

"Don't feel bad. It happens to the best of us."

"You've done it too?"

"Nope."

Maya placed the red cloth back on the display and the spotlight went out. Must have had a sensor somewhere under the drapery, simple enough.

"You said your dad moved El Mismo. So he just unscrewed it and put it in another room?"

"Yep."

"Are you ever afraid someone will steal it?"

"Not really. It's so unique, everyone would know where it came from. No one would be able to sell it."

I pondered the ghost element. "You said there was a camera?"

"Yeah, right up there." She pointed to a corner of the room. I could make out a small black security camera with a wire coming out of it. The camera had a light shield above the lens, like the ones used for outside, but not as big. Near the camera was a small shelf, built specifically for a small black box set atop it. The box was about double the size of a deck of cards. The camera wire disappeared behind the black box. I figured it plugged into it. Another wire came from the back of the black box and into a hole that was cut into the wall. The hole was about an inch wide with a grommet that had a rubber fitting inside of it with a hole for the wire to thread through.

Maya grabbed onto my arm again, startling me. I looked at her. She was even prettier in the flicker of candlelight. "I'm going to go tell Mamita to make us something to eat. I hope you like Mexican food because that's what you're getting." As she was leaving the room, she said, "Meet me at the bar so you can taste the Poison." I was walking out but stopped and looked back at El Mismo and the camera. It was all too weird. Something didn't make sense, but I didn't know what it could be. A chill went up my spine and I made a beeline for the bar.

8 | Pequito

Maya was right. Calavera's Poison tasted awful and packed a punch. I was one and done. I still had to drive Chuck's bus so I didn't want to get sloshed. I figured some food should get me back to square one by the time I had to leave.

Dinner was absolutely, positively amazing! Maya's mom made me a combination plate. And she was right, her mom was good at what she did. The plate was the size of a hubcap and had six different items on it: red enchiladas, green enchiladas, a flauta, a taco, chile con carne, and a thing called a *chile relleno* (which I had never heard of before) as well as beans and rice. There was a little bit of lettuce and tomato, not much. I got guacamole as a bonus. No one would accuse Calavera's of being a health food joint. The best part of the whole thing was the chile relleno. It was a green chile stuffed with cheese then breaded and fried. Like a giant jalapeño popper, only better. Maya said some people even roll them in a tortilla and make a burrito out of them. That sounded like a heart attack waiting to happen. It also sounded delicious.

After dinner, Maya said we needed to stop by her house to pick up some clothes and Piquito. Her house was isolated in a way. It sat by itself in the middle of a big field of trees. The nearest neighbor must have been at least a hundred yards away, maybe two hundred yards. She had me wait outside because she said her dad might not be doing so hot. He wasn't.

"You can meet him tomorrow, OK?" she said as she hopped back into the bus. She had a Chihuahua dog in a big purse which she had slung on one shoulder, a backpack over the other. She held the purse up to me and said, "This is Piquito. Say 'Hi' Piquito!" Piquito said nothing, just shivered.

"He's cute," I said. Piquito barked.

"He's not cute, he's handsome."

"Oh, sorry. He's handsome." Piquito didn't bark at that comment.

"He's super smart too. Aren't you, Piquito?" Piquito looked up and tried to lick Maya's nose. "You'd be surprised how smart he is. If he had thumbs, he could solve one of those Rubik's Cubes." I seriously doubted that, but I could see Maya believed it with all her heart. She fawned over him.

"What does *Piquito* mean?" I asked her.

"Something that pokes, but small. Like a beak or a thorn."

"Why do you call him Piquito?"

She held him up and pointed to his male parts. "See?" she said joyfully, "Piquito!" Piquito barked. "He gets mad when I do that. I think it's because we had him fixed. He's sensitive about his manhood."

"I would be too," I said with all honesty, partly sympathetic for Piquito. Maya shot me a knowing grin and set Piquito, bag and all, in the seat behind us.

"You stay back there," she told him. He didn't put up a fight.

We drove slowly back to the hotel. I wanted to extend our time together. Maya said I drove like an old man, but I told her I was worried that a cop would stop me and arrest me because of the shot of Calavera's Poison that I had. She called me a lightweight.

At the hotel, I parked next to her car and we got out. I walked her around the back of her car to the driver's side. "What are you doing tomorrow?" I asked.

"I don't know. What *am* I doing tomorrow?" She put Piquito and her backpack in her car.

"You're going to tell me about *Día De Los Muertos.*"

"Oh, yeah. And you're going to tell me about the Grateful Dead. And meet Poppy."

"And meet Poppy. And then you and I are going to go out on a date." I tried to look confident and collected.

"Well, where are you going to take me?"

"Do you have a strip bar around these parts?" I smiled at her and she hit me in the arm.

"Are you always this fresh with girls you just met?"

"Honestly? No. Actually, never. Usually, I need to really get to know a girl and she has to really know me before I even try to flirt with her. You're different though. In a good way. I feel comfortable around you. And free to be myself."

"Me too."

"No sex," I said and held up my hand. "High five." She giggled and gave me a high five but then held onto my hand, interlacing her fingers with mine. I pulled her hand around and kissed the back of it. "Have fun with Bibi," I said. "And Piquito." She bit her lip, looked up at me, and breathed in deep. She didn't say anything, just got in her car and drove away. For a moment I thought that maybe I was a bit too forward but then thought, *Hey, what do you have to lose?*

I stood out in the night air for a spell, just going over the day. I didn't know what time it was because my only clock was on my phone. But it must have been ten or eleven. The day I just experienced felt like a lifetime. A good lifetime. I smiled thinking about Maya and remembered that I wanted to look up the word *chulo*. I contemplated running up to my room to look it up on my computer, and checking my email and Facebook and all that. But then I thought, *why ruin this moment by trying to cram social media into it?* Needless to say, I thought better of it. I simply went up to my room and went to bed.

9 | Wednesday

I slept like a log and woke up early, 6:00 AM, and confused as to my surroundings. For a moment I had forgotten where I was and, in a way, thought the whole Maya/El Mismo thing was just some glorious dream. But it was real. I lay there reveling in the moment. I was on the best vacation of my life, and it had only just begun. How could it possibly get any better?

I assumed that Maya wasn't a morning person. She just seemed like the type of girl who would sleep in. I don't know why. Call it stereotyping. We all do it, right? With that in mind, I outlined a brief plan to poke around town until lunchtime. Do some discovering. I had a vehicle after all. Why not make the most of it?

I liked where I was staying and thought that it would be easiest to just stay there. I went to the counter and told the clerk that I wanted to stay for two more nights. The prices were actually pretty cheap, sixty bucks a night. So I was only out one-twenty before taxes, maybe one fifty total. Not bad. That left me with three fifty to eat and have fun, if I wanted to spend it all on the vacation. A big part of me wanted to. By that, I mean I wanted to spend it on doing stuff with Maya.

After taking full advantage of the hotel's continental

breakfast, I headed out in the VW bus. At one point, it dawned on me that the bus might not have a license plate on it. What do people do when they sell a car? Does the old license plate stay on? Do you take it off? I pulled over and jumped out to see. There was a license plate and it was current. I guess Jared didn't care. Then I thought that perhaps it was something Chuck took care of with him to get it back to Colorado. In any case, I was legal.

Not having a phone was actually liberating. I wasn't constantly checking to see if I had texts or playing a game or jumping on Facebook. There was a slight problem with knowing what time it was. I decided that, since I had an extra three hundred plus dollars, maybe I'd pick up a watch. Then I remembered that, eventually, I was going to need another phone. Not to get too deep into it, but the phone plan I have is with this online company that Chuck told me about. It's a way cheaper service but I have to use their phones. And to get one of their phones, I would have to go online and order one. And to do that, I'd have to go and deposit the money I had into the bank and order the phone, which would leave me without much spending money. I split the difference: deposited half of the money, about one hundred seventy-five, into my bank account and pocketed the rest. I'd have to wait for it to clear and, when it did, I could buy one of the cheaper phones. Or just wait and use part of my next paycheck and get the same one I had. All that to say that I decided against a watch or a phone at that moment in time. I went *time naked*.

Even though I was resolved to not try to contact Maya until after noon, that didn't stop me from thinking about her. Kind of hard not to. Here was this beautiful girl who was fun and charming and feisty. And, to add to it, she seemed to like me. For what reason, I don't know but she did. I'm no stud and I don't have money or power, and she could pretty much have any guy she wanted. I winced at the seemingly absurd thought that she liked me romantically. But then I thought, *she doesn't know anything about me other than what she's seen so far. Maybe she* could *like me.* That was empowering and bolstered my confidence. I sat up straight in the driver's seat and drove just a little faster than I had been.

The city of Las Cruces bustled on a Wednesday morning, at least the traffic did. There were lots of cars on the streets. And lots of stoplights. I was surprised at how many. It seemed like every few hundred yards was another stoplight. And it felt like they were all red. Luckily the weather was gorgeous and driving around in a VW bus with the windows down made me something of an attraction. One girl even yelled to me from her car, "Nice ride, dude!" and shot me a peace sign. I shot one back. Why not?

While filling up on gas, I asked someone if there was a mall in town. I felt like spending money on something. I didn't know what, just something so I could say, "Oh, this? I got it in Las Cruces." I was directed in a general location and headed there. Unfortunately, the mall in Las Cruces is not the most hopping place on a Wednesday morning at 10:00 AM. Well, that's not completely true. There were a fair number of old people walking briskly for exercise.

Most of the stores were chains so it wouldn't mean anything if I picked up something like a shirt from any of them as they have the same stores back home. I went into one of the clothing stores to ask a worker there what places were cool to go to in Las Cruces. There was no one in there so I just browsed, waiting for someone to notice me. I thought, *anyone can just come in here and steal stuff and no one would even know.* That made me look around for security cameras. There were three: one in the entryway corner facing in, one in the back of the store facing out, and one facing the cash register. The cameras looked like the one that was fixed on El Mismo, only these were white. I got up as close as I could to one. It had a sticker on the side that said "STAR SERIES 1100." The *T* was a star shape. The sticker was cut along the edges of the letters and star. It was thick and stood out from the surface of the camera.

A girl came out from the back, fixated on her phone. She didn't even notice me until she almost ran into me. "Whoa," she said startled, "how long have you been standing there?"

"Just a few minutes."

"Sorry. Usually no one even shows up until after eleven." She shrugged with a *what do you expect* look on her face. "How can I help you? We have pants on sale, two for one. What are you, a thirty-two waist? Thirty-four?"

"Thirty-four. But I don't need pants. Actually, could I ask you a question?"

"I have a boyfriend."

"No, it's about the security cameras."

"Oh, sorry. Habit. I get a lot of creepers who come in when the store is empty. What about the security cameras? You're not going to rob me, are you? Because that would be dumb to rob a store at opening. No sales, empty register."

"Nothing like that. I just saw a setup just like the one you have here. Well, almost like the one you have, except there was a wire that went from the camera into a little black box, about this size," I recreated the size of the box at Calavera's in the air with my hands. "Then another wire went from the box into a hole in the wall. Do you guys have a little black box? What is it?"

"We don't have a little black box, it's a big computer thingy. The cameras plug into that and the box plugs into the wall. There is one TV that shows all the angles. The computer is a recorder. It stores all the video. I don't know how far back. The manager knows all that stuff because she has to look at it every so often to see if people are stealing."

"All the video is in the box?"

"Yeah. Where else would it be?"

"And the box is big?"

"Yeah. Like a big ol' computer." She formed an imaginary cube in the air in front of her, about the size of a standard desktop computer.

"And the computer is hooked up to a TV with a wire?"

"Yeah."

"So there's a wire from each camera to the box then one wire from the box to a TV and another wire that plugs into the wall?"

"Yeah. I'm no tech geek but even I can figure out how it all works." She walked up close to me. "Are you some plainclothes cop or something?" She was cute and young, around eighteen or nineteen, eager for drama.

I was going to tell her I was just curious but decided to embellish the situation. "Can you keep a secret?" I whispered to her. She looked at me wide-eyed and nodded. "I'm an outside investigator trying to crack a criminal case in Old Mesilla."

"The case of the Sugar Skull Ghost Thief?" she cried out loud.

"Shhh!" I chastised her. "Do you want to blow my cover?" I asked her acting like a cop. I wasn't on the high school drama team for nothing. She shrunk and shook her head. I felt sorry for her. What cover was she going to blow? All I had to do was act and she reacted accordingly, without much thought to the content I was speaking. "Can I see the television that displays the camera feeds?" She looked around to see if anyone was looking at us and then nodded.

She led me into the back of the store. Poor girl. She was gullible. What if I was some guy lying just to lure her into the back of the store? Then I realized I was pretty much that. Well,

I *was* an outside investigator of sorts. And I never claimed to be a cop. Still, this poor girl was naive and I guess I was taking advantage of that fact. She might even get fired for doing what she was doing but my concern was higher for Maya than for this girl. She opened a door that had a plaque on it that read "OFFICE". Inside was a desk with papers littered all over it along with used to-go coffee cups and other random items. Whoever was the manager wasn't too tidy. Nor discreet. And worse yet, absent, which allowed me this privilege.

I looked at the computer. Seemed like a basic PCU. There were USB port wires from the cameras plugged into it, a VGA output, which had the monitor plugged into it, a power source with the wire plugged into the wall, and, in the front, another USB port with a mouse attached to it. The camera wires came in from a hole in one of the tiles of the suspended ceiling. I hadn't paid attention to cameras before then, but I got the gist of it. I looked at the monitor. The image was slightly grainy with a running timestamp on the lower left-hand side. It showed no one in the store.

The girl hovered close over my shoulder. "Have you seen the ghost?" she asked, giddy.

"Not first hand but let's just say I have a source that's close to it all."

"Have you seen El Mismo?"

"Yes."

"It's super crazy, ain't it? All painted and creepy like. A real skull!"

I didn't respond.

"Do you have a badge?" she asked me.

"Don't need one," I replied. "I'm a private investigator, a P.I."

"That's kinda sexy," she said and traced her finger on my back. What was it with this place? Why couldn't girls act like this back home? Then again, I'd never told anyone I was a P.I. back home. Maybe that should be my new approach.

I saw what I needed to see and turned to go. "Listen," I told the girl as she looked up at me with hungry eyes, "I'm on a case. You're a pretty girl and all but I have to focus." Then, in an overly dramatic way and in a deep voice I said, "Old Mesilla needs me." She shivered at that and smiled, tracing her finger up and down my arm. "Besides," I added, looking suspiciously at her, "didn't you say you had a boyfriend?"

"I was just saying that because I thought you were a creeper."

I didn't respond to that directly but instead thanked her for her time and for showing me the computer.

I brushed past her and out of the store. On any other day, I would have done backflips to have a girl come onto me like that. But I kept on thinking about Maya and her promise to herself. There was a purity in it that the mall girl didn't have. She was looking for something I wasn't wanting to give, not then and there. Not with Maya on my mind.

As I left the mall, it hit me. When I went in as just a normal guy possibly interested in her, I was considered a *creeper* as she put it. But, when I misled her to make her think I was something I wasn't—essentially being a *real* creep—she was attracted to me. Maybe it wasn't about being creepy. Food for thought.

10 | Ghost

I still had a couple of hours before my predetermined *find Maya* time so I decided to go back to my hotel room and work on the commercial. I was no further than I was the day before, and my progress wasn't all that far then. I also wanted to check emails and Facebook. And, of course, I wanted to look up that *chulo* word.

When I got back to the hotel, the maids had already cleaned up my room. It was nice to walk into a clean, cool, crisp environment. I threw the keys on the dresser and headed into the bathroom. I turned on the light only to find a figure draped in a white sheet with it's arms up, reaching out to me. "Muahahahaha!" the figure laughed in an eerie deep woman's voice. I just about jumped out of my pants and let out an indistinguishable holler as I instinctively retreated backwards out of the bathroom, tripping on the edging of the carpet where it met the bathroom tile. I fell on my butt and scrambled back as the figure headed toward me, preparing to strike.

Then the figure stood straight up and started laughing heartily. I was confused. What was this? An apparition? A burglar? The cleaning lady playing a trick on me? The figure pulled the sheet off to reveal herself. It was Maya! She continued to laugh, even doubling over. "I got you, *Chulo!* I got you good!"

I got to my feet and composed myself. "That's not funny, Maya. What if I had fallen back and hit my head and died?"

"Then *you* could come scare *me* as a *real* ghost!" She smiled, still chuckling inside. I was legitimately angry but couldn't help but soften up to her, seeing her so playfully happy. I thought of how she planned the whole thing, getting into my room and waiting patiently for me to return. It was actually sweet and endearing. I had to laugh.

"Let me feel how fast your heart is beating," she said and stepped up close to me, placing her fingers on my neck to feel my pulse. "Wow! Must be one hundred eighty beats per second. You're officially a rave!" She looked up at me, into my eyes while still holding her hand on my neck. "Feel mine," she said and held my hand to her neck. "Well?" she inquired.

"Feels fast to me but I don't know how fast it's supposed to be."

"It's fast," she clarified. "It's exciting to scare someone. Almost as exciting as being scared." We stood there feeling each other's pulse and looking into each other's eyes. She lifted her hand to my face and gave me a gentle slap. "You better go use the bathroom. That is, unless you just did in your pants."

"Luckily," I replied, "no, I didn't." I used the bathroom and, when I came out, she was sitting on the bed with the remote control, flipping through channels. Piquito was lying on the bed next to Maya's purse, the one that doubled as his carriage. She must have hid him in the closet or under the bed. He seemed well-behaved and calm.

"I didn't see your car," I said. "Did you drive here?"

"Yeah. I parked in the back so you wouldn't see it." She was fiddling around with the remote. "Do you watch TV? Like *TV* TV? With commercials and everything?"

"No. Usually just Netflix or movies."

"Same here. And now I know why. It's pretty much all commercials and crap. I was watching it earlier while I waited for you. There's absolutely nothing of value on that thing." She gestured toward the TV with the remote control while pushing the power button to turn it off.

"How did you get in here?"

"I know people." She winked at me. "By that I mean that I came up here and waited for the cleaning lady to get to your room and I told her I was staying here and she just let me in, no questions asked."

"That doesn't make me feel safe."

"Safety is an illusion."

"And so is a girl dressed up like a ghost."

"True."

"Where did you get the sheet?"

"From your bed. I took it off and made up the bed without it."

"Oh. So I have to put it back on? Where is it?"

"I already put it on."

That confused me. I was only in the bathroom for a minute, two minutes max. "You already remade the bed with the sheet on it? That was quick."

"My people are quick and efficient," Maya stated proudly then paused and added, "when we want to be."

"Are you Mexican?" As soon as I asked it, I regretted it, felt like it was an offensive question, me being white and everything. It just felt like I was being racist somehow. "Is that," I stammered, trying to recover, "something I can ask?"

"Why not? Mexico is a country like any other country. Would you feel bad about asking someone if they were Canadian or Nigerian? Being Mexican, or of Mexican descent, isn't a bad thing. You know my dad is American since I told you about the Calaveras going back to the nineteen-twenties. My mom, however, was born in Mexico and came over when she was a teenager. So I'm not Mexican really, but that's where my mom and ancestors are from." She noticed I was uncomfortable. "And yes, that's something you can ask."

"I guess there's all this weird stuff about Mexicans and everything. Like immigration and all that. I never know if I'm being racist if I say anything. About anyone, really. Mexicans, black people, Asians…"

"I guess it depends on what you say."

"I just don't say anything. Or try not to say anything. When you say your people are quick and efficient when they want to be, you're making an inside observation. If *I* were to say it, I would be stereotyping."

"I can see that. But there's one thing you have to remember." She looked directly at me. "We are a resilient and diligent people, the Latinos. And we're used to people looking down on us and thinking we're second class citizens. I'm not complaining or being a baby about it. It's just, as you put it, an inside observation. But instead of getting our panties all in a knot, we simply carry on, move forward. We work. We serve. We learn and grow. I can't speak for every Latino out there but I can speak for the ones I know. The basic philosophy is to power through and one day our hard work will pay off. At least that's what I believe."

It was an impassioned speech. I just stood there absorbing it. "Now, here's something else you need to know," she added, "and I'll just speak for myself here. When I work, I work hard, efficiently, effectively, and purposefully. And when I slack, I slack hard, efficiently, effectively, and purposefully. It's a double-edged sword."

Again I said nothing. Just listened.

"And," she said in an exaggerated tone, "I've learned that I can apply my work ethic to whatever I want. It doesn't have to be the restaurant. I don't want it to be the restaurant. I want to go into medicine. I want to be a doctor. That's why I want to go to UNM. Nothing against my parents. They've worked long and hard to make the business work. And they've done everything they could to provide for me. But it's so volatile and fragile. If I were a doctor, I wouldn't have to worry about customers not coming in because of some stupid ghost. At least I seriously doubt any doctor would."

"I never thought of that," I replied. "If you think about it, doctors are anti-ghosts. If there is any profession that is a ghostbuster, it would be doctors. They solve the issue of ghosts by doing what they can to prevent death to begin with."

Maya's eyes widened and glinted. "I like that," she said joyfully. "I'm not going to be a doctor as much as I'll be a real life ghostbuster! I ain't afraid of no patients!" She laughed at her own joke. "Oh, here," she said handing me a slip of paper. "It's your roommate Chuck's phone number. He wants you to call him. He called Jared last night, told him he couldn't get a hold of you. Wanted to know if you ran off with his seven thousand dollars. I told Jared about your phone dying and he let Chuck know. Chuck still wants you to call him to let him know what's going on."

I held the number in my hand. I couldn't remember the last time I had to make a long distance call without my cell phone. How much did that cost? Maya noticed my concern and handed me her phone. "Use my phone," she said. Easy enough.

I called Chuck and told him everything was OK and that I would be staying for a few days and that I'd let him know exactly when I was heading back so that he could be on the lookout in case I stalled or anything. I also thanked him for the opportunity to come to Las Cruces and Old Mesilla. He didn't really care, just wanted to know when I'd be back with his bus.

"Keep it safe, dude," was pretty much all he said.

"Let's go see Poppy," Maya said. "He's feeling better today. And you drive again. I like it when you drive me around in that thing. I feel like a flower child." She started to dance around like a hippy. Piquito looked on contently.

11 | Lalo

The southern New Mexico weather at this time of year was warm with a tinge of cool. Maya was dressed in jeans and a sweater that hugged her form nicely. Part of me thought that she wore it on purpose, knowing I had a weakness for her already. Or maybe she just wore it to wear it. Maybe I think too much.

We headed on down to her house. The fact that I was getting used to the bus, coupled with the fact that Maya mentioned she liked riding around in it, bolstered my confidence. I was driving casually and faster than before with few hiccups, if any. We drove with the windows down. Piquito rode on the floor between us. Sometimes I could hear him jump onto the back seat and stand up against the side panels to look out the window but then he'd hop down and rest again between us. I couldn't figure him out. He was enigmatic, just like Maya.

Maya's house was humble. It was an older home, made of adobe like the restaurant. It wasn't in a neighborhood really, more like a farm. It was set inside of an orchard of sorts. I didn't get a good look at the surroundings the night before because it was dark. Maya told me that the trees were pecan trees and that they harvested the pecans and sold them. I asked her why they were worried about the restaurant if they had the pecans. She said that the pecans didn't bring in enough money for them to live on and that it cost money to harvest them. There was a machine they used to shake the trees so that the pecans dropped and another machine picked them up. Not all the trees were theirs, either. They had sold off part of the farm already because of the lull in business. She said her dad was thinking about selling the rest off as well if things didn't pick up.

If Mr. Calavera was ill, he sure didn't show it. He seemed a bit fatigued, but his attitude seemed bright. Maya introduced me to him and he shook my hand. "Eduardo Calavera," he said cheerfully. "But they call me Lalo." Piquito was at our feet and ran to Lalo who greeted him fondly.

"Percy Kale," I replied, "but they call me Perk."

"Perk?" he asked, "Like coffee?"

"Yes." I couldn't tell if he meant that my name was like a percolator or if he was asking if I liked coffee. He smiled, revealing a silver-capped tooth. I was reminded of El Mismo's silver teeth. "Come in," he added and welcomed me into his kitchen and invited me to sit down. Maya sat next to me and rubbed her knee against mine.

Lalo went to the stove and picked up a sauce pan and poured the contents into a mug and handed it to me. Everything he did was slow and methodical. I thanked him and took a sip, did my best to hide my reaction. It was boiling hot and super strong.

"That's cowboy coffee," he said gruffly.

"It's…" I wanted to lie and say I liked it but I'm no good at lying. "It's hot and strong. I can't say I like it. May take some getting used to. Maybe some cream and sugar?" I took another small sip.

Mr. Calavera looked at Maya and winked. He reached

over and took my cup from me. "You're an honest and humble man," he said as he poured the coffee down the sink drain. He then went to a coffee pot and poured a cup of coffee out of the carafe. He brought cream and sugar and set them down on the table.

Maya was smiling. She looked at me and said, "He does that to all the guys I bring home. It's his test. If they act like they're all manly and pretend like it doesn't bother them, it's a red flag. To Poppy, that is."

"And how many times have I been wrong?" Mr. Calavera asked Maya with pride.

"You're *always* right, Poppy." Maya got up and went to her father and kissed him on the cheek. He happily allowed it, gleaming with pride.

Mr. Calavera then poured his own cup of coffee from the carafe and dumped the cowboy coffee down the drain. "No one drinks cowboy coffee unless they have to," he said as he sat down across from me. Maya sat back down beside me, knee to knee again. She was obviously communicating that she liked me, possibly hinting for me to get on with asking him about our date.

"I like your restaurant, Mr. Calavera," I said.

"Lalo," he replied. I felt odd calling him by his first name but, if he insisted, I wasn't going to deny it.

"Lalo." I said. I didn't mention El Mismo because I didn't want to upset him.

"Did you see El Mismo? He's neat, *que no?*" he asked.

"He's amazing," I replied. "Absolutely amazing. I love the history."

"It's not history, it's a legacy." He shot a glance at Maya but she acted like she didn't notice it. He looked back at me. "But all good things must come to an end, *verdad?*" At that Maya looked quizzically at him. He added enthusiastically,

"We move forward!"

We talked a little about Old Mesilla and Las Cruces. Lalo was enamored with the region and spoke highly of it. Every so often Maya bumped my knee with her knee, hinting at me to get to asking. I liked Lalo but I had never asked a girl's father if I could take his daughter out. When a break in the conversation arose, I said, "Lalo, I would very much like to take Maya out on a date. May I?"

Lalo looked at me as if I was asking the silliest question in the world. "Maya said you are from Colorado and that you are only here for a few days. Is that right?"

"Yes."

"Well, what are your intentions. If you're only here for a few days, what do you hope to accomplish in that time with my daughter?"

"Sir, I don't hope to accomplish anything. I only want to take her out on a date."

"So you're admitting that you have no plans for the future?"

I felt that he was either playing with me or seriously feeling me out. "Well, you're right. I don't have plans for me and your daughter for the future. I can't guarantee the future and, even if I did have big plans, those plans would involve Maya's input as well. All I can say is that you have a beautiful, smart, clever, charming daughter and I would be a fool to *not* try to spend time with her. Even one date would make a memory I would cherish forever. You too are a man so I'm sure you understand."

Lalo looked at me through squinted eyes. "Perk," he said, "I like you. Too bad you didn't come earlier. I could have used a man like you at Calavera's. With Maya leaving to school, *que no?*"

Maya looked at her father again confused.

"Is that a *yes?*" I asked him.

"Claro que si," he said. Maya looked at me and nodded. She

wanted to go. I could see it in her eyes. She loved her father, but she didn't want to spend too much time at her house.

"Thank you," I told Lalo. He sat back in his chair.

Maya and I got up to go. Lalo went to get up as well, albeit with much labor. "Don't get up, Poppy," Maya said as she bent over and kissed his forehead. "I'll be back soon to see you."

"Leave Piquito here," he said to her. "He keeps me company."

12 | Green Chile Cheeseburgers

Maya and I headed nowhere in particular. She was pensive and quiet. I was getting hungry so I just drove and kept my eye out for a restaurant that might catch my interest.

"I don't get it," she said, breaking the silence. "He's been depressed this whole time then, all of a sudden, he's doing OK. And what's with all this past tense talk?"

"Past tense?" I asked.

"Yeah. He said 'All good things come to an end,' and 'Too bad you didn't come earlier.'"

"Hm," I replied simply out of acknowledgement.

"It's like he's given up or something. Or has some sort of plan that he hasn't shared with me. I mean, he even talked about me going to school as if it were no big deal. He's been fighting me on that this whole time."

"Do you think he's just putting on a good face?"

"You don't know Poppy. He may not be the most successful or prominent man on earth but, if anything, he's honest. He'd rather die than lie."

"So you think something's going on?"

"I *know* something's going on."

"Maybe he just got better. Like a miracle. Maybe he's

feeling up to going back to running the restaurant, and he has ideas to make it work."

"It's not like he's just depressed," Maya spoke slowly and quietly. "He's sick for real. Not just psychological, but physical. Mamita and I think it's cirrhosis of the liver. You don't get better, you can only hope to not get worse." She paused for a moment. "He's a drinking man. He had cut back for a while but, with all this ghost stuff, he got back to drinking big time. He's getting worse. He won't see a doctor, but I see all the signs. I'm pre-med, remember?"

"Then what?"

"I don't know. He probably wouldn't tell me if I asked him. He'll just say that everything will be fine. If he's down, everything will be fine. If he's up, everything will be fine. It's his standard answer. Drives me crazy." She looked out her window. I instinctively reached over and squeezed her hand, not romantically, but for comfort. She squeezed back and sighed heavily.

"Can I ask you something?" I said.

"Ask away." She was still looking out of the window.

"Why do you think this is happening? The ghost and all."

"Beats the hell out of me. Maybe the ghost is anxious or angry or who knows."

"You think it's really a ghost?"

"I saw the video. There's a ghost that comes out of the skull and floats away. Floats back after it's done its business."

I noticed a burger joint by some railroad tracks called "Spikes" and pulled in. Maya didn't protest.

"You hungry?" I asked her. She nodded and squeezed my hand and let it go so I could downshift.

We got a table inside. In any other city, that restaurant would be considered a dive, but Las Cruces had a strange rough edge to it which made the place seem right at home. Maya ordered me a green chile cheeseburger with fries. She didn't even look at the menu. Must be a staple around these parts.

"What exactly does the ghost do?" I asked, continuing with my questioning.

"Petty crimes mostly," Maya said. The waitress brought us chips and salsa which I thought was a nice touch. The salsa was hot. Maya attacked the chips. She was small but she could put down some food. "Mostly breaking and entering," she continued, "stealing random stuff like framed pictures and blankets or even flowers. Weird selection. Or it will deface something like a car or a wall or a bathroom. The problem is not the size of the crimes but the frequency. It's been consistently twice a week. Sometimes three times. Weird, though. It hasn't happened for a week now. I didn't even realize it until now."

"Aren't people on the lookout?"

"They are. And that's the problem. People are actually witnessing this thing as it roams through the streets."

"And not one has tackled it or anything?"

"Old Mesilla is a very superstitious town. That and it's filled with old people. Put those two things together and there's not a lot of ghost tackling going on."

"What about pictures?"

"There are a few but it's tough to see since it's always at night."

"How is it described?"

"Are you a cop? You ask questions like a cop." Maya broke a smile.

"No. But I did tell a girl at the mall that I was a private investigator," I admitted.

"You what?"

"I told her I was a private investigator cracking the case of the Sugar Skull Ghost Thief."

"Why did you tell her that? Were you hitting on her?" If I

didn't know better, I would have said that Maya had a hint of jealousy in her voice. I won't lie. It felt good.

"She was working in a store that had security cameras like the one you guys have recording El Mismo. I wanted to see their set up so I told her I was a private investigator. Which is not a lie, really. I *am* private and I *am* investigating…in a way."

Maya gave me a look as if to say, *You dog!*

I shook my head. "I wasn't hitting on her. But she got all hot and bothered when I told her I was a P.I. and she started to come onto me."

Maya raised her eyebrows.

"I told her that Old Mesilla needed me and I left. Then you made me almost piss my pants by scaring me in my hotel room."

That made Maya let out a genuine smile. "I guess I can't blame her. The mall girl, that is. I mean, look at you. ¡*Que chulo!*" She pinched my cheek again and winked at me.

I told Maya how the camera was set up and how it had a big box, not a small box like the one at Calavera's. I told her that the small box may house a Raspberry Pi—basically just a tiny computer that people use for all sorts of things. My roommate Chuck used one to watch movies and TV shows that he downloaded via bit torrent.

"You said Esteban set up the system?" I asked her.

"Yep. And he's the one that showed us the ghost video."

"He's the sommelier?"

"Yep."

"Where did he show you the video?"

"On his laptop. He hooked it up to the back of the little box and showed us. He had to climb up on a ladder because the box is screwed into the shelf it sits on." That seemed odd to me.

"I saw a wire come from that black box, went into a hole in the wall. Do you know what that goes to?"

"Esteban said it's the power wire. He said that he had to hardwire it in since the plug on the wall is covered by the shelves that hold the candles. He also said that he didn't want to have the wire dangling over the paintings on the wall."

That made some sense. Something hit me though. "How did he hardwire it in? Is there a room behind that room?"

"No," Maya answered puzzled. "It's just the back of the building."

"Did he have to tear apart the wall back there?"

"I don't remember him doing that. He was done in like five minutes so I doubt it. That room was an addition. It's not adobe, just regular walls so it probably wasn't that hard to do. I was working that day. I just thought he was super smart."

"I'd like to see the video," I said. "Where is Esteban?"

"He's in town now but he hops back and forth from here to Phoenix where his parents live. He leaves again tonight. Hence my double-double."

"We need to catch him before he goes. I'd like to see that video."

"I'll text him and tell him to meet us at the restaurant," Maya said, pulling out her phone from her back pocket. "He likes showing the videos."

"Quick question: has the ghost struck when Esteban was out of town?"

"Yeah, a bunch of times."

"So you don't think he has anything to do with it?"

"If it's not a ghost and it's just some guy messing with us, no. I know for a fact he went to Phoenix. He even delivered a gift for me to a cousin of mine who lives there when he went once. And the ghost struck that same night he was there."

Maya texted Esteban. He texted back immediately and we were set to meet him at Calavera's shortly. We ate our green chile cheeseburgers (which were awesome, by the way) and headed down to Calavera's to meet up with Esteban.

13 | The Ganchos

We arrived at Calavera's before Esteban. Maya said she wanted to go see her mom. I told her I would hang out and look around.

I went to the bar simply because I wanted to check it out. The couple of times I was there, I was preoccupied. Now, I could just kick back and look at things. I liked bars and pubs. I liked to see how they are decorated and stocked and lit, what sort of bar top and stools they used. Were there games? TVs? Mirrors? I loved all that stuff, how it added up to create a vibe.

There was only one customer in the bar, the pudgy guy with the old black t-shirt. He seemed to be keeping to himself. Jared nodded to me and I nodded back and bellied up. "Want a drink, Traveling Man?" he asked with a grin. He was standing in the middle of the bar, I was towards the end near the entrance.

"Shouldn't," I said. "I'm trying to stretch the few dollars I have left."

"On the house." He slapped the bar top and poured a generous shot of Calavera's Poison into a lowball glass and slid it across the bar. It stopped dead center in front of me. Damn, he was good. I looked at him and he gave me a confident wink, as if to say *Did you expect anything less?*

I sipped on the Poison, choking it down. Wouldn't have been my first choice for a drink but I'm not one to look a gift horse in the mouth. I scanned my surroundings. The room was dark and elegant in an odd way. I couldn't explain it. Almost as if it were a tavern in another country, but I couldn't say where. I swiveled around on my stool to look behind me. There were paintings on the wall, not photographs like in the hall and the other dining room. The paintings were hauntingly strange. They were portraits of people, possibly nobles, possibly family members. The artist was not all that good so the people looked somewhat out of proportion or deformed. One painting depicted a man whose nose lay flat on his face, his nostrils open to the front, like a pig. Another had a woman with her breasts down at her waist. They all had oddities like that.

"Admiring the artwork?" Jared said to my back, startling me.

"Can't say I'm admiring. The artist has a weird way of painting people."

"He paints them exactly as they are, or were. That's what I hear."

I turned to look at Jared to see if he was joking. He looked stoic and serious, peering at the paintings. "I obtained these paintings on a trip to Mexico a few months back," he said. "I visited the village where, as legend has it, El Mismo lived. A little place called *Hoja Ojo*. Means *leaf eye* or *eye leaf*. Whichever. It's a ghost town for the most part. The only people that live there now are transients and rejects, misfits."

"Ghost town?" I said. "How appropriate." I smiled at my own quip. Jared didn't respond, he simply continued.

"You know what a *bruja* is?"

I did. A friend back home, Cal, used that term for women who can put a trance on you. "Means *witch*, right?"

"It does," he said leaning over to me as if speaking

confidentially. "I met one down in Hoja Ojo," he said in a hushed tone. "She was a medium too. Psychic. I'm sure Maya told you the story, right? El Mismo the two-headed man and the skull and the psychic?"

"Yes."

"Well, this was one such psychic but she was a full-on witch. They're for real." At this point he had stood back up straight and abandoned his clandestine manner of speaking. In fact, if anything, he was more gregarious than before. "Don't let Hollywood tell you it's all fake. In any case, I told her that we had El Mismo and she just about fell over with joy. She kept on saying, '*Verdad, verdad!*' Means, 'The truth, the truth!' Turned out the legend was legit as she knew about Lucio Calavera and everything. Unfortunately, after Lucio took the skull, the town started to decline. The elders died off and no one wanted to step up to take their place. It was OK for a while as everyone just did their own thing. However, one day a strange family rode into town and, seeing a void, took control, like self-appointed royalty. They were part of some sort of cult-like religion and had been ousted from everywhere they previously tried to settle. So they traveled on and on for decades. And, because they were so isolated in their traveling caravan, they were all inbred and crazy. They took over Hoja Ojo and tried to make it their little kingdom. Those people in the paintings? Those are the portraits of that crazy family. The witch said they were called *Los Ganchos*. Either that was their last name or the name given to them by the locals."

"You bought the paintings?"

"Even better. The witch *gave* them to me. Told me that those people were a curse on the town. They tried to collect taxes from the townspeople who were already poor. As you could imagine, that pissed everyone off. All the businesses left and, with them, all the families. The Ganchos pillaged the houses and buildings for themselves, taking anything of value. But they were not farmers or ranchers so, in time, their food ran out. The witch said they took to eating dogs and cats. Pretty soon, transients and unfavorables took to hanging out in the town. Also, rejects from other villages. And, of course, witches like her. Then outlaws came in and sacked the Ganchos, taking all their possessions and killing the lot of them. They left the paintings and the witch snagged them. She wanted to burn them but didn't know if that would bring a curse on herself. So she just stored them and waited.

"I came along and started asking questions. She told me the story I just told you. Then she said she would give me a reading for twenty-five bucks. I thought *why the hell not?*"

"What did she tell you?"

"That's between me and her," he said with a wink. "But I *will* tell you this: she said she would sell me a key that would open all the doors I desired to be opened."

"And?"

Jared reached behind his tie and pulled out a key on a chain. It was an old iron skeleton key. He held it up and it dangled in front of my eyes. *"La Llave de la Bruja,"* he said in a dramatic tone. "The Witch's Key."

I sat back skeptical.

"I can see the doubt in your eyes. I know it must sound fantastical but you don't know how mystical people are around these parts. Even more so down south of the border." He tucked the key back behind his tie. "You don't have to believe anything. But I'll tell you this: ever since I got this key, I've been getting what I want. The doors are opening left and right, buddy!"

I didn't respond. I didn't like black magic or witches or curses or any of that stuff. I wanted to believe it was all fake, but part of me had to accept the fact that, if there was a one-percent chance it was real, there was a one in a hundred chance that it worked for someone somewhere. Jared was a charming guy, that's for sure. And I doubted if I could tell if he was lying or not. He seemed to have confidence with everything he said.

"Why did they let you hang the paintings up?" I asked. "They're not attractive."

"Two things," he said holding up two fingers. "One: the story lines up with El Mismo so it's part of the charm of the place. And two: I wanted to hang them up and, like I said, I've been getting what I want." He tapped his chest where the key rested behind his tie.

"Fair enough," I said. I choked down another sip of Poison. "Tell me, since you're getting everything you want, what is it you want now?"

At that Jared stood tall and opened his arms out wide, palms up. "I want it all," he said with a wide smile. His comment didn't necessarily make me feel good and I guess he read it on my face. "But," he said resting his forearm on the bar top and leaning in toward me, "who doesn't? I mean, any man worth his salt has ambition. What are we if we don't have drive? If we don't want to be more than we are now?" It was a rhetorical question yet he paused as if I were supposed to answer. "Don't you want more out of life, Traveling Man?"

"I guess so," I replied rather meekly.

Jared stood up straight. "Of course you do," he said with a smile. He poured a shot of Poison and held it up. "To ambition," he said. I held up mine and we clinked glasses. The guy at the bar held his up too, joining in simply as habit and custom dictated.

We downed our Poison and I thanked Jared. I left a buck. Servers tip other servers, even if the food or drink is free. "Good man," he said picking up the dollar and putting it in a glass vase with several other dollars. "Tell the freak I said 'Hi'," he said with a wink. I didn't ask him who the freak was but I assumed he was talking about Maya, and it wasn't a term of endearment. Whatever they had between them was a mystery to me and I debated whether or not to bring it up the next time I saw her.

I met up with Maya and we headed to El Mismo's room. The door was locked. Maya said that they only open it at night from 8:00 PM to 10:00 PM. She said it made it more special. Also, they conserved candles by showing only in that window of time. Maya flipped on a light switch near the entry door and an overhead light came on. It exposed everything and made the room less scary, less magical.

In the light, I could see that the camera was the same one that I saw in the mall store, only this one was black. The little box didn't look like anything special, although I really couldn't get a good look at it since it was up on the shelf, about seven and a half feet high.

Esteban arrived shortly after we went into the room. He was small, thin, and wiry, well-dressed in fitted clothes, with thick-rimmed glasses and a messenger bag slung over his shoulder and chest. He was carrying a six-foot stepladder. "What's up?" he said to me with a nod. "Esteban."

"Perk."

"You the guy who wants to see the video?"

"Yeah. Sounds creepy."

"Totally. Couldn't believe it myself." He didn't acknowledge Maya. What was with these guys? They all seemed to treat her like crap. Maya stood silently, arms crossed.

Esteban leaned the ladder against the wall, over the candles and made a great show of hiking up it to plug in the USB cord from his computer. He descended the ladder and opened his laptop, set it on a rung, then gestured us over. He had a folder open with a long list of files. He clicked one and set it to full screen. It was black and white and strangely clear, not at all grainy. It showed El Mismo without his covering, the light shining on him.

"Here's one time when the ghost comes out of him," Esteban said as he scrubbed the video playback. I recognized the video player, pretty common application. I guessed that the stored files were compressed into MP4's to save space. There was a small timestamp in the lower right hand corner of the recorded video stating the time as 2:15 AM. Esteban leaned back allowing us to see the screen fully. At 2:16 AM the skull grew a bit darker, then, sure enough, it looked like the skull had a ghost of itself float up out of the set skull. The ghost rose like steam and vanished. The whole thing looked odd. Too clear and clean for a ghost. But, then again, I had never seen a real ghost on video so who's to say?

"Crazy, right?" Esteban said in my direction. "Now check this out." He scrubbed the video forward to around 4:50 AM. At a little after 4:51 AM, the ghost re-entered the skull exactly the same way it went out. Esteban pressed pause and said, "On that night, around three to four o'clock AM, a house was broken into, and the ghost took some of those Russian dolls that fit inside of each other."

"Babushka dolls," I said.

"Yeah, Babushka dolls," Esteban said, as if he knew what they were called all along. The only reason I knew was because my grandma had a set in her house.

Esteban shut his laptop and stood up. "I gotta go," he announced. "I'm leaving in a few hours to Phoenix, and I haven't even packed." He unhooked his computer, pulled the ladder from the wall, and walked out of the room without saying another word.

Maya closed up El Mismo's room and we meandered down the hallway. I held her hand and she held mine back. Just seemed right in the moment. "Sooo," I said slowly.

""Sooo," she replied.

"Want to go out on a date with me tonight?"

Maya grabbed onto my arm and held it tightly. We stopped in the hallway. "Where are you going to take me?" she asked.

"It's a surprise."

"What should I wear?"

"Go naked. I'd like to see that." I was actually being honest. She looked up at me and punched me in the gut. "Do you have a dress?" I asked.

"Of course."

"Wear that. I don't have anything fancy but I'll do my best."

She let go of me and we headed out to the bus. I told her, "I'll drop you off back at the hotel so you can get your car. I've got some stuff to do. Investigating and what not. Oh, by the way, show me the back of that room where Esteban did the electrical work."

She led me around the back of the building and pointed to a blank wall. There was nothing there, no discoloration, no new stucco, nothing. It hadn't been touched since who knows how long. "So he didn't get into the wall from behind and he didn't get into the wall from in front. How exactly did he hardwire the camera into the electric source?"

Maya looked blankly at the wall. "I..." she paused. "I never even thought of it."

"Meet me at my hotel around six thirty tonight," I told her. "I think I have an idea of what's going on but I don't know why. We can talk about it later. Right now I have to check some stuff out. And get ready for our date."

Maya didn't say anything the whole way back to the hotel. It was as if she was in shock. I walked her to her car. "Hey, you OK?" I asked.

"I can't believe I didn't even think to check," she answered.

She looked up at me and said, "All this time and no one has even checked. And you come here and see it right off the bat. Who are you?"

"Private investigator, Ma'am," I replied in a deep, authoritative voice.

Maya pulled me close and gave me a hug that rivaled her mother's hug. She pressed her cheek against mine. "You didn't come here to pick up a bus," she whispered in my ear. "You were brought here to help us." Then she kissed me on the cheek, got into her car, and peeled out of the parking lot.

14 | Jaded

My mind was swirling. When I got back to my room, I noticed that it was already 3:45 PM. That meant I only had two hours and fifteen minutes to get ready for the date with Maya. I had told her it was a surprise, and it was. To me as well. I had no idea what I was going to do. To add to it all, my mind was racing with the Sugar Skull Ghost Thief. I had a few answers but a lot more questions.

The hotel provided a complimentary notepad and pen. I had never used them before. I finally saw their use. I jotted down some items. Basically, I could only do so much so I didn't try to plan for a huge event. I thought that doing something simple on our date might benefit Maya and not add any further complications to her life. Plus it would benefit me because I was lacking in time. I also didn't have a lot of money nor any way of knowing what there was to do in Las Cruces that was fun at a moment's notice. In short, the plan called for me to get some candles, get sandwiches and chips, cookies, wine, some sort of plates, utensils, drinking glasses, and flowers. It was the best that I could come up with on such short notice.

There were complimentary plastic cups from the hotel so that was easy. I went downstairs and asked if they had some paper plates and plastic utensils. They actually had that stuff in stock and they gave it to me for free. Score! I headed out to get candles, wine, food, and flowers in that order. I found a dollar store and stocked up on the candles and some cheap glass globes, bought a lighter too. I could get the wine, food, and flowers at the same grocery store so I decided to do that. There was a small fridge at the hotel so the food would stay cold. Unfortunately, I got carried away with picking the perfect bouquet of flowers that I completely spaced the wine. I didn't realize it until I got back to the hotel room and saw the plastic cups. I looked at the clock. 5:15 PM. Just enough time to go get some wine and head back and take a shower before Maya arrived. Easy enough.

I asked the clerk for the nearest place to buy a bottle of wine. She said there was a package store right down the street. I hadn't seen it. She said I could even walk there, would take me only ten minutes. Cool. On any other day, I would have walked but, since I was already in a hurry, I took the VW bus.

As I pulled into the parking lot of the package store, a tall, blonde girl came stomping out of the store in my general direction. She was wearing a tight tank top and daisy dukes with boots. And she was mad as a hornet.

"I thought I told you to never come 'round here ever again!" she screamed as she looked to the ground, spotted something that looked like a broken brick, and picked it up. "If you get out of that bus, Jared, I'll chuck this through your windshield, so help me God! I don't care if it is a *classic fifty-nine!*" That last part was said very sarcastically, yet she meant every word. "You know what?" she continued, "I think I'm just going to hurl this thing at you anyways. You're a snake!" I sat there not knowing what to do. The girl was livid. There must have been a glare in the windows from where she was standing, obscuring my face from her view.

The window was open and, between her threats and obscenities, I yelled out, "I'm not Jared! I just bought this bus from him!" She didn't quite catch it the first time so I yelled it again. She allowed her brick-wielding hand fall to her side and walked slowly up to the bus trying to look in. She made her way around to the driver's side and looked at me with seething eyes. Then, when she was absolutely sure I wasn't Jared, her face softened.

"You're lucky," she informed me. "I was two seconds from letting you have it." She threw the brick to the side and leaned on her arms in the window. "You better not tell me you're a friend of his, coming to give some stupid message or something." Her mouth moved around like she was chewing gum or trying to get chia seeds out of her teeth. That's the only way I could explain it. I think she was on some sort of drug but I couldn't say for sure. I had just met her. And we hadn't actually met.

"All I want is a bottle of wine," I said. "And all I know of Jared is I gave him seven grand and he gave me the keys to this bus."

"Seven grand?" she said almost yelling. "I knew it! I just knew it!"

"Listen," I said. "I don't know what happened between you and…" I paused. Jared seemed like a cool guy to me but both Maya and now this girl had a beef with him. Curiosity got the best of me and I decided to fish for some info. "You know what? I only met Jared once or twice but, in those meetings, he seemed kind of, I don't know, different." I was hoping she took the bait.

"Different? That's *one* way of putting it. Try completely wacko lunatic sociopath!"

"That's a harsh accusation. Maybe whatever he did to you wasn't so bad," I baited again.

"Oh yeah? You don't know the half of it! This bus, this stupid *classic fifty-nine VW Microbus,* is only one of the many screwed up things that guy has done. Not just to me, but to pretty much everyone he gets in contact with. He's a plague!"

"Are you saying he took me for seven thousand bucks? Because I think this thing is worth a lot more."

"That's the thing! This bus was my grandpa's. Jared wanted it but he didn't have the money, at least not what it was worth. Grampie was going to sell it for fifteen thousand. Jared came along and wanted to buy it for three. Grampie thought he was joking. But Jared persisted, saying he was going to get it for three thousand. Then Grampie started getting harassed: phone calls late at night from random places and no one on the other end, weird threats in letters. One time he got a dead cat sent to him UPS! Grampie couldn't prove it was Jared, but Jared always came around after each prank and told Grampie that he would be wise to sell him the bus. Grampie couldn't take it anymore so, one day, he gave up. Then Jared offered only five hundred. Grampie didn't care at that point, not for the bus, only for his peace. Five hundred dollars and peace of mind is good when you're all old and stuff." The girl paused long enough to light up a cigarette. "So he bought this thing for five hundred and sold it to you for seven thousand." She glared at me.

"Actually, it was my roommate that bought it. I just made the deal."

"Whatever."

"Hey," I said kindly. "I'm just saying I'm Switzerland over here." She shrugged. I pressed forward. "So, basically you're telling me Jared isn't someone to be trusted?"

"I don't trust him as far as I could throw him. Dude got me hooked. I hate him!"

I didn't ask what she got hooked on. Didn't want to know. "I have a friend who is kind of…close to him," I said to her.

"Should I warn her about anything?"

"Her?" the girl basically spit out the words. "Yes, you should. You should warn her to not let that creep take certain pictures in certain situations, and by certain situations I mean naked and doing sex stuff." I winced at her candor. She continued, "Let's just say that he doesn't keep his word. Let's just say that a certain someone—that certain someone being me—let him take such pictures and, when that certain someone asked him to delete them after we broke up, he said he would but he didn't and, to add insult to injury, had them printed and sold them to some pervert friend of his. Does that answer your question?" This girl was unstable for sure but that was no reason to screw her over; neither her nor her grandpa.

"If I can ask, did he do anything else to you?"

"You don't know the half of it. You see this store?" She motioned to the store behind her. "It's my family's. Jared nearly swindled my parents out of the whole thing. He has these delusions of being a billionaire. And he'll probably do it, you know? Jerks always get rich!"

"Hmm," I replied. We sat there for a few moments just staring at each other. She kept on moving her mouth like a cow. "I still need that bottle of wine," I said.

"Oh. Sure," she replied rather chipper. "Come on in. We're running a sale on all our cheap sweet reds."

I purchased a bottle of wine at around six bucks and headed back to the hotel with a head full of new theories. At the same time, I had my mind on Maya. I held onto the thought of her.

15 | Date

My mom used to tell me to always pack a button-up shirt, just in case I had to look "presentable," as she put it. So that's what I wore, a white long-sleeve button-up shirt with jeans and my low-rise Doc Martens. I looked in the mirror. Not horrible but far from elegant. It would have to do.

Maya arrived right on time. For being a pretty girl, she was punctual. I wasn't used to that. She knocked and I made her wait. I wanted to make it look like I wasn't ready. She knocked again and I answered through the door. "Oh," I said with fake surprise, "I was just going to text you to tell you that I wasn't ready."

"Text me with your poopie phone?" She was quick.

I opened the door and my jaw nearly dropped off of my face. She wasn't just wearing a dress, she was wearing the dress to end all dresses. It was deep red and it clung to every minute curve of her body. It had fringes criss-crossing across her front, accentuating her breasts. The hem sat at mid-thigh and the neck hung low enough to make me gulp. She had fashioned her hair in such a way that the curls were big and bold and reflected the light from all angles. She had actually put on some makeup and she wore it well. It wasn't thick but classy. She wore heels but not too high, just enough to showcase the muscles in her legs. And her earrings were little happy faces. Those didn't seem to fit the outfit but, in my mind, they fit her personality. My knees got weak.

"Are we going to go?" she asked. "Or are you just going to stand there drooling all night?" At that she posed for me. Then she bent over and picked up her bag with Piquito in it. "He's coming too but he won't bother us. He can stay in the bus. I just like having him near." I didn't mind.

I composed myself, reached out and held both her hands in mine and said, "There are rare moments in a man's life when he is absolutely, positively, no doubt completely joyous that he is a man. Right here, right now, this is one of those moments for me." Then, almost instinctively, I kissed the back of her hand. As soon as I did it, I thought that maybe it was silly but it went over well with her. Really well. She blushed and looked at me seductively. This was going to be an interesting night.

"Let's go," I said. I held her hand as we made our way down to the bus. Any other time, any other girl, and I would have felt weird about it, but not with Maya. She seemed so natural and real and close. I lamented the fact that I was only in town for another day or so. Then I told myself to enjoy the moment, to enjoy her.

"What's the surprise?" Maya asked as we got into the bus.

"If I told you, it wouldn't be a surprise."

"Well, I'm hungry so I hope this surprise of yours has food in it."

"It does."

Earlier that day I had asked the clerk at the grocery store where she would love to have a guy take her for a picnic. She said there was a park in the center of town called Pioneer Women's Park. She said that it wasn't big but it was charming. The clerk added that there were tables there but they were cruddy. My plan didn't call for tables.

The park was small but charming nonetheless. It had a big gazebo in the middle. That square in Old Mesilla also had a gazebo and my plan was to head there after this place. I guess it was a gazebo-themed evening.

Maya was giddy when she saw that I had all the stuff for our date in one of the back seats of the bus. I had covered it all up with the comforter from my hotel bed. "What's under there?" she asked attempting to lift it up.

I slapped her hand gently. "What did you tell me about patience?" I said. At that, she relented but not without a small pout.

At the park I got us all set up. We sat on the comforter and shared a glass of wine from plastic cups. "To chance encounters," I toasted.

"Chance encounters," she repeated and we tapped our cups together and took a sip.

I set out our food. I had picked up two deli sandwiches: one turkey and Swiss cheese with avocado and one pastrami with provolone. I also got us a bag of tortilla chips. Unable to wait for the official meal, Maya grabbed the bag of chips, tore it open and began to munch. She had the energy of a young girl, happy and excited.

"I like gummy worms," I told her pointedly.

"What does that have to do with anything?"

"You don't understand. I *really* like gummy worms. If there was only one kind of candy left on earth, I would want it to be gummy worms. They are my absolute favorite."

"You're a weirdo." She replied and continued to munch on the chips while she put some mustard on her sandwich from a packet I took from the deli.

I looked her directly in the eye. "If some maniacal madman came here right now," I said, "and told me that I had to choose between giving up gummy worms for life or give up the memory of this exact moment—like he had some memory eraser gun or something—I would choose to lose gummy worms."

"Ahh," Maya cooed. "That's the sweetest and weirdest thing anyone has ever told me." She leaned over and kissed my cheek. "Now can we gorge on these sandwiches already?"

It didn't take long for us to finish our meal as we were both famished. We lay back on our elbows, basking in the afterglow of cold cuts, sipping wine, and enjoying each other's company.

"Can I ask you a question?" I asked.

"Mm-hmm," she affirmed with her mouth to her glass.

"What was the favor? The one you owed Jared that made you obligated to pick me up at the bus stop."

At that she stopped sipping and lowered her cup and her gaze. "I'm not sure I want to say."

"Just a guess, but does it involve photographs?"

Maya looked at me suspiciously. "What do you know?"

"So it does?"

Maya didn't respond, just kept peering at me.

"I met—well, not met, but ran into—a girl earlier today. At the liquor store. She wanted to throw a brick through my windshield."

"Charming," Maya quipped. "Do you have that effect on most women?"

"I wouldn't say *I* do, but *Jared* might." At that, Maya went from looking at me suspiciously to looking at me with angry anticipation. I didn't play around with her. "The girl said that, among other things, Jared took pictures of her, naked pics and stuff, and she asked him to get rid of them. He said he would but, instead, printed them up and sold them to some guy."

Maya sat up abruptly, spilling some of her wine and exclaimed, "He did what?"

"Sold naked pics of that liquor store girl to some guy after he had told her he would get rid of them."

"That bastard!" Maya's nostrils were flaring. I felt like an idiot spoiling the mood but, at the same time, felt that she needed to know. She sat there fuming for a few moments, staring off into the distance. I didn't say anything, just let her work it out in her mind. Then she sighed heavily and looked at me. "I'm sorry. I didn't mean to get so angry and ruin our evening."

"It's not ruined," I said, trying to project calm in my voice. "The night is young."

Maya eased back onto her elbows and sighed. "I told you I made a vow. A vow to not have sex with any guy until marriage." She paused. "A lot of that, maybe *all* of it, has to do with Jared. We used to go out. He was so charming at the beginning. I let him…well, like that girl you met, I let him," she paused again. "I let him take all sorts of pictures of me. I trusted him completely. In my mind, I'd finally found the one. I mean, I was so in love and everything he said led me to believe that he was too, and that we were going to be together forever. It didn't help that, at that time, I drank a lot and…" She set down her wine. "He kinda introduced me to some stuff."

"Drugs?"

"Did the girl say anything about that?"

"Yeah. She said he got her *hooked.*"

"That sucks. But yeah, I can see it. I mean, it was all fun and games, you know? Try new things and live a little on the wild side. Doesn't hurt to experiment. Or maybe it does I guess. Let's just say that I was not in my right mind a lot of the time we were together. Looking back, no, I absolutely wouldn't let him take those pics." She looked at me. "I told you, I'm no angel."

"No one is."

"If he didn't get rid of those pics…" She stared off into the distance again. "You don't know, Perk. I'm embarrassed to even think about them now." She was getting emotional. "Even at my worst, I'm not who I was at that time. I don't know what came over me. Maybe it was the drinking or the drugs he let me try. Or maybe it was that, plus him laying on the charm. All of it together, a perfect storm. That was the favor: he got rid of the pics and I gave him an open favor, nothing illegal, no sex, just a favor when he needed it. Whenever, wherever. When I picked you up, I thought that was it. He and I were square! I wasn't overjoyed about having to drive all over creation but, in my mind, it seemed fair. And I *was* happy. You saw me, I couldn't help it. I was done with that chapter in my life. I just wanted to celebrate somehow. To dance. Thanks, by the way." She caressed my hand. "But hearing this, this news about that girl and her own pictures…" She pulled her hand back and held it in her own. "I just don't want to even think…I mean, if those are still out there. And what if my…" A look of deep concern came over her face. "If my dad were to see them, it would break his heart. It would…it would kill him. Why did I…" Her eyes were welling up.

I set down my cup and sidled up beside her, sat her up and held her. She started crying, sobbing gently. I held her tighter and took out a handkerchief from my back pocket and handed it to her. I held her for a few moments, just giving her time.

"I'm such a puppet," she said through the handkerchief. "I don't know why. I'm weak, I guess."

"You seem like you know what you want and you're doing it."

"*Now* I am. But only after the whole Jared thing. But think about it, if he didn't get rid of those pics, he can still hold that over my head, threaten to show them to people, make me do stuff."

"That's blackmail. It's illegal."

"If you haven't figured it out, Jared really doesn't care about what's legal or not."

"You've got a point."

"Can I blow my nose in this thing?" Maya said looking up at me teary-eyed.

"Be my guest. Just keep it. I've got others."

She blew her nose. "I don't know anyone under the age of fifty who carries around a handkerchief," she said.

"You do now."

"Do you always carry one around?"

"Yeah. When I was seven, my mom bought me a pack of three for my birthday. Along with some other gifts of course. But I remember the handkerchiefs because they seemed so odd. She said that a gentleman always carries one, not only if he needs it, but if a lady needs it, he should willingly offer it up. That stuck with me. Not because I wanted to be some noble gentleman or anything, but because my mom was worthy of a guy who would do that for her."

"You're dad wasn't that guy?"

"No. He and my mom had split up by that point. And my mom never had much luck with guys. They always seemed to treat her like crap. I think it's because she's really nice and trusting and forgiving. She's a hopeless romantic. And maybe that has something to do with it. Like, maybe she's too quick to fall in love. In any case, I never wanted to be like those jerks she used to go out with. Maybe this makes me sound like a mama's boy, but I always wanted my mom to be proud of me. So I always carry a handkerchief."

"That's sweet. I can understand why your mom gets walked all over. Sadly." She sighed again but now she didn't seem angry, just resigned to the fact that things were as they were. "I'm going to go freshen my face. All this crying must have me looking like hell. Plus I want to check on Piquito."

Maya got up and headed to the bus. I sat there letting things roll around in my head. My mind went to Esteban and the camera. Why the fake camera? What motive did he have to fake anything? It didn't make sense for him to use the ghost of El Mismo as a cover-up for petty crimes. Then I started thinking about Jared and what a turd he was. And Rocky taking pics of Maya's butt when she wasn't looking. I started to see why she didn't get along with any of them.

Maya returned and plopped down right next to me, our sides touching each other. "I'm glad you told me," she said and put her head on my shoulder. "You're a really good guy."

"Don't say that," I said feeling irritated.

"What, are you going to tell me how bad you are? Don't try that humble stuff with me. I see right through it."

"That's not it. It's just that," I paused, embarrassed to go on. But I had nothing to lose. "That's what girls tell me right before they friend-zone me."

"Oh." I felt Maya tense up ever so slightly. We just sat there motionless. I felt like a complete idiot.

"It's no big thing," I said trying to act like it wasn't. Then, for some reason, I felt I needed to just be honest about it all. "You know what? It kind of is a big thing. To me, that is." I turned to face Maya, expecting her to have a look of disgust on her face, but she didn't. She actually looked interested in what I had to say. "I like you, Maya. It's probably impossible not to. But I like more about you than just your pretty face and perfect body. I like your humor and your touch and the love you have for your family. And granted I've only known you for a couple of days, but I feel like I've really gotten to know you, probably better than a lot of other girls I've known for a lot longer. And, like I said, I like you. And not just like a friend. In all honesty, I want to grab you and kiss you. I'm not some good guy. I'm a guy who deeply desires you on all your levels."

I was a bit intense and maybe a bit too angry in my manner but there it was. I laid it all out. Never did that before. I took a breath and looked at her, expecting the *I just don't like you in that way* speech. When I looked at her, however, she was giving me a smile. Then she gave me a look that said, *what are you going to do about it?* I leaned over, held her face in my hand, drew her closer to me and kissed her. She welcomed it, kissing me back with gusto. Her lips were soft and full, her breath was warm and heavy. I leaned her on her back and continued kissing her while we lay on the comforter in the grass. She grabbed my hair and pulled me ever closer to her. We pressed against each other and she let out a slight moan. I pulled back and looked in her eyes. She was staring up at me with a longing I could feel, as if her eyes had tractor beams in them and they were set on me. I leaned in and kissed her again, but this time just briefly. I was getting too turned on, and I knew I needed to give myself a breather. I sat up and she looked at me as if I had hurt her.

"What's the matter? Why did you stop?" she asked.

"Because if I didn't stop, I *wouldn't* stop."

She let that sink in for a moment then sat up beside me. I held her hand.

"That's one way to get out of the friend zone," she said squeezing my hand. I looked at her and smirked. But she was right, I had to admit it.

"I've got cookies for us," I said as if it were a substitute for making out.

"Oh, goody," she replied facetiously.

"I also have another part of the date for us. We'll pack up in a bit and then head out."

It was starting to get dark so we made quick work of the cookies. I drove us down to the square in Old Mesilla. The parking lot at the square was just about full and there were actually a few people milling around. I wasn't anticipating that. Maya said that there was a bar that wasn't open Mondays or Tuesdays, which is why there weren't many people the previous night. The bar brought them out.

It didn't thwart my plan though. I had a bag with the candles and the hand-crank radio in it. Maya left Piquito in the bus again. He seemed fine with it. It wasn't too cool outside so we kept the windows open. She said he wouldn't jump out.

I led her by the hand to the gazebo in the middle of the square. Luckily no one was there.

"What are you doing?" she asked.

"You'll see." The gazebo was an octagon, each side had a ledge. On each ledge I set a candle in its little glass globe. Then I lit all the candles. They didn't give much light but they created a romantic effect. Then I got the hand-crank radio out of the bag and turned it on. I had cranked it earlier to power it up and selected a station that I thought had the best slow music for dancing. It was a Spanish station but that seemed appropriate in the setting. I set the radio down on one of the ledges and turned it up. Then I held out my hand and said, "May I have this dance?"

Maya gave me a knowing smile and accepted. I held her close as we danced to song after song, slightly altering our moves with the cadence and timing of the music. A couple of times I kissed her on the neck. She seemed to enjoy that; she even shuddered once and held me closer to her.

We took a break and sat on one of the ledges. All the anger and sadness had evaporated from Maya. She now seemed content and pleased. We watched people walk by and they looked at us and smiled.

"I've never had a date like this," she said to me.

"Me either. I think it's awesome."

"Me too."

"And we haven't even gotten to the *Día De Los Muertos* part yet."

"Oh, yeah," Maya said as if waking from a dream. "So the *Día de los Muertos* is a Mexican holiday. It's really big around here. It lands on November first or second or sometimes both depending on who you talk to. Basically, it's a time for people to remember those whom they have loved but lost. But it's not a morbid thing, if that makes sense. It's more of a celebration. Traditionally, people decorate the graves of their loved ones with flowers and other stuff. Like, kids' graves will get decorated with toys and adults graves with pictures or food or even liquor. Especially tequila. Old Mesilla holds a huge celebration for it every year. There's dancing and music, face painting, food, and partying. Sometimes there are even rides. It can get crazy but it's a lot of fun."

"What's with the skeletons?"

"*Día de los Muertos* is all about skeletons. They're everywhere. Especially skulls. That's where we get the sugar skulls from. A sugar skull could either be a little replica skull that's made out of sugar or a clay skull that is painted. Usually all the skulls are painted with flowers and designs."

"So El Mismo is a sugar skull? Hence the Sugar Skull Ghost Thief?"

"It's not really a sugar skull in the strict sense. It's not sugar or clay. Well, I guess it was *believed* to be clay way back when, but everyone knows it's real. I don't think Grandpa Tavo actually meant for people to think it was a sugar skull. I believe he was just trying to fool that priest, make him believe it was clay, and the only way to do that was to paint it."

"But other people think it's a sugar skull?" I asked, still trying to understand it all.

"I guess it is, in a way. It's a skull that's painted. To tell you the truth, I don't know who first came up with the name *Sugar*

Skull Ghost Thief. I think the newspaper did." Maya sat back a bit on the ledge of the gazebo, signaling that there was nothing more to say about *Día de los Muertos*.

"That sounds like a weird holiday," I said. "Weird but cool."

Maya held onto my arm and put her head on my shoulder as we sat in the soft glow of the evening lights. The radio was losing power and the music from the bar was getting louder. Maya said, "Come here," and she slid down to the floor of the gazebo. I followed suit. The side walls were wood and gave us a little privacy, like ducking behind a small wall. She kissed me, first soft then harder. I followed suit again. She was grabbing my shirt from the front, pulling me as close as possible. I had my hand on her waist and pulled her to me as well. Time seemed to stand still. Who knows how long we sat there kissing each other. It only seemed like a moment but, before we knew it, the radio had died and a couple of candles had completely burned out.

"What time is it?" I asked her.

"You have somewhere to be?" She pulled me to her again.

"Just curious."

She pecked me on the lips and hiked her dress up along her right leg, revealing a lacy leg band which also had a pouch on it. She opened the pouch and pulled out her phone. "Handy, *que no?*" she said.

"Sexy," I countered.

She looked at her phone with astonishment. "I don't believe it!" she said. "It's past ten!"

"Really? How long have we been down here?"

She nestled up beside me again and said, "Not long enough." She kissed my neck. It was like a magic trigger that made my whole body tingle.

Just then, we heard the high pitch of Piquito barking in

the bus. He was going crazy. "Piquito!" Maya cried and we both hopped up to see what was making him bark so vigorously. The bus was parked in such a way that it was facing us but at an angle. The driver's side was on the opposite side from our view. It was roughly fifty yards away. We could see Piquito bouncing up and down in the bus, still barking up a storm. Then, through the windows, I saw a head pop up on the other side of the bus with an arm up next to it. It was holding something and moving in a strange looping motion.

"Hey!" I yelled, "Get away from that bus!" The figure stopped and, even though I couldn't see its eyes, I could tell it was looking in our direction. And while the light was soft and yellow, it still lit up the parking lot. The figure started moving to the back of the bus then it poked out from behind it. I couldn't believe it. It was him. The Sugar Skull Ghost Thief, in the flesh!

"It's him," Maya and I said at the same time which made us look at each other in disbelief. Instinctively, I started moving toward him. He saw me and began running away. He wasn't tall, but, from what I could see, a bit shorter than me. And his skull head was big. He didn't run very well, mostly because of the big black robe he wore, which he held up as he ran. I could see his legs and feet, pants and sneakers. Not a ghost at all.

"Go check on Piquito," I said as I turned back to Maya and pitched her the keys, realizing, as they were in the air, that we left the windows open and the doors unlocked. I had just wasted a few precious seconds for nothing. Dammit! "I'm going to see if I can catch him!" He wasn't running fast at all but there was a lot of distance for me to cover. All he had to do was duck behind the right building and I wouldn't be able to find him. Not in the dark. Luckily I had two things going for me: first, I may not have the most endurance when it comes to running but I am quick; second, he had a large gap between the bus and the nearest building. I put on the afterburners and headed straight for him. He was getting closer to the building, looking back at me every so often with his deep empty skull eye holes. I was gaining on him. Strangely, he didn't take the first street beside the building he was heading toward, opting instead to run in front of the building to take the alley on the far end. I could hear him breathing heavily. I was too. "Stop!" I yelled, as if he would somehow obey my voice. He didn't, of course.

He was ten feet from the alley on the side of the building when I got to about five feet from him. I reached out to grab the back of his black robe but he was just fast enough to elude me. He turned quickly down the alleyway and, when I got to it, I realized why he went that way. It was completely void of any light. I stood there not knowing what do. Should I run after him? What was down there? He obviously knew his way around. Maybe it was a trap. Then, like magic, a light shone bright from behind me. I saw the Sugar Skull Ghost Thief with his back to the wall just waiting. I assumed he was waiting for me to run past him so that he could trip me, maybe hit me over the head with something. When the light hit, he took off down the alley. I turned around to see where the light was coming from. Maya had gotten in the bus and pulled up with the lights on. "Go get him!" she yelled. Piquito barked and I assumed he was telling me to do the same.

The alley was long but there was nothing in it other than a few items here and there. The guy was running slower, obviously winded from just that short run. I ran after him with all the speed I could muster. I thought about how I asked Maya if anyone had tried to tackle him yet and how she said that old people weren't built for that. I was not really built for tackling a thief either but I didn't let that stop me.

As we approached the end of the alley, I could see that it let out into a dark open field then some more buildings farther up ahead. I caught up with the ghost thief and I lunged at him, aiming my shoulder for his lower back. I hit him pretty hard and I wrapped my arms around him and tackled him. He was soft around the middle, pudgy. I heard him grunt as he hit the ground. Definitely a guy. Unfortunately, I landed on his foot and it knocked the wind out of me. I let loose my grip ever so slightly and he started kicking wildly. Before I knew it, he kicked me twice: once in the temple and another in the mouth. And while his kicks were wild, they were not powerful. Still, a kick is a kick. The strike to my temple disoriented me and the one to my mouth startled me. It took me a few seconds to collect myself and, in that short time, the ghost thief took off into the darkness, outside of the beam of the bus's headlights. I squinted in the direction that I thought he ran and listened, but I could only hear music from the bar behind us a ways back. Then I heard a *clip-clap* of someone running toward me. It was Maya.

"Perk!" she yelled. "Are you OK?"

I sat up and looked her way. Piquito was running alongside her.

I was still out of breath so I nodded unconvincingly. "He got away," I strained to say, stating the obvious.

"You're bleeding," Maya said bending down beside me and looking at my mouth. "Come on, let's go. Let's get you cleaned up."

We walked back up the alley. A small group of people silhouetted in the headlights of the bus could be seen ahead of us. When we arrived at the mouth of the alley, there must have been ten to fifteen people standing there. They gawked at us and drilled us with questions.

"Did you get him?"

"Did the ghost disappear?"

"Did he hurt you?"

We didn't answer anyone, just picked up our stuff from the gazebo and drove away.

16 | La Llave de la Bruja

Maya drove us to her house. She said she could fix me up there. She also told me to be prepared for her dad, that he might be drinking. She explained that he had good days and bad days but pretty much all the days were drinking days. "He seemed to be in a good mood earlier," she said. "Let's hope it's a good day. Just play along with him. And please don't judge him. He's worked hard for us and he's in pain." Her voice wavered at that last statement. It seemed as though *she* was the one in pain with the whole situation.

"You love him a lot, don't you?" I asked knowing the answer.

"Of course. He's my Poppy."

"Some people don't love their dads. Some people don't have dads or the dads they have are crap."

"I'm sorry," she said looking at me. "Don't you have a good relationship with your dad?"

"It's OK, I guess. We get along."

"Oh, I thought maybe you were talking about yourself and I was being ungrateful for even having a dad."

"Not at all. I was just saying that some people don't like their dads. You seem to like your dad all right. Love him, I mean."

"I do. I just wish this whole ghost thing wasn't going on. It put him over the edge. Maybe he was heading there, but this thing just sped everything up. He probably had another good twenty years in him. Now? *¿Quien sabe?*"

I didn't ask for a translation.

We rode in silence, the cool air gently flowing through the windows. I didn't mind it. I was still worked up from the run and the air felt good on my face. My lip was swollen and I knew I was bleeding. I felt for my handkerchief to hold over my mouth then remembered I gave it to Maya. She must have read my actions because she said, "Your handkerchief. I used it up on all my *mocos*. Sorry." She pointed at her nose and I took it that *mocos* meant snot.

I was wearing a white T-shirt under the button up shirt and I pulled that up to my mouth to catch any blood. It might ruin the shirt but, oh well.

We arrived at Maya's house and she told me to wait in the bus so that she could see how things were at the house. I started to realize that this was standard practice for her. I had never lived with a parent who drank, much less drank heavily. The way I sensed it, every day was similar yet, at the same time, every day was completely unique. A wildcard among wildcards. On the surface, Maya was this hot Latina chick with a knack for spontaneity. Deeper down, she was racked by demons, some big, some small, but demons nonetheless. It pricked my heart, and I wanted to hug her. But now wasn't the time, not with me all bloody.

Maya came out and said we were OK to go in. She picked up Piquito and we headed inside. Her mom had already gathered some first aid stuff on her kitchen table. I could hear music coming from the back room and her dad singing along with it. He sounded drunk. Maya looked at me and shrugged.

I gave her a knowing half smile, something to say *I understand,* even though there was no way I could.

"*Ay, mijo,*" Mrs. Calavera said as she looked at my mouth. "What happened?" She dabbed my lip with a cotton ball doused with alcohol. It stung but I tried not to wince.

I looked at Maya. Should we tell her? The Sugar Skull Ghost Thief was a sensitive subject. Would it cause some sort of stir in her house?

"It was the ghost, Mamita," Maya said. "We saw it. Perk chased him and tackled him."

"You caught him?" Mrs. Calavera sat up straight in wonder.

"He kicked me and got away," I said.

"He has feet?" Mrs. Calavera was intrigued. "Or maybe hooves like *el diablo.* Did he have hooves?"

"He has feet," Maya said. "Human feet with sneakers."

"Why does the ghost have sneakers?" Mrs. Calavera was genuinely confused.

There was a clink behind me that gave us a start. Lalo had dropped an empty beer bottle into the trash. It clinked against the other empites.

"*¿Qué pasa con el fantasma?*" he said, sounding unhappy about it. I didn't understand Spanish but I could tell his words were slurred.

Maya stood up and approached him. He was swaying. She held onto him, steadying him. "We saw him, Poppy," she told him. "Just a few minutes ago. Perk chased him."

"*Esta noche?*"

"*Si, Poppy. Horita.* We saw him. Perk chased him and tackled him but the ghost kicked Perk in the mouth."

"*Horita?*" Lalo said again. He had a look of confusion on his face.

"Just a few minutes ago," Maya said.

Lalo's face went pale as he stood there staring off into

space. He swayed gently, his lips moving ever so slightly.

"Poppy?" Maya said concerned.

Lalo began mouthing something inaudibly. *"La llave de la bruja,"* he whispered, his voice rising. *"La llave de la bruja… la llave de la bruja…"* He pushed Maya's hands off of him and stumbled out of the room repeating the phrase. Maya looked at me and her mom and shrugged.

"What does he mean?" Maya asked us.

"No se, mija," Mrs. Calavera answered.

I remembered Jared and his necklace. I looked to Mrs. Calavera. "Could you give me and Maya a moment alone please?" I requested. She didn't say anything, just got up and headed to the back room where Lalo had retreated.

Maya sat down and peered at me in anticipation. "Well?" she asked.

"Jared's key. He showed it to me."

"His what?"

"The skeleton key. *La Llave de la Bruja.* The Witch's Key. Haven't you seen it? You said you and he used to go together."

"He never showed me any key. He showed it to you?"

"Yeah. Earlier today. When we were meeting Esteban. I went to the bar. He gave me a shot of the Poison. Then he told me about the paintings on the wall and the key he got from the witch."

"He got a key from that witch in Mexico?"

"Yeah. What, he didn't tell you?"

"He went after we broke it off. Since then, he doesn't tell me much of anything." Maya sat back in her chair and mouthed indecipherable words like her father. Turned out she was saying the same thing as her voice rose. *"La llave de la bruja… la llave de la bruja…"* She seemed to be in a trance. Then she looked directly at me. "Why does Poppy know about this key?" she asked. "Why did it bother him so much? And why is he talking about it when we told him we saw the ghost?"

We sat there in stunned silence. What did it all mean? I had a theory but this shot holes in all that. Essentially, I thought Esteban was the guy behind this. The camera and video looked suspicious. But this fat ghost and now the Witch's Key? And those paintings in the bar. Jared said that the witch told him they were a curse. I thought I was close. Now I felt a million miles away.

"Poppy knows something," Maya said as she got up and went into the back room. I sat there with nothing to do but contemplate the whole situation. In less than two minutes she came back into the kitchen. "He's passed out. Mamita is crying in her room." I felt horrible. Had I said something wrong?

I drove us back to the hotel to pick up Maya's car. We traveled in silence, both of us trying to process the events of the evening. When we arrived, I got out and noticed something I hadn't seen before when we were in the darkness of Maya's driveway. Across the driver's side of the bus in red spray paint was scrawled "EL MISMO," in all caps. "Dammit!" I said to myself under my breath.

Maya came around to my side. "I didn't want to tell you," she said. "Not after you got kicked and everything." I just shook my head. What could I do? File a police report against a ghost for vandalizing an unregistered vehicle that wasn't even mine? I would have to find a way to work something out with Chuck. I was, after all, responsible for the bus' safe delivery.

I walked Maya to her car. She opened it up and got in. Then she stopped and stood back up and turned to face me. "I'm sorry I got you into all of this," she said as she gently touched the cut on my mouth.

"I'm sorry I upset your mom and dad," I replied.

"They were already upset."

I nodded. "Not the best ending for our first date," I said

stupidly.

Maya looked up at me. I could see tears welling up in her eyes. I felt so bad to have made her cry. She grabbed the front of my shirt and buried her face in my chest and sobbed. I held her tight.

"I'm such a crybaby," she said into my chest.

"You're going through a lot," I assured her. "I think you're holding yourself together. You could crumble but you don't. You're staying strong for your family. And for yourself."

She looked up at me and pulled my face to hers and kissed me. "You see into my heart," she said and hugged me tightly. Then her hand trailed across my chest and she gently tweaked my nipple. "You know what that's for, *Chulo,*" she whispered in my ear. She pulled back and looked up, smiling weakly. "Tomorrow I work a double," she said. "Come see me. Anytime, after we open at eleven. I'll hook you up with a *relleno.*" Then she got into her car and drove off.

17 | Thursday

I slept eight solid hours and had healed up nicely. My lip was still swollen but not as bad as the night before. I had showered and tended to the few scrapes I had from the tackle but, all in all, I was no worse for the wear.

I grabbed my laptop and headed down to the lobby to piddle around with the video software and have some breakfast. Unfortunately, my extended slumber left me with a late start on the complimentary continental breakfast buffet. Slim pickings. I kicked myself for missing out on free food since I was running low on funds. At the same time, I was thankful for the sleep and what little scraps I scrounged up.

I set up shop at a table with coffee and a shabby-looking muffin, intent on making massive progress on the commercial for Mr. Argyle. I realized that, in the midst of all the commotion and mystery of the Sugar Skull Ghost Thief, I hadn't even opened my laptop since I had left Colorado. That meant that I hadn't checked my email or Facebook.

I logged into both expecting a barrage of messages. My email inbox only had four messages: two of which were throwaway newsletters and the other two were from Chuck. One of

his simply said, "Dude. Can't get a hold of you. Call me. C."
The second said, "Never mind. I figured it out. C."

My Facebook was equally meager. I had a bunch of notifications but they were mostly telling me that other people commented on posts that I had commented on days earlier. Since I hadn't posted anything in a few days, there was nothing new for me. Facebook is a fickle friend in and of itself. I had two Facebook messages from Chuck but they were the exact same as the emails. I replied to his latest Facebook message, to let him know my phone was broken but I had made the deal. I didn't mention the fact that his bus was tagged by a ghost. That's not something you share in a Facebook message.

I opened the video editing program and continued to play around with it. I already had Adobe Photoshop and was learning how to work with graphics. I had a picture of my boss Mr. Argyle and I decided to put him in front of a background image of the café. In Photoshop, you can cut out a shape — in this case, Mr. Argyle — and save it as a PNG. This makes it so that you can paste it over other images as a cutout. The video editing software also worked in layers so I could do things with the picture of Mr. Argyle on one layer without affecting the background layer. I had some fun using various effects on my boss. I could make him magically appear in front of the café or disappear if I ran the effect backwards. I could make his image image swirl and flip and distort. I thought that it might be funny to have my boss swoop in from the side and then have him swoop out. Of course, he wouldn't think it was funny and probably wouldn't pay for such a commercial. I tried an effect called "Melt" and the image of Mr. Argyle seemed to melt like wax down to the bottom of the screen. That was cool. Then I tried "Butterfly" which made his image fold in half and fly away like a butterfly. Ha! Then I tried "Vaporize" which made him dissolve and float away like steam.

I stopped and stared at the screen.

I scrubbed backwards through the playback to take another look. He floated away like steam again. I added another PNG of him, just like the first but put it on another layer behind the one that was already on the screen with the *vaporize* effect added to it. I played the video. Sure enough, one image of Mr. Argyle stayed put while the other image, the overlaying image, floated up and away.

Just like steam.

Just like a ghost.

Exactly like the video of El Mismo.

I closed my laptop and quickly finished my coffee and muffin. I had to show Maya. But it was still early, only around 9:30 AM. The restaurant wouldn't open until another hour and a half. I sat and fumed, not wanting to wait but not wanting to go to her house and bother her and her family in the morning.

I decided to go for a walk. I needed to figure out why Esteban faked the video. I had my suspicions with the power cord and the clarity of the video, but now I had proof of how it could be done. I wasn't sure if he used the same program but it sure looked like he did. It was a simple enough effect to pull off. But again, why?

And why was Lalo so upset the previous night? Why did he mention the Witch's Key? How did that fit into everything? And the big question: why was any of this happening at all?

18 | Mr. Argyle

My walk yielded no revelations. The excitement of figuring out Esteban's method of faking the video had worn off. I had nothing else. And I couldn't figure out why Esteban would do it, so it seemed stupid to bring it up to Maya, other than the fact that I was pretty sure it was faked.

On another down note, my walk made me think about my stay in Las Cruces and Old Mesilla. Chuck had paid for Tuesday night and I had paid for Wednesday and Thursday. Another night was unlikely. Not only was I running low on funds, I had to consider what it might take to get Chuck's bus repainted. Sure, there was a chance he wouldn't like the restored paint job and want to have it repainted anyway, but I doubted it. He saw the pictures and bought it as-is. I decided that I didn't have anything to lose by asking him. Maybe I could tell him that the colors were ugly and it would look better another color. Regardless, none of that solved my problem of not having a place to stay after Thursday.

I concluded that after lunch would be a better time to go see Maya. Maybe she could take a break and eat with me. I resigned to working on the commercial. But I still had no concept. I remember reading a book once where the writer said something like, "When in doubt, just ask." That's a novel idea. Why not ask Mr. Argyle? Maybe he already had an idea of what he'd like to see.

I found a convenience store, bought some gummy worms and had the clerk give me my change in quarters, for the pay phone. I called the café, the only number I really knew. Maybe he would be there by chance. He wasn't but Compa gave me his cell phone number.

"Mr. Perk," he said curtly. "Have you finished the commercial yet?"

"Not yet, sir. That's why I'm calling. I've been learning the program and now I'm ready to move forward with making it. Only thing is, I'm not sure what to put in it. Did you have any ideas of what you wanted it to look like? Or not look like? Anything?"

"Hmm…" Mr. Argyle went silent. I allowed him time to ponder. "Whatever you do should be fine."

"Well, you wouldn't want anything like a girl in a string bikini, right?"

"Absolutely not!"

"OK, then. That's what I'm getting at. Boundaries for me to work within. Or a general idea. Like…what is your vision for the café? Why did you start it? Maybe if I knew that, I could have something to run with."

"It was a no-brainer. I purchased the office building and the lobby was just a large open space with a desk for a general receptionist. Originally, the building was supposed to house one business. But, at the time I bought it, there wasn't a business large enough to fill the whole thing. So I rented it out as office space to various businesses. That left me with no need for a general receptionist. And, instead of having an empty desk in the lobby, I built in the café with the idea that the workers in the businesses upstairs would also eat at the café for convenience sake."

"Smart," I said.

"Thank you."

"So it wasn't just to make money?"

"I had thought it would but I had never run an eatery before. The margins are slim if any. My goal these days it to just stay in the black. Gives you guys a job and my commercial tenants get a benefit to renting in the building. That's why we do promotions like Chorizo Monday and such."

"Ah," I said, soaking it in. He had never laid it out like that before. I thought of how Maya said that her parents worked hard and how she lived in that humble house. And how hard it must be now that business was down. "Mr. A," I continued, "do all restaurants run at such low margins?"

"Can't say for certain. I suppose not all of them. Most of them, yes. I have friends in the restaurant industry, and they all tell me the same thing: they get hammered on food costs and upkeep, not to mention utilities and labor. But things can go good though. Like any business, large amounts of small margins make for an overall large bottom line." Mr. Argyle cleared his throat, which meant he was going to give an example. I knew his mannerisms. "Say Old Boy has a restaurant that brings in twenty thousand a month," he began. He had a way of using the term *Old Boy* for any generic businessman in his hypothetical scenarios. "If he clears ten percent, he makes two thousand, right? Before taxes mind you. But that's factoring in labor and raw materials, food and other items. If he is able to recoup his initial expense on all that, the margin expands with every unit sold. You get where I'm going? Thing is, as it stands now, I'm not showing much of a profit or a loss. And Uncle Sam doesn't like that. Looks like I'm not reporting all my profits."

As fascinating as it all sounded, it didn't give me any ideas. I was curious about something though. I asked him, "Doesn't the office building have a good margin?"

"Excellent margin. I own the building outright. All rents are profit. But the café and the building are under two different businesses."

"Why couldn't you just even out the money between the two?"

"You mean move around the money so one business shows a higher profit and the other shows lower? I could pull money from one and inject it into the other, but I wouldn't be able to count it as profit. If I did, that would be considered laundering."

"Oh," I remarked. I hadn't ever thought about what laundering money actually was. Just thought it was something people did on TV.

"However," Mr. Argyle continued. "There are lots of folks out there who launder money through restaurants. Not hard to do, really. Just record more food sales and get rid of the food somehow. Not that I've thought about doing it or anything." Obviously he had. "But, if I were to launder money—not saying I would, mind you—I wouldn't go the route of a restaurant. Too many hands in it. No, instead I'd use an entertainment venue of sorts. Ticketed events and such. Circus or the like. Why, you could hide thousands of dollars in ticket sales and no one would be the wiser. Who's going to prove that a couple of thousand people *didn't* show up to an event? Who would you ask? The people that didn't show up? Easy as pie. Redirect the money into ticket sales, tear the tickets, keep the house stubs, and burn the customers' stubs. Now the numbers are on the books and there's no product to get rid of. Not that I've put much thought into it."

"I think I have an idea for the commercial."

"Don't mention money laundering," Mr. Argyle said abruptly. "That was all hypothetical."

"No, not at all. I was thinking of interviewing regulars like

Moxy and Henna. Cute girls. And they'd say good things about the place. I know they would."

"Sounds like a plan. Get to it." With that, Mr. Argyle hung up.

I had the bones of an idea but not the meat. I would have to get home and do some testimonials for content. Couldn't do anything more, being out of town.

I had some time to kill so I thought that YouTube might help me out. I opened up my browser and then remembered Maya's name for me. *Chulo*. I had wanted to look that up on Google Translate and just hadn't had a chance. She had called me that again the night before. I opened Google Translate and typed it in. Needless to say, that made me even more confused than the whole El Mismo ghost stuff.

19 | Scorpion

The thought of driving around town to explore crossed my mind. But then I remembered that the bus had "EL MISMO" spray-painted across the driver's side. Also, it wasn't my bus and driving it around only increased the likelihood of more stuff happening to it. I vowed only to drive it when I had to. That meant when I was going to see Maya. Had to do that.

With that in mind, I decided that I could do one of two things: 1) stick around the hotel, maybe get in a workout at the little gym they had (which only had a treadmill and a stationary bike), or 2) drive down to Old Mesilla and explore the area on foot. If someone told me they had those two choices and chose option #1, I would kick them in the groin. Why pass up culture? I hopped into the bus and drove down to Old Mesilla.

I parked at the square since it was the only place I was familiar with. I didn't think the ghost would make a daytime appearance so Chuck's bus should be safe.

Everything outside of the square and Calavera's was unventured territory. The little park with the gazebo was hemmed in by streets, and on the other side of those streets were small shops. And while I felt like I had been in southern New Mexico for a lifetime, I was still a tourist. I set my mind to tourist mode and walked around with fresh eyes.

Most of the shops were boutiques. They sold jewelry or novelty items, souvenirs of the region. Apparently Billy the Kid was big in these parts. I strolled into one of the shops and browsed. I came across some scorpions encased in glass. Even though scorpions were also in Colorado, I had never seen them displayed like this. At least not myself. Part of me thought it was cruel to put this animal in glass. It was posed as if it were alive. Maybe it was. Maybe putting it in glass was what killed it. If that were the case, then the exact moment of death was captured forever in the glass.

I thought about El Mismo and how he was also encased in glass, or plastic, whatever it was. The skull had been tilted slightly upward which gave it the appearance of pleading or yearning. When I first saw it, I thought it was a cool effect. Now, looking at the scorpions, I felt different. Basically, by placing El Mismo in the glass, he was being told that he was never going to be reunited with his brother. He was now a showpiece, an attraction. And, even if his brother's skull were to come back around somehow, this half of him, the El Mismo that was in Calavera's, was here to stay. The thought of the Ganchos entered my mind as well. Could the combination of encasing the skull along with the introduction of the Ganchos paintings have some sort of strange paranormal effect? There was no doubt that the Sugar Skull Ghost Thief that I tackled was human. But, just because he was physical, didn't mean that he wasn't influenced by the spiritual.

It seemed like this whole thing was both spiritual and physical. That thought bounced around in my brain. I had thought that I had traction with Esteban. Now I had more possibilities than proof.

"Cool, huh," came a voice from nearby. It was the clerk in the store. A girl. I turned to see the source. She was young and blonde. I wouldn't say pretty, but I wouldn't say she was without her charms. I like to see beauty in all sorts of girls.

"It's different, I'll give you that," I replied. "Do they kill the scorpion while they do this?"

"I don't know. I guess so. Yeah."

"Do you think that's cruel?"

"Have you ever been stung by a scorpion?"

"No."

"Well, I have. A bunch of times. And I have no sympathy for those little bastards."

"How much?" I asked, holding the globe up.

"Flip it over."

I turned it over. A sticker read "$3", no zeroes.

"I'll take it," I said. She rang me up and that was that. I put the scorpion in my pocket and headed on out to explore more sights of Old Mesilla.

20 | The Mug

Beyond the immediate plaza square of Old Mesilla was a random assortment of buildings, some of them commercial, some of them residential houses. There seemed to be no delineation of zoning. But all the structures were old, so my guess was that everything was grandfathered in. There was a small theater that featured independent movies, none of which I had heard of. It was closed until later in the day. There was a wine bar that looked charming and cozy. Also closed.

I wove through a neighborhood going nowhere in particular. I encountered no less than five Chihuahua dogs running loose at their leisure. A couple of them barked at me. None of them attacked. They simply meandered close enough then ran away when I got near, tail between their legs. Strange breed.

I estimated that I had about forty-five minutes to kill before I could head over to see Maya. I kept walking. Before long, I happened upon a coffee shop on the side of a main road. It was called "The Mug." I went in. The place was charming enough, independent and artsy. There were two girls working. Both of them were young, college-aged. Both looked like hippies.

I didn't want to spend much money but how much could

a cup of coffee cost? I found out that, at that place, a cup of coffee cost three dollars. For that price, I could get another scorpion!

One of the regulars at the café back home, Wren, once told me that he got free coffee from girls at coffee shops by making them laugh and he gave me a few of his routines. I had nothing to lose so I decided to give it a shot.

"Hi," I said to one of the girls at the counter. "I'm traveling and running low on funds but," I held up my finger to emphasize my next statement. "If I can guess your age to the exact day, can I get a free cup of coffee?"

"Give it your best shot," she replied with a hint of a snicker.

I closed my eyes as if I was consulting another dimension. I opened my eyes, smiled, and said, "You are exactly seventy-three years, five months, and two days old!"

She couldn't help but smile and shook her head. "Nope," she said.

"Dammit!" I exclaimed as if I were really upset with myself. I even slapped the counter top. "But tell me," I said to her earnestly, "was I over or under?" Then I smiled at her. She laughed.

"Fine," she relented. She poured a cup of coffee and handed it to me. "I'm a sucker for hoboes and cheesy humor," she said. I didn't say I was a hobo, only that I was traveling and low on funds. Oh, yeah. I guess that's the definition of a hobo. I thanked her and sat down, prepared to do nothing but think. And drink coffee, of course.

There was a painting on the wall with a skull decorated with flowers. A sugar skull. It didn't look like El Mismo, just a regular skull with flowers. I stared at it, working things out in my head.

"I painted that," came a voice from over my shoulder. It was the girl that gave me the coffee.

"I like it," I said.

"It's for sale. Two hundred bucks. Cash money, no paying with jokes."

"I'm sure it will sell. It's worth twice that much." I sipped my coffee. She refilled it without asking me if I wanted it refilled.

"So you're traveling? Where are you from?"

"Colorado."

"Nice up there. And what brought you here?"

"A Greyhound bus." I couldn't help it, too easy. She smirked. "You said you liked cheesy jokes. But, truthfully, it's a…" What was it that I was doing? "A delivery thing. Did a deal with a guy down here. Jared. Works at Calavera's, right around the corner. Know him?"

She rolled her eyes. "Who *doesn't* know Jared." Then she looked at me as if I was an alien lifeform. "You came from *Colorado* for a *delivery?* Ha! Makes sense." She sat down beside me and leaned in close. "I'm cool," she said. "I mean, I buy from Jared too so it's not like I'm going to rat him out or anything." She looked from side to side to make sure no one was listening in. "I've always been at the tail end of it all, buying a stash here and there. I know these guys make money, but I never know how much. You know? Guys like Jared have to buy it at a certain price and sell it for more to make money. Even I can understand that. But how much more? I mean, you're probably getting paid just to deliver it."

At that point, I realized we were not talking about a VW bus but, rather, drugs. I wanted to correct her. At the same time, this was some interesting information.

"I have no idea what you're talking about," I said flatly, pretending to cast aside her comment. "But," I continued, "let's just say Guy Number One in one state was purchasing something from Guy Number Two in another state. And

Guy Number One couldn't make the trip. Well, I guess Guy Number One would hire another person, Guy Number Three, to make the deal."

The hippie girl's eyes widened.

I continued, "And, yes, Guy Number Three should be compensated for the inconvenience of traveling to take care of the business."

The girl leaned in even closer. She smelled faintly of patchouli. "Don't tell me specifics. Just how much, in dollars, are we talking about? How big of a load?"

"Let's just say that a person like Guy Number Three would deliver seven grand."

"Seven thousand dollars!" The hippie girl realized she yelled it and hushed herself. "You brought all that with you on a Greyhound bus? How?"

"Let's just say Guy Number Three has his ways," I sat back in my chair as if I was some seasoned veteran of drug dealings. The girl sat back as well, astonished.

"You know there's talk of legalizing it down here too," she said. "I think that's why he's getting into the harder stuff."

"Harder stuff? This is all news to me," I said looking concerned.

She picked up on it and took my bait. "You didn't hear it from me, OK? But Jared's been dealing some crazy crap out there. Some sort of new stuff. Like ecstasy mixed with coke mixed with meth. Acts like some crazy aphrodisiac. Jared calls it *ganchos*."

"Ganchos? Like the freaks in the paintings?"

"You've seen them then," she stated. "Yeah, the way I hear it, it's kind of code. You go in and ask Jared to tell you about the Ganchos. Then he asks you, 'Which one?' and you say, 'The sexy one,' which is the real code because they're all butt ugly. Then he'll ask if you're a cop and when you say no, he'll hook you up."

"Have you tried it?"

"Nope. I'm not that hard core. I hear the stuff is intense." She looked at me sideways. "You're not delivering *that* stuff, are you?"

"No. I can honestly say I'm not delivering ganchos to Jared." And I was honest too.

"Good. It's all messed up. I mean, I have fun too. I party now and then. But the stuff he's putting out there is…it's just too much. I know of a few people who are hooked. Sad, you know? I mean stuff's there for fun, not to get all strung out."

I didn't reply.

"Nothing against what you do," she said as if she felt her comment had insulted me.

"Do me a favor," I said. "Don't tell anyone that you saw me."

"You're a ghost," she replied.

A ghost. How appropriate.

21 | Rocky

I headed back to Calavera's. I still had a few minutes to kill so I looped around another part of the village just to take in more sights, think about El Mismo, and do some Chihuahua dog watching. I ended up on a street that ran along the backside of Calavera's. I recognized the back of the building from when Maya and I were looking for the work that Esteban supposedly had done. It was still about a hundred yards ahead. I saw a guy leaning against the back wall. I squinted and realized it was Rocky. He was smoking a cigarette. I decided to go up and talk to him. Maybe I could get him to tell me something, anything. Maybe he had some sort of information that would help me figure this whole thing out.

I started to walk his way and stopped when another guy came from around the side of the building. It was Jared. I thought better of approaching, opting to eavesdrop instead. I snuck around to where I was not visible to them and quickly approached the side of the restaurant, backing up against the wall and leaning my ear toward their direction. They were speaking in hushed tones so I couldn't make anything out. I strained to hear. Then Jared's voice grew louder. "Honestly, Rocky, I couldn't give a rat's ass! We had a deal. You hold up your end, I hold up mine. But you didn't hold up your end, did you? So I don't have to hold up *my* end."

"Come on, Jared," Rocky pleaded. "You don't understand. I need to have—"

"You don't *need* to have anything," Jared sneered back at him. "You can't control yourself. You think you *need* but you *want*. That's what this is all about, right? Don't you see? You're doing this to yourself."

"You can't just not give me…I mean, not after all this time! All I've done!"

"I can do whatever I want. That means I *don't* do what I *don't* want to do." Jared had a steely calm to his voice.

"But Jared, I'll tell—" Rocky's words were interrupted by a harsh slapping sound. Then there was a strange tussling sound followed by a thump.

"You'll keep your mouth shut, you idiot!" Jared demanded. "Or I'll shut you up like I shut up Zoey. You want that?"

There was a low "Uh-uh," Rocky grunting in the negative. Then I heard footsteps walking away. I peered around the corner to see Rocky on the ground looking at his hands. There were scrapes on them.

I took a few steps back then started whistling casually, as if I was just walking around. I rounded the back of the restaurant and acted surprised to see Rocky on the ground.

"Rocky?" I said with mock concern.

"What are you doing back here?" he asked. He was not happy. Probably about getting roughed up by Jared. Or maybe he was just not happy to see me. Probably both.

"Just taking a walk before I go in and see Maya."

At that he bounded up and walked right up to me and got in my face. "This is all your fault, you know? You came around here and got mixed up with Maya and El Mismo and now look!" He showed me scrapes on his forearms. They didn't seem that bad, they weren't even bleeding.

"You're just a jerk like every other jerk she goes out with," he said, almost getting emotional. "She should be with me! I'm glad El Mismo tagged that stupid bus of yours. And I'm glad he kicked you in the mouth. Good luck kissing Maya with that busted lip!" He turned around and stomped away.

Weird guy. Disillusioned guy too. And, above all, jealous.

I ventured into Calavera's to meet Maya. There were only a few tables occupied with customers, all looked like tourists of course. There was no hostess so I sat myself. I figured Maya would spot me.

She did.

She smiled and pinched her fingers together in a *give me just a tiny moment* gesture. No worries. I had to process the Rocky encounter.

Before long she showed up with some water and chips and salsa. She came up beside me and scratched my back gently. "Hi," she said. "I've got Mamita making you lunch. You *are* hungry, right?"

"Absolutely." I squeezed her hand. She squeezed back. This was nice. But, in my mind, and probably in hers, our time together was limited. Make the best of it.

The other tables finished up and Maya cleaned up after them. I was alone in the dining room. Maya appeared from the kitchen with two plates and set them down at my table, one for me, one for her. It was the same plate I had last time. She was eating a salad. She got herself some water and sat down beside me.

"I was hoping you would come earlier," she said. "I mean, I just wanted to see you."

"I thought I'd come after the rush." I felt bad right after I said it, as if I had inadvertently insulted her.

"We were actually busy for once. I guess it's good that you

came when you did. Now we get to eat together." She leaned over and kissed my cheek and then dove into her food with reckless abandon.

I ate the relleno first. I figured that, if the proverbial end-of-the-world asteroid hit, at least I got that relleno in my belly. I usually eat all my meals like that, best first. After I got that out of the way, I decided to get to some business. "Did you see Rocky today?" I asked.

"Yeah. Just a minute ago. I saw him come in and go straight to the locker room. He looked rushed."

"Is he still here?"

"I don't know. I just saw him come in, and I really wasn't paying that much attention. And, if you can't tell by now, I'm not too interested in Rocky."

"Might be a good time to start being interested," I said, lowering my voice.

Maya looked at me seriously. "Why?" She asked, matching my hushed tone.

"I wanted to come see you after lunch so we could visit. But I got anxious and just wanted to be near you. So I came down here earlier than I had planned. I just walked around, wandered, explored. I got a cup of coffee at that place, The Mug. I talked to a girl there and she told me about Jared and *ganchos.*" When I said *ganchos,* Maya froze mid-chew and grew pale.

"The girl said it's bad stuff. The only reason I bring it up is because I heard Jared and Rocky talking behind the restaurant."

Maya had recovered her composure but stopped eating. She moved some food around on her plate and was silent. I could see the wheels turning in her head as she looked at her plate.

"Jared was pissed at Rocky for not making good on a deal," I continued. "Rocky was just begging for whatever Jared was supposed to be giving him. Then Jared roughed him up."

"So you think Rocky and Jared had some sort of drug deal?"

"Can't say for sure. All I know is what that girl at The Mug told me. She said that *ganchos* act like some crazy aphrodisiac."

Maya set her fork down gently. "They do," she said softly. "It's a lot of the reason, you know, for my stupid decisions. The pictures. All that. I don't blame the drug. Not for everything. I mean, I took it, right? I just didn't expect it to..." She looked guilty. I wanted to ask about this Zoey girl that Jared said he shut up, but it didn't seem to be a good time. I tabled it in my mind for later.

I took Maya's hand in mine. "Look, it's all in the past," I reassured her.

"Not if—" She stopped.

"What?"

"Nothing." She poked at her food and nibbled a bit. Her eating gusto now gone.

"Not to dampen the mood any more but tonight is my last night at the hotel," I said. "I don't have enough money to stay any longer than tonight."

She looked up at me and cocked her head to the side.

"I can probably leave later tomorrow evening and drive all night so that I don't have to get a hotel," I said. "Maybe sleep in the bus at a rest stop."

She was still looking at me like I was insane. "I can't believe I didn't think about it," she said as if she just realized I had to leave.

"Well, I can't stay here forever, Maya," I said. "I have to get the bus back to Chuck. That's why I'm here."

"No, not that. I know you have to leave. But I forgot about the casita." She beamed at me.

"I haven't said anything about it before, Maya, but I really don't know much Spanish."

"I'm sorry," she said with a shake of her head. "A *casita* is a little house behind a house, in the backyard. For guests."

"Oh, like a *mother-in-law* house?"

"Kind of. But usually a casita doesn't have a full kitchen. It's more like a hotel room. We have one." She put down her fork and yelled over her shoulder, "Mamita?"

Maya's mother came out of the kitchen wiping her hands on her towel. Somehow she heard Maya's voice over her music. But, then again, they say parents hear their children even in loud environments.

"Que quieres?" Mrs. Calavera asked.

"La casita, Mamita," Maya said holding onto her mother's hand. "Can Perk stay there?"

"OK with me," Mrs. Calavera said as she winked at me. "Maybe I visit him at night," she cooed in accented, slightly broken English. "Take him fresh baked sopapillas *con* honey, no?" She spoke loudly. I hadn't noticed it in the kitchen when the music was blaring. I felt a bit embarrassed hearing her talk to me like that even though there didn't seem to be anyone else around.

"Mamita!" Maya said and spanked her mother on the butt. They had a weird relationship.

Mrs. Calavera giggled and told Maya, "You ask Poppy. If he says it is OK, I say it is OK. *Sopas o no sopas."* She winked at me again and turned around and went back into the kitchen.

Maya said, "I'll call Poppy. He should be up by now. I'm sure he'll say yes. He likes you. But it's not like he has to be your biggest fan or anything. I mean, he even let Rocky stay there a week one time when he was between places. Much to my chagrin, mind you. I made sure I had extra thick drapes put up on my windows before he showed up, if you catch my drift."

"Smart move," I said. She was no stranger to Rocky's pervy ways. "He took a pic of your butt, you know. Yesterday."

"Doesn't surprise me. He's always taking pics of me. I can't wear certain shirts around him or he tries to catch me bending over. If I catch him, he always says the same thing: 'Oh Maya, you're so pretty. You should be a model.'" That last part was spoken as if it were being said by slime. Nope, Rocky never stood a chance with Maya.

"Are there extra thick drapes on the casita?" I asked. "For *my* protection of course. Wouldn't want you sneaking around trying to catch me in the buff."

Maya kicked my shin under the table. It hurt, but I didn't let on that it did. She grinned at me with a mouth full of food. She was back in a good mood and her eating proved it. "No," she said with food in her mouth. "Just blinds. And, even if they're closed, I can still peek through them. They're not that good. Please wear the Speedos." I liked her humor.

We finished up and Maya began gathering up the plates. "Before we go," I said, "I'd like to look at that camera one more time. Up close. Do you have the stepladder?"

"Yeah. It's in the locker room. I'll get it after I drop these off. Meet me at El Mismo." She took off into the kitchen. A moment later, I sensed someone going through the front door. I couldn't see from my angle, but the idea that a patron would come in this late in the afternoon to a restaurant that hadn't been too busy felt odd. But then, no one came in. Maybe someone went out, Jared or someone at his bar. All in all, it shouldn't matter. I guess it just felt weird. Maybe I was letting the whole mystery get to me, make me paranoid.

I got up and made my way to El Mismo's room. A moment later, Maya arrived with the ladder, carrying it easily. She was small but strong. She handed me the ladder and opened the door, turned on the light. I placed the ladder up against the wall, like Esteban had done, and ascended it. The first thing I did was pull on the wire going into the wall. It was loose and I could pull it easily until it stopped itself. The grommet was fitted so I couldn't see inside. But I could loosen the whole grommet and remove it from the hole; it wasn't glued in from what I could tell. I pulled it out only to find that, on the other end, was a standard electrical plug.

I showed it to Maya and said, "Just what I thought. Not hardwired at all. It's a dummy."

Maya stepped up to take a closer look then looked at me with concern in her eyes. "But I saw the video," she said. "We all saw it. You did too."

I placed everything back the way it was and stepped down. "I've got something to show you," I said. "Who's here working right now?"

"Just me and Mamita. And Jared. Jared's always here these days. Doubles every day."

"And Esteban? When does he get back?"

"Tomorrow. He's on the schedule for the night shift."

"OK. Let me get my laptop." I hauled the ladder to the room they called the locker room. Maya let me in. It was like a master bedroom with a bench in the middle. There was a line of footlockers against one wall, eight total, four on top, four on bottom. All of them except one had a combination lock. There were a couple of armchairs and a loveseat set up like a small lounge. There was also a sturdy coffee table. In the far right of the room was a bathroom. There was no window and no pictures on the walls, just a simple lounge area. I thought it was a nice touch. Back home, Mr. Argyle got us footlockers but then took them back for a refund. He thought we would abuse them. I guess these things can be abused. It had never occurred to me to be suspicious about what was in them until my boss took them away. Now I was looking at the locked lockers and wondering what secrets lay within.

I was staring at the lockers when Maya came up behind me and put her arms around me, hands on my chest and pulled herself close to me. I turned around and looked at her. She gazed up at me and I kissed her. "I don't want you to go," she said quietly. "I would never have imagined, not in a million years, that a guy like you would capture my heart."

"I don't want to go either. I'm a lucky guy, if only for a few days." I kissed her again and said, "I have to go back to the hotel to get my laptop I'll be right back."

"Wait!" She took out her phone and made a call. The whole conversation was in Spanish. I understood *Poppy, casita,* and *gracias.* She had called her dad about me staying in the casita. "He says it's OK with him. I told him that you would stay starting tonight. I thought that maybe you could get a refund on your room and that maybe we could spend some more time together after I close tonight." She clinched the front of my shirt in her hand.

"I like that idea," I said, kissing her again. I couldn't get enough of her. And it seemed as though she couldn't get enough of me. It was powerful. Then I thought of being close to her tonight. And I thought of her vow. Even so, I kissed her harder.

22 | FX

The clerk at the hotel was hesitant to give me a refund. She said that, since I didn't check out by 10:30 AM, I was obligated to pay for the night. I didn't want to stay that night. Or, rather, I wanted to stay near Maya. After some back and forth, we came to a compromise. I offered to pay twenty bucks and get a refund on the rest. Not the best deal but forty bucks is better than nothing. I gathered my stuff, checked out, and headed back to Calavera's.

When I arrived, I purposely made my way quickly past Jared. I didn't want anything to do with him. And I wasn't too big on him anyway because of the photographs he may or may not have deleted. No one was in the dining area so I just went into the kitchen. Why not? Maya was in there talking to her mom. Her mom wasn't as jovial as she had been before. They both looked at me when I got in as if I was interrupting something. "I'm back," I said. "I'll wait for you out here." And I backed out of the kitchen.

I sat down, got my laptop out, and opened the video editing program and the file with Mr. Argyle turning into a ghost. Within a couple of minutes, Maya made her way to my table and sat down. She looked concerned.

"Is everything OK?" I asked.

"It's Poppy. Mamita is worried about him. We both are."
Maya sat down at the table with me. "She just called him and
he's already started drinking. Usually he waits until evening.
He sounded down earlier when I asked him if you could stay
in the casita. I just thought he was more hungover than usual.
But Mamita is saying she's never heard him this depressed.
She called him just a few minutes ago. He was telling her that
we were better off without him, that he ruined our lives or
something."

"Did she ask him about the key?"

"No. She doesn't want to upset him. I want to ask him but,
by the time I get home, he'll probably be passed out."

"Can you call him?"

"Not when he's drinking. I mean I can but he always gives
me the runaround. Tells me everything will be OK."

I could see that she really didn't want to talk to him so I
didn't press it. I switched the subject. "Look at this." I turned
the laptop so that she could see it and played the video of Mr.
Argyle and his ghost.

"Whoa!" she exclaimed. "That's just like the El Mismo
ghost. Where did you get this?"

"I made it myself with a video editing program I have."

Maya sat silent for a moment, processing this information.
Her eyes darted from side to side. "So Esteban put up a dummy
camera and faked the ghost video? But why?" she shrugged and
frowned, confused. "So that he could run around town stealing
babushka dolls and tagging VW busses?"

"That wasn't him I tackled." I said. "The ghost—the guy
dressed as the ghost—was pudgy around the middle. Kind
of chubby. Esteban is thin. He wears those tight-fitted shirts.
There's no way to hide fat in those. Plus he's in Phoenix, right?"

"As far as we know, yes. I saw some of his pics on Facebook.

Every time he goes to Phoenix these days, he posts like a hundred pictures of himself there."

"Those could be faked too."

"I doubt it," Maya said. "They're selfies with people there and he's tagged them and they commented on the pics, about what they did. It would take some sort of large cover up to make all his Phoenix friends fake it. And their friends would know. You can't fake partying on Facebook. People call you out on that."

"Let's think about this for a second," I said. "We know that Esteban faked the videos but he's not the ghost."

"That's assuming there's only *one* guy dressed up as the ghost," Maya retorted pointedly. She was quick on the draw.

"How have people described him when they have seen him?"

"Basically how he was when we saw him. Not too tall and didn't move too fast. He's always described with that big black robe so no one can say if he's skinny or fat. There's no real way to tell. At least not in the dark."

"Well, the one I tackled was kind of fat," I said. "Let's just assume that there's only one guy who dresses as the ghost. That gives us two guys involved in this thing. And think about it, if there were a bunch of people involved, it could get complicated. Also, it thins out the take."

"The *take?*" Maya was intensely intrigued, leaning in toward me.

"Yeah. Think of a band that plays a gig at a bar," I said. "If they get paid a hundred bucks to play that gig, it gets split up between the band members. If there's only two of them, each gets fifty. If there's four, they each get twenty-five. In the case of the Sugar Skull Ghost Thief gig, they're splitting a pot full of small items. Would a bunch of guys risk their necks for some dolls or pictures or whatever else is stolen. What's the value?"

"OK, so two guys. Esteban and someone else. But who?"

"Who's the fat man?" I asked rhetorically. We sat and thought for a moment.

"It would be easier if we knew *why* they were doing it," I said, breaking the silence.

No response from Maya.

"This is probably not the best place to talk about all this," I said. "When do you get off?"

"We close at ten. I'm usually done around that time. We pre-close everything and, since we're not too busy, we usually get out right about ten fifteen."

"I'll be back here at ten, and I can follow you home. This place is dark, and I'd probably get lost without GPS."

"That works," she said. "What will you do until then?"

"My boss is paying me to make a commercial for the café where I work. That's why I have all this time off. He bought me the video editing program, the one I used to make that ghost, and he's paying me one week's wages to create it. So far all I have is my boss vaporizing. I have to get it done by Monday morning or I'm toast." I put my laptop away and started to get up. "Tomorrow's already Friday and, in all honesty, I'd like to spend as much time with you as possible."

"Me too," she replied looking up at me.

"If I can get this commercial done, I can put it behind me." I looked Maya straight in the eye. "This ghost thing? It's no small deal," I said. "Your dad, witches, Esteban's fake video, your whole restaurant at risk. This is big stuff. And I think we're close to figuring it all out. We *have* to figure it out."

"I know," she said softly.

"I can't just leave you in this mess. I like you too much for that. Plus it would drive me crazy for the rest of my life."

She didn't say anything, just nodded looking down. She was the same girl I met when I got here but she had changed.

And I guess I had too. Together we changed. I liked us. Too bad it couldn't last.

23 | Geode

The commercial for my boss loomed over everything. I had to get that done, no way around it. It didn't occur to me that I didn't have a place to work. I was in limbo, not at the hotel and not yet at Maya's family's casita. And I had around seven hours until ten tonight. And while I was determined to not drive Chuck's bus around unnecessarily, I was, for all intents and purposes, living out of the thing. At least for the next seven hours.

I needed two things: electricity and wi-fi. My laptop was low on battery and I needed internet access. The obvious decision was a coffee shop. But not The Mug. That would be weird going back there, especially with that girl who thought I was a drug runner. So I drove around.

There was a university in Las Cruces. New Mexico State University. In my experience, where there's a university, there are places for students to go hang out and work. I stopped off at a gas station and went in and asked the clerk how I could get to the university. She directed me to the southern end of town near a mountain range. She also gave me a tip: park off-campus or take a bunch of quarters for a meter. I had no intention on parking on campus so the idea of spending money to park there sounded stupid. But then something hit me. All college campuses have a library and I assumed such places would be quiet and have electrical outlets and wi-fi. For the same three bucks I would spend on a cup of coffee and fight for a table near an electrical outlet, I could feed a meter and set myself up for a couple of hours at least and mooch off of the library's resources. Plus, the energy of being around focused students diligently studying might rub off on me, yield a better video. Sometimes coffee shops can be distracting.

I got five bucks worth of quarters from the clerk. Holding the quarters in my hand led me to think about doing a load of laundry. I was on my last set of clean clothes. I under-packed and I didn't want to stink in front of Maya. My plan was to get as much content for the commercial as I could from my time at the library then assemble it at a laundromat. Made sense.

After some driving around and asking people, I found the library. There was a parking lot nearby with meters. The meter rates were fifty cents per hour. Twenty five cents cheaper than home. Not huge savings but, when you're running low on funds, every quarter counts. Plus I needed to buy laundry detergent and such. I guess I could ask Maya if I could use their washer and dryer but they were already letting me stay there for free. My mom always told me not to wear out my welcome, and not to use other people's things without them offering first. I thought about my mooching off of the library and concluded that, by leaving the resources open to everyone, they were, in fact, offering.

I fed the meter enough quarters for two hours and headed into the library. It was three stories tall and my plan was to go to the third floor, presumably the quietest. When I walked into the lobby, I was struck by the fact that they had an exhibit of sorts. Displayed were specimens of petrified wood, all different kinds and colors. In addition, there were geodes and fossils. I was drawn to them. I walked around looking at the different specimens. Some were huge tree trunks. Others were slices. They had been treated so they were glossy like glass. There was a giant geode, taller than me. It was sliced in half and the crystals inside were magnificent. I gazed at the crystals lining the inner walls and thought they looked like jewels as they sparkled in the light. How much did something like that cost? That made me think of value. When the geode was closed, it must have looked like just any other big rock. No one would buy a big rock unless they needed it for something. But a rock is a rock. A geode, however, is not a rock. There is treasure inside. And that's the difference.

Value.

The geode was on display in the library because it had value. It had been shipped to Las Cruces, and that couldn't have been a cheap undertaking. It took effort to make this happen, from finding the geode to displaying it. People spent time and money to make that happen. Value. Worth something. Incentive and effort. Risk.

What exactly was *so* valuable to compel someone to don the El Mismo mask and run around at night stealing small items and vandalizing, all at the risk of being arrested? The payoff was just too small for that. In fact, the payoff was so small that it would only be worth it if someone paid you to do it. Or if there was some bigger payoff over and above the value of the items that outweighed the risk of going to jail.

Esteban was risking something with the fake videos. The fat dude was risking something with the crimes. Where was the value? What was the take? I stared at the crystals in the geode. Hidden. The value was *hidden*. The prize was a mystery, unknown until made known.

I tucked the thought in the back of my mind and headed up to the third floor to start work on the commercial. I would have stood there thinking about the Sugar Skull Ghost Thief for two hours, but the meter was running out. Also, my clothes weren't getting any cleaner as the day wore on.

When I reached the third floor, I found a table and set up shop. I had to do some finagling to hook onto the wi-fi. By "finagling" I mean I had to convince some girl to let me piggy back on her account. They verify if you're a student or not. I told her that I was traveling from Colorado and needed to get on to make a commercial for back home. She didn't hesitate to let me use her credentials. In fact, the mere mention of my origins in Colorado endeared me to her. Don't know why. My guess is that desert people like the forest feel of Colorado. I like to think that she thought I was cute. I'll leave it at that.

My plan was to gather positive feedback from patrons. The only problem was, I had no way of getting in touch with them and it was later in the day on Thursday. I would need testimonials, preferably at the café, by tomorrow. We were closed over the weekend so there would be no way of getting that content after Friday, 5:00 PM.

The earbuds I used were supplied with a microphone, good for hands-free phone calls. I plugged them into the computer and set up a Google Voice account so that I could make phone calls. I called the Argyle Café. Candy would be manning the front and Compa would be cooking in back. I had the café's number memorized, been working there for a while. I dialed it and waited to see which of my coworkers answered.

"Café," came a female voice from the other end. It was Candy. Good.

"Candy, it's Perk," I said.

"You didn't text me back," she said gruffly.

"You texted me? My phone is completely done for. I haven't been able to use it since Tuesday morning. Sorry. Was it important?"

"No. I just wanted to know how you were. It's like you dropped off the face of the earth. Where are you?"

"Old Mesilla," I replied as a matter of fact. Then I realized she (like me before my visit) probably had no idea where Old Mesilla was. "Well, actually I'm in Las Cruces, New Mexico. Old Mesilla is a small town next to it."

"What the hell are you doing down there?"

"It's a long story," I said. "A really long story. And it's not done yet."

"Did you get the commercial done? Mr. A said you wanted to put girls in bikinis and money laundering in it. What's with that?"

I missed her strange sarcasm. I never knew if she was serious or kidding.

"I've got an idea for the commercial but I need your help. Only you can help me."

She didn't respond. I filled the void by saying, "I need some quick testimonials. Things like people saying how much they like the café. Regulars, if you can catch them."

"What will you do for me if I get these testimonials you so desperately need?"

"I'll buy you a burger." I knew that she would up the ante so I started small.

"A burger and you come with me to *Eighties Night* at The Dub Club."

Candy was big on the eighties and had been pressing me to go with her to The Dub Club, a bar/dancehall that had a "radical" eighties night. She said most of her friends wouldn't go.

"Deal," I replied.

"So what exactly do you need?"

"Videos. Tell them that we're making a commercial and we want to feature our most loved and valued customers."

"That's laying it on thick, don't you think?"

"Put your own spin on it. Whatever you need to do to get them to say something. I've only got to fill thirty seconds so they need to be brief. Still, more video is better. I can cut out all the stuff that I can't use."

"What if I did a little bit where I talked about some of our specials?" Candy asked. I picked up on her hint. She wanted to be featured. Why not? I had nothing at that point.

"You wouldn't mind doing that?" I was leading her.

"No, not at all. I mean, you could use it or not. Better to have more stuff than less, right?"

"Smart," I said. The more I thought about it, the better the whole idea sounded. And if Candy was willing to help me out, I was willing to put her in the video.

"You know what?" I said, "I think it's a great idea to feature you. If anyone should be the face of the café, it should be the prettiest face. That's you." I could hear her smiling on the other end.

"I'll get some vids," she said. "How do you want me to get them to you?"

"I've got a Dropbox account. I'll create a folder and send you an invite. Just put them in there. I can retrieve them here on my end."

"Retrieve," she said with a snort. "You're so weird."

I ignored the comment. "Can you get these before close tomorrow?" I asked.

"I'm already on it. I've got my eye on the door. As soon as Short-Shorts Guy comes in, I'm taking a video of him." Short-Shorts Guy was a guy who came in regularly wearing super short shorts.

"I don't think I will use him," I said.

"I don't care. He needs to be recorded."

I thanked Candy again and ended the call. Strangely, the

faint memory of Short-Shorts Guy made me homesick. Then I thought of Maya. She trumped Short-Shorts Guy by a long shot.

After poking around the program, I found that it provided themed templates. It basically did all the work for me. All I had to do was plug in some clips and the theme would do all the fancy transitions. Just so happened that one of the themes was called "Café" and had images of old french cafés and bistros in the transitions along with chalkboard "signs" with drawings of coffee and pastries that I could add text to in a chalk font. The commercial was going to be easier to complete than I had anticipated. Then I thought that the universe had a weird way of balancing things out. Something difficult this way comes.

24 | Trade-Off

I did my best to shake the feeling of impending doom. With some time left in the meter, I decided to walk around the campus, get some exercise. Why not? School was in session so there were plenty of people walking around. But I didn't want to talk to anyone, really. I just wanted to work out the whole Sugar Skull Ghost Thief in my mind.

After walking for about a half hour and not really coming to any conclusion, I sat down on a bench, determined to use up every last cent in the parking meter. Behind me two girls talked about their class. From what I could hear, they were talking about Economics, specifically trade. One girl was complaining about not understanding a concept. The other girl told her, "They call it *opportunity cost* but it's not so much a cost but a trade-off. It's all about trade. No one buys anything; they trade money for it. Same thing with time and energy. You trade one thing for another. Like if you're going to go to the game, you're not going to be in your room studying. It's a trade-off. The cost of going to the game is the time you lose studying."

I liked how she put it. A *trade-off* and that everything is a trade. I thought about Jared and Rocky and Esteban and Maya and her Dad. I thought about what each of them were doing and what they were trading for it. And I thought about trade just by itself. The pieces started to come together.

I went back to the library with the precious few minutes I had left in the parking meter. Maybe Candy got me something to work with. Turns out I got even more than I had anticipated. Candy sent me an email. She had already recorded some videos and uploaded them. I was impressed. Then again, she could be very efficient when she put her mind to it.

After the files synced, I packed up and left. I used the time at the laundromat to trim the videos and pop them into the theme. The whole process was quick and painless. What was supposed to be a week-long project took all of two hours. With the help of Candy and a theme, of course. But still.

I felt that I was getting close to figuring out this whole ghost thing. I decided to get my thoughts together on paper. I went to a store and bought a spiral notebook. I found a taproom by the university, procured a pint of beer, and set myself to work, ignoring the crowd around me.

I wrote down everything I knew about the case of the Sugar Skull Ghost Thief. I noted all the people and all the occurrences. I even noted all that Maya had told me, the personal stuff. That might play a role. I didn't leave anything out. Then I started connecting the dots. And they began to reveal an ugly picture. Even uglier than those Ganchos folks.

25 | Casita

I arrived at the square in Old Mesilla around 10:00 PM. I waited in the bus. I figured that Maya would look for me and pull up to lead me to her house, which she did with minimal fanfare, just a wave.

When we got to her house, I grabbed my stuff out of the bus and met up with her in the darkness. She led me around the side of the house, through a chainlink gate to her backyard. We didn't talk. She simply led me by the hand briskly. Obviously she didn't want to go through the house. No sense in that.

The casita sat far off from the main house. Probably a half a football field from what I could tell. There was a large yard with trees in between. Needless to say, it was secluded.

She said, "Wait here. I'll go get the key." She ran off toward her house, guided only by the light of a crescent moon. She returned in no less than two minutes, according to my estimated guess. Efficient and competent.

She unlocked the door and handed me the key. "Here," she said. "Hold onto it. Stay for a while." She leaned into me and gave me a peck on the lips. "I'm going to go take a shower," she said, pulling away from me. "I smell like grease and armpit." She raised up her hand and sniffed her armpit then scrunched up her nose. To me she smelled just perfect. But maybe I was blinded by my fondness of her. "Are you hungry?" she asked.

I hadn't thought about it but, yes, I was. I hadn't eaten since lunch. "I am," I said.

"I was hoping you were. I didn't eat either. I'll have Mamita mix something up for us real quick. I've got a bottle of wine too. I'll be back." Maya trotted back to her house and left me there with my thoughts.

My mind was all over the place. I had a faint idea of what I thought might be going on, but it didn't make complete sense. There were some dots connecting but not all. And there were multiple and loose connections. I stood there thinking about it all but it ended up going in circles. I figured I would talk it over with Maya when she came back.

I decided to get the casita prepared for her return. There wasn't much to do, the casita only had a bed and a nightstand. It also had a small wet bar on one side of the room with cabinets above and a small refrigerator below. It really was like a hotel room. Only there were no chairs for seating, only the bed. I fitted the clean sheets on the bed and did some light dusting with a washrag, one of many that Maya had supplied me with. I remembered our date and the candles. They were still in the bus. I went and got them, along with the lighter and the crank emergency flashlight/radio. I set up the candles all over the room and lit them. I cranked the radio and turned it on and set it off to the side. There was a lamp beside the bed, and I turned that on and turned off the overhead light. This made a soft glow of light throughout the room.

Upon a full inspection of the casita, I concluded that, yes, the blinds were, in fact, sparse. Ill-fitted at best. The windows dwarfed the blinds by a long shot. I wondered why they were even there. They provided no privacy whatsoever. They hung insufficiently three-quarters of the way down with at least a half a foot of exposed window on each side. Luckily, the bathroom had a door on it. I could change in there without worry of anyone getting an eyeful. Then again, the casita was so secluded, who would see me anyway?

I decided that I could do with a shower and got to it.

When I came out, Maya had already returned and was leaning back on the bed. She was wearing an oversized maroon sweatshirt with a black and white logo of the mascot from her university on the front as well as some tight-fitting, small, pink shorts. She was barefoot. I looked toward the door. Two flip flops lay haphazardly as if kicked off violently. On my end, I was only wearing a towel, nothing underneath. She looked at me and raised her eyebrows. "Hey there, sexy," she said. She twirled her wet hair with her fingers.

"I, uh…" I stammered. "I thought you would take longer."

"Screw all that drawn out stuff. Get to business. That's what I say."

I blushed. She noticed it and got up and made a beeline to me. She grabbed the front of my towel and said, "You don't know how sexy you are to me." Then she kissed me hard. I held onto my towel as I felt it coming loose from her grip.

I pulled away. "I need to get dressed," I said.

"If you insist," she snickered.

I picked out some underwear, cargo shorts, and a t-shirt and got dressed in the bathroom. When I came out, Maya was still on the bed but now she had two glasses of wine and a couple of cold cut sandwiches along with a bag of potato chips. I joined her. Where else was I to sit?

"Let's make a toast," she said. "To the night. May it be filled with us." She held up her glass, and I clinked mine against hers and we sipped.

I ran my fingers through my hair. I felt a bit self-conscious with my hair uncombed and unruly. Maya had no qualms about her own hair. Her hair was still damp but not wet. It was drying and gaining volume. She wasn't wearing any makeup and still looked amazing. Probably more so because she was so natural.

"I was thinking…" she said, "maybe you could stay until Sunday morning." She immediately put her glass to her mouth to shut herself up.

"Two more days?" I asked, obviously. We both dove into our meals, eating ravenously.

"Tomorrow I work a double. Like today," she said with her mouth full but holding her hand over it in an attempt at manners. "We won't get a chance to hang out much. But, if you stay Saturday, I don't work. We could hang out then."

"I don't know," I said, feigning concern. "I've got a turtle in my backyard at home. She misses me something awful."

She gave me a smart grin and slapped my arm hard. "I must be prettier than that turtle," she said playfully.

"I haven't decided yet. I'll let you know."

We sipped our wine and something came to me. "Who's Zoey?" I asked, bluntly.

"How do you know about Zoey?" she asked suspiciously.

"From that conversation I overheard between Jared and Rocky. Actually, Jared was the only one talking at that point. He mentioned Zoey."

"She works at the restaurant too." Maya answered. "Well, I don't know if she still does. She's not on the schedule. Probably because she's had her shifts covered for the last two weeks. I tried to text her to check on her but no response."

"Have you gone to see her?"

"I told you, she hasn't answered my texts. Besides, she and Jared go together now. At least they were the last time I talked to her. If anything happened to her, Jared would know."

Jared *would* know, I thought.

"Maybe she and Jared aren't seeing each other anymore. He doesn't seem like a long-term type of guy," I added.

"Maybe they're not," she replied casually.

We finished our food and Maya picked up our plates and stacked them on the wet bar. "You didn't really answer my question," I said. "I asked if you have gone to see her. In *person*."

"I don't go see people unless they answer my texts. Seems rude."

"And nearly giving a person a heart attack by scaring them dressed like a ghost is somehow *good* manners?"

"That's different," she said, slapping my arm again.

"Do you know where she lives?"

"No. But I can ask Jared."

"Don't," I said. "Can you get her address from your files at work?"

"I guess. Why don't you want me to ask Jared? You want to go hit on her yourself, player?" Maya gave me a wry smile. It was fun and all, but this was serious, and she had no idea that something was happening right under her nose. Part of me wanted to just lay everything out there for her. Then another part of me wanted to just keep things friendly for now. I liked her mood and our current location on the bed.

I faked a chuckle then shrugged. "Let's just say that, the more I learn about Jared, the less I trust him."

Maya just looked at me sideways. "Because of the pics?" she asked.

"Well," I said, "I think I need to *see* the pics first before I make any snap judgements." Then I winked at her.

She gave me a wide-eyed look and nearly spit out her wine. "You *would*, you perv!" Then she smiled at me. "Who needs pictures?" she asked. She set her wine glass on the floor and, in one elegant move, approached me and grasped my shirt, pulling herself close to me. Then she kissed me. I clumsily set my own wine glass down to free both my hands so I could grab hold of her. I was leaning with my back against the wall. I pulled her onto my lap and held her face with one hand and grabbed a handful of her hair with my other hand, both pulling her to me. She moaned with delight, kissing me back all the more.

She inched herself up onto my lap, closer to me, our bodies rubbing up against each other. I pulled her away from me to look at her. She was so beautiful I couldn't believe it. Seriously. I couldn't believe that this wonderful, beautiful, fiery girl was here with me, kissing me and wanting me. She looked back at me with pain in her eyes. She wanted to kiss me and I was keeping her from it. But I had to keep looking at her. I was entranced.

I allowed her to bridge the gap and she kissed me with vigor, rubbing her entire body up against mine. The radio played a song in Spanish. I had no idea of its meaning. It didn't matter. It was romantic and bold and fit the situation perfectly.

I pulled Maya even closer and attacked her neck, biting then sucking on it, trying to avoid hickeys but, at the same time, letting her know how much I desired her. She moaned with pleasure and held my head close to her. She smelled of vanilla. I guessed that she had put that on for me. She drew herself even nearer. I was fully aroused and she had to have known it because she moved her hips accordingly. It was one part torture and one part ecstasy. Her breath was heavy and warm on my neck. I figured mine was too. The music played on and we continued loving on each other. At one point, I recognized the song *"Quizas, quizas, quizas."* I had heard it before but it seemed odd and strange. The sound of that song along with Maya on top of me made me feel like I was in a dream. If it was a dream, I didn't want to wake up from it.

Maya got up from me, gathered our wine glasses, and went

to the wet bar to pour us more. As much as I was upset that she left, I was relieved. I thought of her vow. I was in no place to control myself. Not with her.

She came back to the bed. I had sat up and she sat near me. She said, "Do you know what this song means? *Quizas, quizas, quizas?*"

"No," I admitted.

"It means *Perhaps, perhaps, perhaps.* Or *Maybe, maybe, maybe.* It's about love that never comes to full fruition." She sipped her wine.

I didn't say anything, just took a sip myself.

We sat there silently sipping our wine, just being with each other. Maya downed her wine and set her glass on the nightstand. Then she reached for mine and set it beside hers. She straddled me then placed her hands on my shoulders. I grabbed onto her hips securely. She leaned down, wrapped her arms around my neck, and kissed me with full force. I wrapped my arms around her thin waist and pulled her as close as I could. Her breaths were stuttered and heavy. I drew her even closer.

She sat up and stared down at me, her dark hair a riot about her face. She grabbed the bottom hem of her sweatshirt and began slowly pulling it up, staring deep into my eyes the whole time. Underneath I saw the hint of a thin silk camisole. The only reason I knew that term was because I was a fan of pictures of women in their underwear. And I have to say I was a fan of Maya's choice of undergarments.

She tucked her elbows into the hem of the sweatshirt to pull it over her head, but she went slow and easy. Teasing. I liked it. She smiled and I smiled back. I could see that she was working the moment.

She pulled the sweatshirt up, hiding her face and, at the same time, revealing the spaghetti string camisole which hung loosely over her beautiful, ample breasts. She must have been struggling to get the sweatshirt off because I heard a knock and something of a whimper/grunt; low, hollow, and unintentional. Maybe her shoulder popped and it hurt a bit.

Maya finally pulled the sweatshirt completely off and flung it to the floor. She shook her hair out of her face and looked at me, deep into my eyes, smiling. "That was a weird sound," she said.

"You're telling me," I replied. I wrapped my arm around her waist and pulled her to me and kissed her. She held onto my face and moved her hips. I let out a low moan and she let out a higher moan. Then came the knock again, followed by the same low hollow whimper/grunt but it didn't come from her. It sounded like it came from outside.

I lowered my mouth to her neck and kissed her softly, all the while holding her hair in such a way that I could look through it to the windows. Nothing was in the first window, the one to the right of the door. I panned to the window on the other side of the door, having to maneuver my making out as well as her hair to get a better look.

Then I saw it.

In the lower right hand side of the second window, below the bottom of the short blinds, peering in, face pressed against the glass, was the unmistakeable face of the Sugar Skull Ghost Thief. I couldn't see any eyes behind the mask, but I knew they were there somewhere.

My body tensed up involuntarily and I held my breath.

"Oh," Maya said sadly, breathing into my neck. "Already?"

"It's not that," I whispered in her ear. "Don't stop what you're doing."

She said nothing, just went back to work on my neck.

I whispered, "I'm going to tell you something but, when I do, do your best to act like I told you something other than what I told you. Maybe act like I told you something dirty."

"That's a weird game," she said. "Why not just tell me something dirty to begin with?"

I got close to her ear and whispered clearly, "Don't look, but ol' El Mismo is getting an eyeful of us from outside the window."

Now it was her turn to tense up and hold her breath. She recovered quickly. "Ooo, that's…dirty!" she said loudly.

I whispered in her ear again, "We need to find a way to get closer to the door so that I can get outside quickly and catch him before he gets too much of a head start."

She pulled away and looked at me. "What do you want me to do?" she asked.

I knew there was no way for the ghost to hear us when we talked in low tones. The music was loud enough to cover it up, and he was outside. "I need to get my shoes on first," I said. "Get up and act like you're going to give me a striptease. He's at the bottom left hand corner of the window to the left of the door. Make it so that you stand in front of him there, close but not too close. I doubt he'll move if he thinks we don't notice him. As soon as you block his view, I'll put my shoes on really quick. But don't stop dancing around."

Maya nodded and played the part. She got up slowly from the bed and inched away, keeping her back to the ghost and her eyes on me the whole time. She began to dance around, holding her hair up above her head. She backed up toward the window just a little bit more. I grabbed my shoes. Doc Martens. Not the best running shoes on earth but better than going barefoot. They were the only shoes I had. I was able to catch the ghost in them last time so I was confident I could do it again.

I bent over to lace my shoes which was difficult since Maya was really putting on a show. I wanted to look at her. She teased as if she was going to undress then wagged her finger at me. She would pull her shorts down just enough to show the strings of her underwear then brought them back up again. I heard the hollow whimper/grunt a few times during the show. The ghost was making the noises. I hoped that it was all he was doing out there.

I laced up my shoes and sat by the side of the bed. Maya turned, which gave me a view of the window. The ghost was gone. I instinctively looked to the other window. He was there. But this time, he noticed me spot him. His face was pressed up to the front of the mask which was pressed up to the window. I could see his eyes now, but they were faint, hidden behind some covering in the mask. We both froze. Maya continued to dance. Then he bolted.

I jumped up and ran to the door. "He knows we know!" I yelled. Maya scrambled to put on her flip flops as I made it through the front door. I stopped and listened in the night. I could hear him running, not to the front of the house but around and to the back.

The sound of his footsteps grew dim as the sound of the music got louder. Maya came up beside me and shoved something in my hand. "Here," she said. I looked down. She had handed me the radio, still playing music.

For a split second I thought to myself, *What am I going to do with this? Throw it at him?* Then I remembered that the radio had the flashlight on it too. I flipped it on and looked at Maya in complete appreciation one second before I took off after the ghost.

I could hear the general direction that he was going: deeper into the pecan tree orchard. I ran after him while doing my best to scan my surroundings. I saw a lot of trees, but no ghost. Then, about forty yards away, I saw one tree that had a wider trunk than the rest. I focused in on it. He was hiding behind one of the trees. Or trying to hide, rather. His sides came out from either side of the tree at least four inches on each side. Once he realized I was onto him, he took off again, lumbering and bumbling, holding his black robe up. He ran slow, slower than when I chased him before.

I knew I had him. I couldn't see that far past him, but I was pretty sure there weren't any buildings for him to hide behind there in the orchard. I set my course for him, running at full speed.

My adrenaline kicked in. I thought about him kicking me in the face. I thought about what he was doing to Maya and her family. I thought about the history of El Mismo being marred by his stupid actions. And I thought about him peeping in on me and Maya making out. I wanted to bust his jaw.

The forty yards between us dwindled quickly. He was slowing down, and I was going top speed. The radio was now playing *Besame Mucho.* I knew that one. It meant "Kiss me much," or something like that. Kiss. I altered my plan from tackling him again to pushing him high on the back, a kiss in its own right. A bully had done that to me back in elementary school while I was running on a track. It offset my center of gravity and I toppled forward. It should work with the ghost.

Thirty yards, twenty yards. He started trying to dodge between the trees which was stupid since he was still going in the same general direction. It only slowed him down more. I ran harder. Ten yards. Five. At two yards away, I dropped the radio and thrusted myself toward him, arms out in front of me. I caught him squarely at the top of his shoulders and he lost his balance. I couldn't see much without the light, but I could make out his arms windmilling as he fell forward. Then he ran into the tree with a thud, and I heard his body slowly slide down to the ground. I stood still. Was he out for the count?

I doubled back to retrieve the light. *Bésame Mucho* kept

playing in the stillness, the light cast on the ground in front of it. I picked it up and dusted it off as I turned around to go inspect the ghost. I looked up and realized that no, he wasn't out for the count. He was on his feet, glaring at me some twenty yards ahead. I shone the light in his eyes. I could see the pale skin of his face through the holes in the mask. He squinted his eyes below furrowed eyebrows.

It was clear that he was not able to outrun me. He realized this. So he decided to attack. He lifted up his robe and started running at me clumsily. I didn't know exactly what to do. Should I move aside and trip him? No, he'd just keep coming back. He had nothing to lose. Should I try to punch him? I wasn't a punching person and he was wearing a mask. What if the mask was made out of metal or something. I'd mess up my hand. Wouldn't want that. Hit him with the flashlight/radio? I'd lose the light.

It's weird what goes through your mind when you only have a second to process something and make a split decision. When I was a kid, my favorite professional wrestler was a guy who went by the name Boss Boot. He wore big army boots. He had a signature move where he flung his opponent against the ropes and, as his opponent was flung back from the ropes, Boss Boot stuck out leg straight and his opponent ran into it with his gut.

If it worked for Boss Boot, it should probably work for me.

The ghost was closing the gap between us. I stood my ground until the moment seemed perfect. Then I took a small step forward with my left leg and then swung my right leg up in front of me, hoping to catch the ghost square in his belly. However, the ghost tripped and started falling toward me. My steel-toed Doc Marten was heading upward while his face was heading downward. The two met with a satisfying *CRACK!*

The ghost's head snapped back and his body fell limp to the ground, face down. I stood over him like a victorious warrior. *Bésame Mucho* came to a climactic end on the emergency radio/flashlight. *Kiss my foot, ghost!*

26 | Capture

I heard steps coming up behind me, flopping as they tread. It was Maya. I stood there, shining the light on the ghost as she ran up beside me.

"Did you see that?" I asked proudly.

"What did you do?" she said in distress as she knelt beside him.

"I kicked him in his freakin' face," I said. I was satisfied that I had done it. He deserved it.

"Did you kill him?" Maya was frantic. I didn't really kick him that hard. I wasn't trying to kick him, only trying to lift up my leg. But he was falling pretty fast. Even so, I doubted he was dead.

Maya knelt beside the ghost and felt his wrist. "He has a pulse," she said. "But I'm afraid to move him." She looked up at me. "I saw what you did. The human body is both incredibly resilient and, at the same time, fragile. His neck might be broken."

"*You* saw him," I said. "He was attacking me. What did you want me to do? Grab him and handcuff him?"

"You didn't have to try to *kill* him!" Maya seemed angry with me. I thought I was protecting her; both her and her family, not to mention her family's business and everyone involved. And now she was mad at me because I may have put this stupid ghost out of commission?

"I wasn't trying to kill him," I said. "I was trying to stick my foot out so that he would run into it. Like Boss Boot."

Maya looked up at me. "Who the hell is Boss Boot?"

"A wrestler." I shrugged. I never said I was some great martial artist or anything.

"That stuff's not real, you know. People get hurt." She started pulling out her phone.

"Who you gonna call? Ghostbusters?" I smirked.

Maya didn't find my joke amusing. "Seriously?" she exclaimed irritated. "This is no time for jokes. I'm calling 911."

The ghost started grunting and rolling about like he wanted to get up but didn't know where he was. "Wait!" I said to Maya, catching her before she hit send on her phone. "He's moving. His neck isn't broken."

"You don't know that. What, do you have x-ray vision or something?" She still seemed a bit irritated, but I could tell that she was relieved that he was moving on his own. The ghost groped around wearily, like he was half awake.

"I thought if you broke your neck, you were either paralyzed or dead," I said with the utmost confidence. "I mean, that's what happens in the movies."

"Only if there is severe damage to the spinal cord. Still, he could have a broken vertebrae or have a dislocated vertebrae."

"And he could still move?"

"Yes. Unless he tries to move his head around and messes up his spinal cord."

This was all news to me.

"Can we at least take the mask off to see who he is?"

"No. That could do the same thing as if he moved his neck." She swiped her phone to make the call. The ghost rose up onto his hands and knees and shook his head.

"Wait!" I cried out to Maya once again.

She looked at the ghost and jumped away from him. Then she kicked him in the face hard. This time it was less of a crack as much as it was a crunch. The ghost went down. Maya hopped on one foot, holding the other in her hands. "Ow, ow, ow," she said as she hopped. I shone the light on her foot. "I forgot I was wearing only *chanclas!*" she said putting her foot down and stepping on it gingerly.

"What if *you* killed him this time?"

"If he died from a *chancla* to the face, that would be a first." She knelt down beside him and checked his pulse again, just to make sure. "He's fine," she said.

"We should tie him up," I suggested. "I mean, we can still call the cops, but what if he tries to get away again? It's probably not the best idea to keep kicking him in the face until we figure out what to do."

Maya stood up and came close beside me, hugging my arm. "I guess we could," she said.

"I'm thinking we *should*," I said. "You need to know what's going on, and this seems to be the person to ask about it."

She looked at the ghost without making a comment.

"Look," I said, turning Maya to face me. "He's not the only one involved, we know that much. And I'm thinking he's not the big dog in this whole thing. He's just a pawn. If the cops get to him, that doesn't change anything. Let's see if we can't get some info out of him first, and then we can hand him over to the cops."

"How should we do it?" she asked.

I thought for a second and came up with the perfect answer. "Does your dad have tools and all that?"

"Of course."

"Go see if you can find some zip ties," I said. "The thicker, the better. Get a bunch of them. And if you have a chair with armrests, get that too. I'll get the ghost to the casita. Meet me there."

The ghost wasn't moving. I felt pretty confident that he was OK, only knocked out. I turned him over and dragged him by his arms back to the casita. He was heavy. It was harder and took longer than I had imagined. By the time I got back to the casita, Maya was already inside with a wooden chair with armrests as requested.

"Help me sit him up there," I said. We picked him up under his arms and sat him on the chair. "Did you get zip ties?" I asked. She held a handful up in front of me. They would suffice.

My friend Cal back home told me a story about how he had once been tied up with zip ties. According to him, a few bigger ones pulled tight enough will keep a person from escaping.

I applied one zip tie to each of the ghost's wrists and ankles. Then I went around again adding more until there were five on each limb He was wearing gloves. I removed his gloves and his shoes, just in case he somehow got loose and tried to run again, although that didn't seem likely. He wasn't going anywhere. He sat with his head hanging down.

"Now can we take off the mask?" I asked Maya. She nodded.

I raised the ghost's head to look at what we were working with. The mask was an amazingly similar replica to the actual El Mismo, only a little bigger and in one big piece—meaning that it was a shell more than a skull. The places that would have been empty, like around the jawbone, were part of the face of the mask, only recessed a bit and painted black. The front of the mask was cracked where Maya and I had kicked him. I looked closer at the cracks and noticed that the material it was made out of was a lime green plastic. The markings on the mask matched El Mismo's more or less. They weren't as intricate but they were of the same markings at roughly the same places. The eyes were cut out but the holes were lined with a black mesh, like form a screen door. That's why I had trouble seeing the eyes clearly before. I had to hand it to whoever made the mask. It was nicely crafted. Part of me felt bad that we cracked it.

I pulled up on the mask but it didn't come off. I yanked harder but I was just yanking the guy's head up. I put my hand under the mask and felt a strap with a latch. I recognized it as the same type of strap from a bicycle helmet.

I undid the latch and was able to pull the mask off. Maya and I stood back and looked at the now exposed (and slightly bloodied) face of the Sugar Skull Ghost Thief.

"Yup," I said.

"Yup," said Maya.

27 | Interrogation

I had my suspicions and, as it turned out, so did Maya. We just never talked about it. Maybe we didn't have the time. Or maybe we were just focused on each other. Regardless, we now knew who the chubby Sugar Skull Ghost Thief was. And there he sat, head hung down unconscious with his long, strawberry blond hair bunched up in a hairnet. It was Rocky.

Maya said, "I knew it. Ever since you said he was fat and soft around the middle. I mean, who else could it have been?"

"I kinda thought it was that guy who hangs out at the bar," I said, "the older guy with that worn out black shirt."

"Louie?" Maya said. "He's an ex-cop."

I had not reply. An ex-cop didn't make someone a saint but the point was moot so there was nothing for me to add.

I motioned to Maya that we should go outside to talk. She looked at me confused but I didn't let up. I just went outside and she followed me.

I pulled the door shut behind us. "We don't know if he's actually out," I whispered. "He could just be faking it at this point. And waiting to hear what we know."

"Ah," she said leaning back to peer through the window at Rocky.

"I had my suspicions about him too," I said, "but I wasn't one hundred percent sure. Just because he works at the restaurant doesn't mean he's tied into this thing. Well, I guess he is, but you get what I'm saying.

"Here's what we know: we know that Esteban faked the video so he's in on it. We know that Rocky is the guy in the mask so he's obviously in on it too. I'm pretty sure Jared might be in on it. Probably Zoey too. That's why I was wondering if you had seen her."

"But you don't even know Zoey."

"No, but I heard Jared tell Rocky that he would, as he put it, *shut him up like he shut Zoey up.* Maybe that has something to do with drugs or maybe with the ghost. I'm thinking the ghost because Rocky doesn't strike me as the druggie type. And now we know Rocky *is* the ghost."

"So what do we do now?" Maya asked.

"We try to get some information from Rocky about Jared and Zoey and anyone else involved that we may not know about."

"How are we supposed to do that? I think we're already outside of the law by tying him up."

"We're just restraining him," I assured her. "Until the cops can come."

"We haven't even called the cops yet." She swiped her phone to unlock it.

"Don't," I said, covering the face of her phone with my hand. "Maybe we can make a deal with him. If we call the cops now, they'll come and take over. We won't have another chance like this to get information from the source."

Maya put her phone back in a tiny side pocket of her short shorts. It hung low in the white pocket below the hem of her shorts. That made me look at her legs and I had to fight to stay focused on the task at hand.

"I have an idea," I said. "I used to be in theater in high school. I had a part in a play called *Six of One, Half a Dozen of Another.* I played this cop whose wife and five kids were killed as a message for him to back off of the crime syndicate. Anyway, long story short, the cop catches the guy who killed his family and tries to get information out of him, about the person who put the hit out. So the cop tells the killer guy that he's going to start cutting off six pieces of him, one for each family member killed. Like a pinky for his kid and a foot for his wife and so on."

Maya looked at me like I was insane.

"I'm not going to cut up Rocky, don't worry. But maybe I can scare him. Make him *think* I might do something like that."

"What happened after six?"

"After six what?"

"After the cop cuts off the six pieces?"

"Well, the last piece was going to be the guy's head so the guy spills the beans. In the end, the cop shoots the guy. It wasn't a very good play, but we got to use special effects like a dummy body with parts that came off and red ribbons pulled by string to show blood. It was pretty cool."

"You're a weird dude," Maya said. "You know that?"

I got into the character of the cop and replied, "Weird but effective." With that, I turned to go back inside the casita. Then I remembered something. "Wait," I said to Maya. "Can you get me something sharp like a knife or a cleaver or a straight razor if you have one?"

Maya's eyes widened. "Are you crazy?" she said more than asked.

"I told you I'm not going to cut him but I need something to threaten him with if he doesn't talk. And I doubt your flip flop would do the trick."

Maya pulled off her flip flop and smacked me on the arm. "It's called a *chancla, Chulo.*" She gracefully placed it back on her foot and headed toward her house to fulfill my request.

I paced outside working over my approach and my words. All the lines in the play wouldn't work in this case but I could figure out how to work with them in a roundabout way. Maya came jogging back with a big kitchen knife.

"You might not want to run with that," I said. "Especially in the dark."

"Oh, yeah," she conceded. "I guess you're right." I wondered why she was the one going to graduate school for medicine and I was a college flunky. Nothing against her, just a thought.

We went back inside. Rocky was still out. I put the knife on the wet bar directly behind me where I would be standing, which was in front of Rocky. It was going to be a reveal to him, just like in the play. I told Maya to get me a washcloth soaked with cold water. She brought it back and handed it to me. I said, "Squeeze it out on his head."

She looked at me like I was asking her to do backflips for my entertainment.

"Just play along," I whispered to her. "He needs to know I have a level of power and influence. Like I mean business." I grabbed the El Mismo mask and held it under my arm.

Maya shrugged and wrung out the washcloth over Rocky. The cold water dripped over his face, which made him start. He shook his head and struggled to move his arms and legs. Then he looked up at me.

"You," Rocky sneered. "You kicked me in the face."

"You deserved it," I said back in a low and even tone.

Rocky looked around the room and saw Maya. "Maya," he said. "Get me out of here! Come on, cut these off!"

"Are you kidding me? You're peeping in on me and you

want my mercy?" Maya said, seething.

"You can't—" Rocky stammered, "can't blame me. You know how much I love you."

"Rocky!" I said in a loud domineering voice. "Peeping Tom is at the bottom of the list of what you have to answer for." I held up the mask.

"I found that," he said.

"You're lying," I said. "It was you. It's been you, all along hasn't it?" I threw the mask hard against the floor and heard it crack. Then I stomped right up to him and poked his belly with my finger. "What? Did you forget that I tackled you? Are you *that* stupid?"

Rocky didn't say anything, just looked away.

"I knew it was you, Rocky," I said. I wanted to add *doesn't take a Rocky scientist* simply because I liked puns but it didn't fit the character nor the moment. "You told me you were glad I got kicked in the mouth by the ghost. But no one told you that."

Rocky looked up at me. "So what are you going to do?" he asked smugly. "Call the cops?"

I stood up and crossed my arms. "Maybe," I said. "Maybe not. Depends."

"On what?"

"On what you tell me."

"I'm not telling you anything. And I'm not telling the cops anything either. What are they going to get me on? Petty theft and vandalism?"

"Fine," I said and turned my back to him. "Then it depends on what you're *not* going to tell me." I walked slowly to the wet bar and picked up the knife and held it up high, looking at the reflection of myself with Rocky in the background. Much like a psychopath might do. Then I spun around and showed him the knife. "If you don't tell me what I want to hear, I may have to use this. And if I use this, the last thing I want is to have a cop come around. Do you catch my drift?"

"You won't use that." Rocky scoffed. I was afraid he would say that. In the play, the killer guy also tried to call the cop's bluff but the cop cooly cut his own finger to let the killer know that he wasn't joking. I had cut my finger with a sharp knife like this before. It bled like crazy even though it was a shallow wound. I remember it didn't really hurt that bad when I was getting cut, only afterward.

I smirked and held up the knife close to Rocky's face. Then I gathered all my courage and acting skills and cut my finger right in front of him. It was my index finger, cut on the side near the thumb. Maya gasped. Rocky's eyes grew large. I am not a fan of cutting or blood, especially my own, but I do like method acting and really getting into character. I acted as if the cut didn't have any effect on me. I knew that it would hurt after the fact and that I should get the cut cleaned up quick. Then I wondered if the knife was clean. Oh well, too late to un-cut myself.

I held up my bleeding finger for Rocky to see. Blood dripped off of it onto his black cloak which, in the light, looked like a judge's robe. "Cut's clean," I said cooly. "If it cuts me this easily, it should cut you just as easily."

Rocky looked toward Maya. "Is this guy for real?" he asked, his voice warbling.

Maya stood tall and crossed her arms. "What do *you* think?"

My finger started to hurt. The cutting hadn't hurt, just felt like a foreign object inside of my skin. But now the sting was coming on strong. I looked at Maya and said in a demanding voice, "It's not *my* blood that's going to get me the information I need, but his. Get me something to wrap this up in." Maya played along and went to the bathroom to get me something for my finger.

"You don't know me, Rocky," I said to him bluntly. "You don't know who I am, what I do, what I'm capable of doing. I don't live here and I'm not staying here. At this point I have only one interest and one interest alone." Maya came back with a wad of toilet paper and a zip tie. Not exactly elegant but it would do. I held out my finger for her to dress it. "Can you guess what that interest is, Rocky? You seem like a smart enough guy. Not the smartest, not by a long shot, but smart enough. What's my interest?"

Rocky looked at Maya.

"Bingo!" I said loud and wild. "You're looking right at her!" Then I grabbed the front of his cloak roughly. "Just look at her. Because that's what you do, right? You *look* at her. And *drool* over her." I let him go and stood up, back straight. Maya had finished with her makeshift bandage.

"But she's a big girl," I said. "She can make her own choices. And she obviously hasn't chosen you, has she?" I peered at Rocky with steely eyes. I had to practice that look for hours to get it right for the play. It had an effect on Rocky. He started to look dejected. He played it as though it didn't affect him but I knew the expression. I had seen it on other guys, and I've probably had it too many times myself to even count.

"Look," I said backing off, "Normally I keep to myself. Stay out of trouble. But you see, I got myself all tangled up with Maya here. Can't blame me, she's perfect. But she came with a problem. Not *her* problem, mind you, but a problem with her family, with their restaurant. Thus making it a problem with her. And then she and I got friendly. Needless to say, the problem is now with me. And I don't like problems. But, you see, *you* are at the center of the problem, am I right?"

Rocky looked up at me inquisitively.

"Ah," I said confidently. "Your eyes betray you." That line

was a direct rip off from the play. "You are most certainly not the center are you? There's someone else involved, isn't there?" It was a guess but I thought it was worth a shot. Maybe Rocky would give me some information on Esteban or something.

He didn't reply.

"You *do* realize that the guy asking the questions is the guy holding the knife, don't you?" Another ripped off line, but I liked that one.

Rocky didn't say anything.

"Tell you what, Rocky," I said. "Why don't we play a game of 'Did you know?' Do you know how to play that game?"

Rocky sat silent in defiance.

"I'm going to ask you a question and I'll frame it by saying, 'Did you know…' If the answer is yes then you say yes. If no, then no. And you have to answer honestly or you get cut. If you don't answer, you get cut. Understand?"

Rocky didn't say anything.

"Good. So let's play. Did you know that I know you are *not* the only one in on this whole Sugar Skull Ghost Thief mess?"

Rocky didn't say anything. Secretly, I was afraid of that. I didn't want to cut him. Actually, I did, as sick as that sounds. But I didn't want Maya to see it.

I called to Maya and she came by my side. I whispered in her ear, "Looks like I have to make good on my word. I may have to cut him to make this work."

"Perk, no," she pleaded, whispering back to me. "Let's just call the cops."

"He knows something. And I need to get it out of him." Listening to myself talk was surreal. I felt that maybe I had watched too many crime dramas on TV.

"I won't hurt him if he talks," I said. "But if he keeps quiet, he's protecting someone. And that someone is messing with your family. That someone is killing your father." That was sensitive ground but, ultimately, was the truth.

"This is too weird," she said shaking her head, but she didn't fight me on it. She just left the casita. Rocky and I were alone.

I held the blade up to my face for effect. "Now that she's gone, we can really get down to business. Let's see... what to cut first. Hmm..."

I traced the point of the blade across various parts of Rocky's body: his arms, his legs, his fingers. In all honesty, I was stalling, hoping he would break.

"Don't cut me," Rocky pleaded, much to my relief. "I don't know why he asked me to do it,"

I raised my eyebrows to indicate that I was interested but not satisfied with his answer. "Who is 'he'?"

Rocky hesitated.

"Let me ask you something," I said. "What are you getting out of this? Is it worth it?"

Rocky looked angry.

"Or," I continued, "are you not getting *any* payment for this. And tonight, well, tonight was not for the job, it was for the jollies of seeing Maya get it on."

Who would pay for Rocky to be a peeping tom? Regardless, I suspected Rocky of being in cahoots with Jared since 1) I suspected that Rocky might have been the fat guy in the disguise, and 2) the conversation I heard him having with Jared. I knew whatever Jared had was so valuable to Rocky that he would do whatever was needed to get it. A trade. But what could be so—

I froze. Then I went outside to talk with Maya.

"The pics," I whispered to her.

"What pics?" she asked.

"*Your* pics. The ones Jared took of you."

"What about them?"

"That's the deal. Rocky gets the pics."

"Jared is selling Rocky the pics? Rocky admitted it?"

"No. I figured it out. And it's not a sale, it's a trade. Jared gives Rocky the pics if Rocky holds up his end of the deal."

"That bastard!" Maya's face crunched up.

"But he never got the pics," I said. "That was what Jared was getting on him about. Rocky didn't hold up his end of whatever bargain they had."

"What was the trade?" Maya asked.

"I'm almost positive it has something to do with Rocky running around as the ghost."

Maya thought for a second then said, "But how then does Esteban fit in?"

"That's a different deal. But I'm pretty sure it's also with Jared. Or maybe something with Zoey. I don't know just yet."

"Did you cut him?" Maya asked.

"No. Not yet."

"Has he said anything?"

"No. Not yet."

Maya breathed deep through her nose. "Well," she said finally, "go in there and get some answers."

I went back into the casita. Rocky was still tied to his chair, looking unsettled.

"You chose this," I said to Rocky. Then I approached him with the knife and put it against his finger, ready to cut him as I cut myself.

"Wait!" Rocky exclaimed. I froze. "Wait, I'll tell you. But you have to promise to let me go."

"My mouth don't make promises this knife can't keep," I said. It was another line from the play. Not as good, it didn't make sense. But I didn't know what else to say.

Rocky breathed deeply a few times. "I'm not getting anything from this," he said.

"From what? Dressing as the ghost?"

"Yes. Well, not for tonight. Tonight I was doing it for, like you said," he paused, "for myself."

"And the other nights?"

"They were for something else. I had a deal."

"So," I said, "you had a deal. The deal was that you dressed up as a ghost and committed petty crimes and, in return, you got what?"

Rocky didn't answer.

"You got pictures, didn't you, Rocky?" I looked down at him. "You got pictures of Maya from Jared. Dirty pictures. Dirtier than the pic that you took of her butt when I met you the first time."

Rocky winced.

The next thing I did was a complete gamble, but I thought it would work. And I didn't want to go the alternate route of continuing on the same route, if that makes sense. Then I knelt down beside Rocky and said, "Listen, I'm not going to cut you. It was all for show. That's not me. And this," I tugged at the black cloak, "this isn't you, is it? Not deep down inside."

Rocky squinted at me then down at the knife. My guess is that he thought I was messing with him.

I lowered my voice to a whisper. "I understand. I know. It must be torture to work with someone you like so much but they won't return that adoration. Believe me, I know. I've been there. And I've fantasized. Over and over, I've done it myself."

Rocky still looked unsure.

"All this," I held up the knife, "is drama. Theater. I did it in high school."

"But you cut yourself," Rocky said.

"Don't you think I know that?" I gave him a half smile. "I appreciate authentic acting. But all that set aside, I need your help. And, the way I see it, we could be enemies or allies." I got up and went to the door and opened it, called Maya back in. I told her everything was OK.

"I know you're not at the center of all this, Rocky," I said. "But, if you help us find out why this is happening, we'll let you go." I could feel Maya's eyes burning into me. "All we want is to know who the big dog is and why he's doing it."

Rocky sat motionless, breathing heavily. He sat there for at least two minutes. I thought maybe he wouldn't say a thing, but he finally raised his head. "Like you said, it's Jared," he said pathetically. "We made a deal: I dress as the ghost and commit the crimes and he…"

"It's OK," I said. "She already knows. I filled her in."

"I get the pics of Maya."

Maya stomped up to Rocky and slapped him hard across his face. He didn't seem to mind it. In fact, it looked to me like he accepted it willfully, like justice and punishment.

"Don't you know what this has done to my family?" Maya exclaimed. "Our business? My dad? He's drinking himself to death because of all this."

"I didn't mean for that to happen," Rocky said sadly.

"Well, it did," Maya returned. "And, by you taking a part in this, you're partly responsible for my dad's death, which is going to come soon!"

Rocky sat silent and rueful. I held Maya's hand and led her outside again. "Give me just a few minutes with him," I said. "Alone."

I came back inside and knelt beside Rocky. "Rocky," I said, "I need your help. Maya needs your help."

"What do I get out of it?" Rocky asked, avoiding eye contact with me.

"It's not about what you get. You're not getting anything now and you've got some crimes under your belt. We could call the police right now. And maybe you won't confess anything but there are witnesses. And they'll get you on something. Right now I'm asking you for help. You *could* help us, you know."

Rocky sat silent for a moment then asked, "How?"

"Do you know why Jared wanted you to dress up like the ghost?"

"I told you, no, I don't."

"You must have an idea," I said. "Couldn't be random. And the downturn of business hurts him too, right? He gets fewer tips. So there must be a reason."

"He's smart," Rocky stated flatly.

I didn't reply to that. Mostly because I shared that opinion of Jared but didn't want to admit it.

"He didn't tell me why," Rocky continued. "He just told me about the pictures. But they weren't just Maya. He had a bunch of them, of a bunch of different girls. Girls I know or have seen him with. So it's not like I was doing all of this just for the pictures of Maya." Maybe, in his mind, that justified his actions or lessened the stigma of Maya's pictures. It didn't. But it did give me an indication of the kind of guy Rocky was.

"You don't seem like a bad guy to me," I said. "But you seem lonely."

Rocky smirked.

"Like I said, I know. I do stupid things when I'm lonely too," I said. "And I get lonely a lot. This whole Maya thing is not normal for me. Usually girls like her won't give me the time of day. But she has."

"Is that supposed to make me feel better? That you finally got a hot chick like Maya to like you?"

"It's supposed to tell you the kind of girl she is. Maybe she's not all about superficial stuff."

Rocky still didn't look happy.

"So here's how you can help us," I said. "We need to know exactly what's going on and who exactly is involved. We know

Jared's involved, of course. We also know Esteban set up that dummy camera and the fake video."

Rocky looked at me inquisitively, as if he couldn't believe we would have figured it out.

"We know Jared sells drugs and that he's got one he calls *ganchos* and it's powerful stuff." I paused to let that sink in and to see how he would respond.

"So what do you need me to find out?" Rocky asked. "Sounds like you're figuring it all out yourself."

"We need you to act like we never spoke. And you need to figure out what Esteban is getting. And how Zoey fits in."

"Esteban is getting three thousand and a shot at a restaurant in Chicago as a sommelier." Rocky said this with disdain, as if Esteban may have received a better deal. Either that or Rocky didn't like Esteban. Or both.

"And Zoey?"

"Zoey's just…gone," Rocky said, his voice a bit strained. "She was going to tell Maya that Jared was up to something. She has a good heart. But Jared, well, he got rid of her somehow."

"Got rid of? How?" This new fact was scary. How does a person just get *rid* of someone? Did Jared kill her? Was he capable of that? And, if so, what is so important? I thought of the geode in the university library. Value. *Extreme* value. *Hidden* value.

"I don't know," Rocky said. "One day she was here and the next, poof, she's gone. Just vanished." He adjusted himself in his chair, hinting that he was uncomfortable. I left him tied up.

"So that's what Jared meant when he said he'd shut you up like he shut up Zoey?"

"You heard that?"

"Yes," I said. "And you don't know what Jared is capable of either, right?"

Rocky sat silent.

"So you can choose to help us out," I said in my best persuasive tone. "If you don't, you choose to assist Jared in whatever scheme he's running. And you get nothing for helping him. By helping us, you get to be a part of bringing him to justice and helping Maya and her family."

"What, like some act of nobility?" he snickered.

"Not *like* an act of nobility. An *actual* act of nobility. And when you're done helping us, you should help out the people you have hurt in the process. And you get nothing for it. In fact, you may have to pay in some way. You'll have to pay for the VW bus, that's for sure."

Rocky looked as if he was processing everything in his mind, tallying up everything he had done and what it might cost to fix the bus.

"It's the right thing to do," I said. "Don't you think?"

"So I get nothing?" Rocky asked.

"Wrong, Rocky, you get everything. If you truly like Maya, you get to see this whole thing work out for the best. You get to see her achieve her dreams. You get to be a part of her family recovering. Not to mention the business."

Rocky nodded. "Sorry for watching you," he said.

"How did you know we would be back here?" I asked.

"I heard you two talking today. At the restaurant. I heard her telling you about the casita and how I stayed here and when you guys were going to meet up."

"Ah," I said. Then something hit me and I went and got Maya from outside. I filled her in on what Rocky had told me. Then, in Maya's presence, I asked Rocky, "What did you do or not do to make Jared give up on the deal?"

"I was supposed to stop running around as the ghost until he told me otherwise."

"And you defied him by going out the night you tagged my bus?"

He nodded.

"Do you know why you were supposed to hold up on it?" I asked.

"Jared didn't tell me," Rocky replied. "But it was about the time he started wearing that stupid key around his neck."

Maya and I looked at each other and knew each other's thoughts without saying a word. The *key* was the *key*.

We cut Rocky loose but not before Maya took a bunch of pictures of him with the mask, just in case we had to show the cops, as insurance when the day came. We kept the mask just for good measure. Rocky left with little fanfare, just strolled off into the darkness.

"Do you think he'll tell Jared about all this?" Maya asked.

"Maybe. Maybe not. But I don't think it will make a difference. I think Jared's further along than we think. And Rocky was just a pawn, like Esteban. Jared's working on something bigger and I'm pretty sure it involves that key."

Maya's eyebrows furrowed in thought.

"And," I said, "I'm pretty sure this whole thing revolves around your dad."

28 | Friday

After the whole Rocky incident, Maya and I called it a night. She had to work a double the next day and I was beat. Chasing ghosts can do that to you.

My plan for Friday was to talk to Lalo. Maya said he got up early but poked around for a few hours before he revved up his mental motor. I assumed that was her way of saying he was working off the alcohol from the night before and took it as a hint to not talk about anything too intense until around ten o'clock AM.

On a lighter note, I was invited to breakfast. Maya's mom made breakfast every morning. I couldn't believe it. That woman made breakfast in the morning, then worked a twelve hour day, cooking, then came home and took care of things around her house until she went to bed. Then she did it all over again. She was amazing. I could see where Maya got her resilience from and, at the same time, why she wanted out of the business.

I woke up early and just lay in bed thinking. The pieces were coming together. The mystery of the Sugar Skull Ghost Thief was no longer a mystery of *who* but *why*. I guess it had always been about *why* but, in this case, the *why* was still a total mystery to me.

Maya rapped on my door and simply said, "Breakfast," and left. That was my cue. I got up and washed my face, brushed my teeth, tried to tame my hair, and made my way to the main house.

Breakfast at Maya's house was the closest thing to heaven that I could imagine. I came in to the sounds of melodic music while Maya handed me a cup of hot coffee and sat me at the table. Maya's mom was at the stove, cooking. She said to Maya, *"Pan dulce, mija. Dárle una concha por favor."*

Maya didn't reply to her mother but handed me a strange donut like piece of bread with a weird frosting on the top. I didn't ask questions, just took a bite. It was a bit dry but tasty, especially with hot coffee. I could smell freshly made tortillas as well as *chorizo*. "Thank you," I said but received no reply from Mrs. Calavera.

"She doesn't see it as a gift to you," Maya said to me in a hushed voice, "just an obligation on her part to provide. Not to say you can't say thank you but it's part of her nature. It seems strange to her to be thanked for doing what she feels is necessary."

"Oh," I said. "Well, it's a gift to *me.*"

Maya leaned over and kissed my cheek.

"Oo, qué la," Mrs. Calavera said with her back to us. "No kissy at the table." I couldn't believe it. Maya's mom somehow heard Maya kiss my cheek over the sound of the food cooking and music in the background.

Maya leaned into me and whispered, "Latina mothers have eyes in the back of their head."

"Y orejas también," Mrs. Calavera said, still with her back to us.

Breakfast was *huevos con chorizo* with freshly made *tortillas* and *papas con chile verde.* That means eggs and chorizo, tortillas, and fried potatoes smothered with green chile. And lots of coffee. Easily the best breakfast I ever had. Lalo came in every so often and picked at some food and poured some coffee and headed out. He was downtrodden. No one spoke to him, just gave him his space. It wasn't until we were all done that he came in and sat down at the table and ate. I excused myself and went to get ready. Maya and her mom were going to do the same.

After I showered, I took a walk around the pecan orchard, killing time until I could go in and talk to Lalo. I followed the path I took to catch Rocky the night before. In the daylight, it didn't seem like we went all that far. I guess the darkness of night plays tricks on us.

The air was cool and crisp and there was a slight breeze that rustled through the trees. It had a calming effect. The sun cast morning shadows with streaks of sunlight in between. I could feel the difference of temperature on my skin from sun to shade, more prevalent than in summer. The hairs on my arm stood up. It felt good.

I had never been in a pecan orchard before. Was it an orchard or a farm? I had no idea. In my mind, a pecan is like a fruit and fruit trees are in orchards so I just went with that. It also occurred to me that I didn't know what pecans looked like on the tree. Actually, I didn't even know if they grew on a tree or a bush or possibly underground. I was surprised to see what they actually looked like. They grew in clusters of three or four. But they weren't small and brown but big and green. They kind of looked like alien cocoons. I wanted to grab one and peel it open, but I decided not to.

I thought about the inside of the pecan. That's why all these trees in the orchard exist. That's why pecan farmers do all this work. They do it because there is a nut inside of the shell of each of these pecans. A treasure. And in this case, a treasure within a shell within that green cocoon. Value. Hidden value. A theory formulated in my mind and the fog of the Sugar Skull Ghost Thief started to dissipate.

29 | Drag and Blade

I didn't know what to say to Lalo. He wasn't open about things with his family, why would he be open with me? But people seemed to open up to me for one reason or another. I've been told I have that gift. I went into Maya's house to see if my gift worked with Lalo.

The back door of their house entered directly into the kitchen. I rapped on the door twice quickly and simply went in. Lalo was sitting at the table drinking coffee and looking at a newspaper. It didn't look like he was reading it, just looking at it. He wasn't in any better spirits than he had been earlier that morning.

"Coffee?" he asked me not looking up.

"As long as it's not that cowboy coffee again," I answered. This made him give a silent chuckle, his round body bobbing on his chair. He got up and got me a mug of coffee and set it down on the table next to him. It was an invitation.

I sat down and took a sip. We sat in silence for a moment. "I like your place," I said. "The orchard. It's beautiful. I've never seen pecans on the tree, never knew they grew inside of those big green things."

"Husk," Lalo said, educating me.

"Husk," I repeated. "I wanted to grab one and peel it to see the pecan inside."

"But you didn't," he said instead of inquiring.

"No. How did you know?"

"If you did, your hands would be black. Or they would be turning black now."

"They have black liquid inside?"

"No. It's not black at all. Maybe a bit clear or green. But it makes your hands black." He took a sip of his coffee. "It's the pecan's way of punishing you for trying to bring it out too early."

"Ah," I said. "So if I had, you would have caught me black handed."

Lalo simply nodded. Either he hadn't got the joke or he hadn't found it amusing.

"When is harvest?" I asked.

"November, December *más o menos*. After two freezes. The first freeze will turn that green husk brown. The second will bust it open." He craned his head to look out of the window at the trees in the orchard behind his house. Then he sighed heavily. "I'll need to go over the dirt with the drag and blade soon, get it ready for the harvest machines."

"Can you show me the machines?"

"I don't have them. Too expensive. I use a harvesting company. They have the tools and the workers. They come in, we harvest, and they get a piece of the pie."

I wanted to say *Pecan pie?* but Lalo didn't seem to be in a joking mood.

"But you said you had to use a, what was it? A dragging blade?" I asked.

"A drag *and* a blade. Two things. The drag goes first, then the blade. Those I have. They hitch onto the tractor. It's the shaker and harvester that is expensive."

"Can you show me the drag and the blade?"

Lalo was pensive for a few moments. Then he said, *"Bueno.* After coffee."

We sat and sipped coffee. "Maya said you sold part of your farm," I stated.

"Leased. It's different. But she thinks it's the same thing, from the standpoint of money. I don't get as much money as if I were to harvest it myself, but I don't have to put up as much money to hire the harvesters," he paused. "I had to pull back."

I had always thought that having a farm was just simple and straightforward. Water trees, feed animals, then sit on a porch and drink lemonade. Lalo was making it sound like a business, which it was.

30 | Curse

After coffee, Lalo took me out to a large shed and showed me the tools he used for his farm. He decided that, since he was already there, he might as well hook up the equipment and do some work. Over the next few hours he and I worked at pulling the drag across the ground. He taught me how to hook up the equipment and drive the tractor. His whole demeanor had changed as he was working and teaching me. It was like he had come back to life. I didn't want to bring up the ghost but I needed the information.

"Lalo," I said during a water break with both of us covered in dust, "you said something about the Witch's Key the other night. The night Maya and I ran into the ghost."

Lalo sighed heavily but said nothing.

"I've seen the key," I said. Lalo looked at me askance. "Jared showed it to me."

We were standing in the shade of the orchard beside the tractor. Lalo leaned back against it. "I don't know anymore," he said.

"Don't know what?"

"*La llave.* Jared said—" he paused, as if he didn't want to say anything. Then he asked me, "That night, you said you saw him? That you chased him and he kicked you? The ghost?"

"I chased him and tackled him. *Then* he kicked me."

"What was it like? Being kicked by a ghost."

"He wasn't a ghost. *Isn't* a ghost. He's..." I didn't know if I wanted to tell Lalo that it was Rocky. Not just yet. I thought that if I told him, he might do something to Rocky and I'd lose out on any further information. Also, I didn't know how he would take it. And I preferred to have Maya by my side when we told him. We would leave out the making out stuff, of course.

I must have zoned out thinking about all those angles and forgot to finish my sentence. Lalo asked, "He's what?"

"Oh," I said, realizing I had left him hanging. "He's a guy. A man. Flesh and bone."

Lalo looked down pensively. After a moment he said, "Or maybe a guy playing a trick, dressing up like the ghost for some reason. Because it *couldn't* be the ghost."

"Why couldn't it be the ghost?"

"Because of *La Llave de la Bruja.*"

"What does that have to do with anything?" I felt that I was getting close to some good information.

"It's nothing," Lalo said brushing the subject aside with his hand in the air and shaking his head.

"Lalo," I said, "it's not nothing. And the ghost is not a ghost. Never was. It's a guy."

We stood at an impasse. Lalo not wanting to share anything more and me insisting that the ghost wasn't a ghost. His eyes shifted from side to side, gears turning in his head.

"OK," he said, relenting. "You say the ghost is not a ghost, *verdad?*" It sounded more like *reh-tha* but I knew what he was saying. Compa said it every so often. Meant *true*.

"Yes," I answered.

"But the key made it all stop," Lalo said emphatically as he chopped the air with his hand for emphasis.

"Made what stop?"

"The ghost. When Jared got the key, the ghost stopped making trouble."

"I thought Jared went to Mexico a few months ago."

"*Sí,*" Lalo said. "But he didn't know it had the effect on the ghost until last week. We figured it out, me and him. Every time he wore the key, the ghost would not go out on that night. So Jared has been working every day and wearing the key. We had a deal."

"A deal?"

Lalo looked at me out of the corner of his eyes again, as if he was wondering if he could trust me. He said, "Jared won't sell me the key. But I need that key to keep the ghost from going out. So Jared and I made a deal."

"But Lalo, the ghost is a fake. You don't need the key."

"It can't be fake because it's more than a just a ghost. It's a curse." He sunk into himself. "It's always been a curse. A blessing and a curse. Or more like a blessing *then* a curse. It was bound to happen. I'm sure Maya told you all about the history, what happened to my father and grandfather, and great grandfather."

"She did."

"So it was bound to happen to me." Lalo was shaking his head in regret.

I thought about the story for a moment and realized something. "But with your father and grandfather and great grandfather, there was something that brought on the curse, as you say. Right? Prohibition, the priest, gambling. They were circumstances and actions, not necessarily curses."

"They were curses," he insisted. "Or why else would they have happened?"

"But prohibition happened to everyone," I pointed out.

"The priest was just being a priest. And the gambling, well, no disrespect to your father but wouldn't you say he brought that on himself?"

"And I brought this on myself too," he said with a sigh.

"How? I don't understand."

"I trapped him. Forever."

"Who?"

"El Mismo. I trapped him in that plastic glass. Don't you see? It's irreversible, final. Like laminating paper. You can't undo it. I trapped him in there and now he wants out." There was a sense of relief in Lalo's voice, like a confession. Maybe it was his Catholic belief system. Maybe it was just the relief we all feel when we expose something about ourselves that we're not proud of. It wasn't until then that I remembered Maya saying that her dad got the whole El Mismo glass head and podium set-up right before the ghost events started happening.

"So you think that ghost of El Mismo is terrorizing the community because you put the skull in the glass?" I asked.

"Yes."

"Do you really think the ghost is real?"

Lalo looked down, sweeping the dirt with his feet. "He's a ghost and a curse," he replied. "And the only way to stop him is with *La Llave de la Bruja.*"

"Because Jared told you so?"

"Yes."

"And what if Jared is lying?"

"But the ghost stopped when he had the key. Like I said, we figured it out."

"But Lalo, if Jared has someone acting as the ghost, he could simply tell him to not go out on any night that he had the key, right?"

Lalo's eyes shifted from side to side. He was thinking. "But Jared, he's been good to us. Works hard. He's been pulling doubles for a while now to help us out. And he's got ideas about how to promote the restaurant. He even made up a prototype little El Mismo skull from a 3D printer. He said we can sell them; price them high and people will pay for them. Says he *already* has people wanting to buy them. He's thinking of the business. But he wants to make sure he gets his share, of course, most of it actually. And I'm not against it. Hey, a small percentage of something for me is better than one hundred percent of nothing. Which is what I have now. That's why we made the deal."

"I get that. But he's still lying. I just know it."

Lalo didn't respond. I could see in his eyes that he didn't know if he should trust me. And I couldn't blame him. Here I was, some guy who came into town and knew nothing about anything. And to top it off, I was hooking up with his daughter—no one told him but he was no fool. So I could understand how hearing that his loyal employee and future business partner Jared was lying must seem weak coming from me. At the same time, I could see conflict in his eyes. He wasn't completely disregarding what I was saying but he wasn't completely convinced.

"Jared had the key the other night and the ghost went out, right?" I asked. "When I chased him? That's why you were so freaked out when Maya and I told you we saw him."

"The key keeps him from going out."

I couldn't tell if Lalo was so dense that he actually believed in that stupid key of Jared's or if he was honestly trying to believe in a curse and a ghost. "I never believed in ghosts before," he said with a sigh.

"Then why do you now?"

"I was destined to be cursed. It runs in my blood. And if I was going to be cursed from this skull, it's like a ghost, right?"

That didn't make any sense to me. I looked him in the eye.

"There is no ghost," I said, punctuating each word for effect. "There's only Jared. And a couple of other people. They're the ones behind this whole thing."

"A couple of other people?" His eyebrows furrowed.

I debated whether I should tell him about Rocky or not. He might ask what Maya and I were doing together so late at night. I thought about Maya. I thought about her whole family. They were all involved. And they all needed to be part of this conversation.

"I'll go answer it," Lalo said out of nowhere and he started walking toward his house. It wasn't until he was halfway there that I realized the phone was ringing. It was faint and low. How did he hear it? His ears must have been attuned to listen for it.

I watched him go into the house. It was pretty far off. Then I saw him come out. He whistled loudly and waved for me to come inside with him. When I got to him, he said, "It's Maya. She's asking for you."

They had a landline and Lalo handed the bulky receiver to me. "Yes?" I said.

"You have to help us," Maya sounded frantic on the other end.

"What do you need?"

"Rocky and Esteban both called in and quit. Rocky said he was sorry for everything he did and that he just couldn't be around any of us or Jared. Esteban gave me some story about getting his dream job and having to leave immediately. And, as luck would have it, they're both on the schedule for tonight."

"I thought you guys weren't busy."

"There's some event in the square tonight and we're picking up. That plus the fact that the whole Sugar Skull Ghost Thief has taken some time off has upped business. Maybe just a little but still. Thing is, I'm the only one serving. And tonight I don't just serve, I help cook and give El Mismo tours. And yes, we're not busy regularly but weekends are different. Busier. That's why we have Rocky and Esteban on the schedule. *Had* them on the schedule."

"So what are you saying?"

"We need you to come in and work. Serve tables. You said you know how, right?"

"What? I don't know your menu. I can barely speak a word of Spanish!"

"I'll help out too. Maybe you can give some El Mismo tours. You know the story."

I thought about it for a moment. I had two options: 1) say no and let Maya and her mom suffer, or 2) say yes. No contest. "OK," I said. "But you have to help me. What do you need me to do?"

Maya told me to buy some black pants and a black button-up, long-sleeve shirt and the restaurant would reimburse me. She also told me to be quick about it. Apparently, they were getting busy and she was panicking.

I told Lalo what Maya needed and got to it.

I wish I could recall that shift but it was a blur. I don't know how I kept up but I did. It was frantic but, at the same time, a lot of fun. And, to be honest, I missed the pace of work. Plus I made bank. One twenty-five. Not bad. And while I couldn't stand Jared, that didn't stop Maya and me from allowing him to pour us a couple of end-of-shift shots of the Poison. It was a strange feeling, everyone working together. It felt good. It also felt like it couldn't last. And, of course it couldn't.

I felt I was ready to tell Maya and her whole family that I had figured it out. I knew what was going on.

31 | Chulo

After work, we all regrouped in Maya's family's kitchen. The air was thick with unease. We all felt it. I should say Maya, her mom, and I felt it. Lalo had checked out for the night. My guess was that the work she and I had done earlier had used up his energy. I knew I was feeling it.

Maya's mom heated up some leftovers for us and we sat at the table. I told them about how Lalo and I had worked on the farm. That really made Maya dig me. She sat with her elbows on the table, hands under her chin, just staring at me and smiling.

I didn't know how much I wanted to share with Mrs. Calavera. I guess I felt like it would be disrespectful to Lalo to talk to her without him there. She told us that she was going to head onto bed without eating, that she had eaten at the restaurant. Under my breath I told Maya that she needed to have a family meeting in the morning and a staff meeting at the restaurant.

"Staff?" she whispered back. "With Rocky and Esteban gone, it's only me, my mom and Jared."

"And your dad," I added. Maya grimaced.

Maya went to kiss her mom and told her about the

meeting. Her mom nodded agreeably and headed off to bed. I assumed she'd let Lalo know somehow. Maya texted someone, probably Jared to tell him about the meeting. Then she slid her phone back into her pocket.

She returned to the table and grabbed my hand and we went back to the casita without saying anything to each other. When we got to the door, she stood there silently with her head down.

"Are you OK?" I asked.

"I don't want you to leave," she said. "But I'm not even staying here myself. Well, not if I can help it. I really like you. And you're the only person who seems to have shaken my dad from his depression, even if just for a little while. That's huge. At least to us it's huge." She stepped up on her toes, put her hands on my shoulders and kissed me, slowly at first, then passionately. "Let's go inside," she said opening the door and leading me in.

When we got in, we made straight for the bed. We were all over each other, clothes started flying off, we were down to our underwear. It was amazing. That is, until my stupid conscience got the best of me.

"Wait," I said, pulling back with every ounce of strength I could muster.

"What is it?" She was kissing on my neck.

"Your vow. About not doing this until, you know, you're married."

She stopped kissing my neck and I regretted saying anything. Yet, at the same time, I felt I needed to. The room was dark, only the soft blue moonlight shone in through the windows. She sat up on the bed, as did I. She poked around in the darkness to find her clothes. I followed suit. There was just enough moonlight to allow us to find things without bumbling around in the darkness. She put her shirt on and buttoned a few buttons. She went to one of the candles and lit it. Then she lit the others. Ironic how romantic the candles made the room feel, even when the momentum of the mood was hindered.

"I didn't want to think about it," She said. "I kind of wished you forgot."

"Forgot? Trust me, guys don't forget things like that." We sat in silence for a moment. "Believe me, I wish I *had* forgotten. Or never knew at all."

Maya leaned in close to me. I thought she was going to kiss me but she didn't. She just nestled up against me, her head on my chest. I hugged her. We sat like that for a few minutes. Then she said, "You know what?"

"What?"

"It's because you would hold me to my vow that makes me want to break it. For you. Does that make sense?"

I held her tighter. I could feel her petite fingers gripping my shirt as she drew closer.

"Maybe it's not that I don't want to wait until I'm married," she said. "Maybe I just wanted to wait until the right guy came along."

"Maybe the right guy would want you to wait." It felt painful saying it. Like I was a schmuck. I mean, any other guy would take advantage of the situation. But then again, that was it. I felt that I would be taking advantage of the situation. Maybe she was totally ready to go on her end. And maybe in the long run, it wouldn't matter—she'd go her way and I'd go mine. But I liked her too much for that. For just a casual thing that happens and is over. I guess I allowed myself to care too much. Maybe that made me less of a guy. I know some guys would think so. I just didn't know how to act any other way.

"You're right," she said, her voice muffled by my chest. "The right guy would not be just the right guy at that moment, but the right guy for longer. You know? For life. And this, you and me, we already know it has to end. Unless *you* move or *I* move and neither of us even knows what's going to happen one way or another."

I didn't respond, just held her.

"And long distance things are always tough," she said. "But maybe it would work out, right?"

"They're tough," I said as a matter of fact. I didn't know what to say. I wasn't too keen on a long distance thing. If I was going to be with someone, I wanted it to be there all the time. I know other people could do it, I just didn't feel I could. Not even with a girl like Maya. *Especially* with a girl like Maya. I'd go crazy thinking about all the guys hitting on her. I wasn't confident enough to not be jealous.

"You know what's weird?" she asked.

"What?"

"This is kind of nice. You holding me like this. In a way, it's like the afterglow, only not after anything. I just realized that's what I like, that closeness after the fact. After sex. Where you lay there and hold each other, tell each other secrets because you trust each other."

"You've got secrets you want to spill?" I jested. "Lay them on me!"

She pinched me ever so gently. "That *is* a secret. Me telling you how I like this part of it."

I held her tight.

"What are you going to talk about tomorrow morning?" she asked. "With my family."

"I figured it out. The whole Sugar Skull Ghost Thief."

Maya pushed away from me and sat up. "What?" she said surprised.

"At least I *think* I figured it out. And I wanted to have all of you there when I lay it out. I could be wrong and I wanted you guys there to point that out if that were the case."

"What it is?" she asked excitedly.

"Here's what I think," I said with a pause. "I think you should wait until morning. I need my beauty sleep." She slapped me hard in the arm. I grinned at her, loving the fact that I had her in suspense.

I reached up and held her face in my hands. I said, "You are so beautiful. And you have so much going for you. You and your family are going to be OK, but you're going to have to pull together. And maybe do something crazy. Maybe, maybe not. But things are about to get crazy and weird and make all sorts of sense."

Maya looked me straight in the eye. "If you don't come out with it within the next ten seconds," she said, "I'm going to give you the tittie twister from hell."

"OK, OK. How about a deal? I'll tell you everything and you tell me why you call me your pimp."

"What?" She seemed taken aback.

"You keep calling me your pimp."

"I have never called you, nor will I ever call anyone my pimp!"

She was earnest. Either she was a great actress or she truly didn't know what I was talking about.

"You keep calling me '*chulo*'," I said. "I put it in Google Translate. It means 'pimp'."

"No it doesn't. It means 'cute'. I'm calling you cute."

"Not according to Google."

Her phone was in her pants and her pants were on the floor, a casualty of our passion. She rummaged around and found them and extracted her phone. She pecked at the phone's screen, the light illuminating her pretty face like a spotlight. Then came the look. A look of total bewilderment. "Bah!" she said and turned the phone to me. She had pulled up Google Translate and, sure enough, "*chulo*" translated as "pimp". She turned the phone to herself again and said, "That is weird. What else don't I know?"

"So I guess that answers that, right?" I said. "You just didn't know."

"I had no idea, believe me." She tucked a lock of hair behind her ear. "If I would have known, I wouldn't have said it. Pimp? Wow." She threw her phone on the bed, face down. She shook the idea away, clearing her mind. "OK, I did my part. Your turn. Tell me."

"We still have wine from last night," I said. "Let's pour us a glass. And then I'll tell you my big fat El Mismo theory."

32 | Poison

I retrieved my notebook and cranked the emergency radio/ flashlight. I tuned into a station playing jazz. Turns out it was the local NPR affiliate, the public radio station being pumped out of the university. Good music for the moment.

Maya and I sat on the bed facing each other. I asked her to lay out what we knew already. She outlined the fake video, Rocky running around in that goofy outfit, and something about the Witch's Key. She had some of the pieces but none of the strings that bound them together.

I said, "You've got to look at the bigger picture. It all starts and ends with the same thing."

Maya slowly turned her head to the side, keeping her eyes on me the whole time. Either she doubted that I could have figured the whole thing out or she was cranking her brain in preparation of my theory.

She said, "What thing?"

"Poison," I said.

Everything in the room seemed to shrink away. Maya squared her body to face me directly. Her eyebrows furrowed as she continued to stare at me.

"What was it that started Calavera's to begin with?" I asked.

"Isidro?"

"Yes. What did he do to get business pumping?"

"The Poison?"

"Exactly. Calavera's Poison. Why was it called 'poison'?"

"Rats?"

"Because it was a cover. It wasn't for rats, right? No one believed it was for rats. But it was a cover. Marketing the liquor as rat poison allowed Isidro to sell it. That's how Calavera's got on the map, so to speak."

"OK. Sure. So what?"

"Everything is hidden and displayed in plain sight. Just like Calavera's Poison back during prohibition."

"You're going to have to explain what exactly you're trying to say. I know all this."

"The poison was sold at Calavera's. And it was illegal. Yet, because there was a legal aspect to it—that it was rat poison—business was allowed to continue. You've got the same thing happening right now."

"We don't sell anything illegal. Unless you count my mom's food as dangerous to your health." Maya laughed with a snort.

"Not the food," I said. "Drugs."

"That's crazy. We don't sell drugs. If we did, we wouldn't be hurting for cash, I'll tell you that much." She sipped her wine.

"That's it exactly! Cash! But I'm not talking about you guys, your family. I'm talking about Jared."

"Jared's always kept his, well, his *business* separate from ours. When we were seeing each other people would come over to his house to make a deal or drop off cash. Or he was going to someone's house or some random meeting place."

"Let me ask you something. In the past few weeks, has he taken long extended breaks? Anything that would lead you to believe that he was making deliveries?"

Maya stared off into space for a while, trying to recall.

"Um, no, I guess not. He's been working doubles non-stop."

"So if he's working doubles, he can't be delivering, right?" I wanted to lay it all out for her, but I needed her to see where I was coming from so she wouldn't think I was crazy. "If he can't deliver, he either has to have the customer come to him or send someone to the customer. But, if he sends someone to the customer, he incurs a cost. And why should he? Everyone knows where he's at. Might as well use Calavera's as a home base. I think he's selling his *ganchos* crap at the restaurant. Remember? That girl told me how to get my hands on it if I wanted some."

Maya's face grew tense, gears turning in her head. "What does this have to do with the ghost?" she asked with a shrug.

"It has everything to do with the ghost. I don't know Jared that well, but I get the sense that he's smart, always a few moves ahead. And he's all about himself. That's a dangerous combination. I talked with your dad earlier today. Now, he told me that you didn't know this so, when I tell you, just remember that I'm not supposed to tell you. But, if I'm right about all this, it really doesn't matter. Anyway, your dad said that he and Jared are in a deal. It's about the restaurant."

"What?" She was surprised.

"Yeah. Your dad is transferring some of the business ownership to Jared."

"No way, I don't think so." She shook her head in disagreement. "There's no reason. No reason at all. He doesn't even like Jared that much."

"Doesn't matter," I said. "It's about the key. That Witch's Key he wears on a necklace."

"That's stupid."

"Not to your dad. He believes that he's cursed, like his father and grandfather and great grandfather. He thinks that El Mismo is cursing him for encapsulating him in that glass globe.

Or plastic dome. Whatever it is. Jared told him that the Witch's Key kept the ghost at bay. But Jared didn't want to sell the key so they worked out a deal where Jared keeps the key, wears it all the time, and, in return, gets a share of the business."

Maya sat there dumfounded.

"Your dad is at the end of his rope," I said. "He's believing the curse and everything. I told him that the ghost wasn't real, but he still believes in the curse. Even more than the ghost."

"OK. So let's just say you're right. That doesn't explain the ghost."

"It does. It's leverage. But in a strange, negative way. The ghost hobbled the business. Jared came in and was a hero for starting to bring it back to life. I mean, you said it yourself, business started increased once the ghost quit popping up. Jared used that key as a bargaining chip."

"But why?"

"To get the business," I said. "So that he can sell ganchos."

Maya fell silent. She was processing everything in her head.

"Let me make this simple," I said. "Jared has a product that he wants to sell. And he's selling it, a little of it. He can't sell more because, if he does, he starts to show up on Uncle Sam's radar. Right now he's probably dealing in all cash so it's not traceable. But I think he's stuck between having the potential to sell a lot of it and not having a clean way to account for it all. He needs to launder the money through something so that it looks legit.

"When I talked with my boss the other day, I asked him if he could just move money from one business to another to make it look like one showed a smaller profit and the other showed a bigger one. He said that would be laundering the money. He also said that, if he were to ever launder money, he would do it through a show or attraction, something where he could sell tickets and not have to have anything to physically show for it. Maybe it's a concert where only twenty people came but, if he recorded that a hundred people came, he could make all that cash account for something and be able to use it."

"Your boss sounds like a crook," Maya said.

"Well, maybe we both do. I came up with the last little example on my own. But only because it helped me figure this whole thing out. El Mismo is an attraction, one that's only open at specific times. What if you sold tickets to see him? Even as little as a buck a person?"

"People wouldn't pay to see him, would they?"

"*I* would. And I'd even pay for a friend to see him. But that's not really the point. The point is that there is a dollar amount to the whole thing. Even if no one paid to see him, Jared could claim that, say, twenty people paid. Or more. Think about it, if the IRS were to ask, he could just say that a busload of tourists stopped in just to see El Mismo and no one would know if they had or hadn't. But no one would ask because the books would look legit." Maya pressed her lips together tightly. I could tell that she was running the scenario in her head.

"And I just thought of another thing," I said. "I bet that mask that Rocky was wearing was made from a 3D printer. It was green plastic on the inside. I wondered how it was made but then your dad said that Jared had little El Mismo skulls made from a 3D printer. He told your dad they could sell them as souvenirs and that he already had a bunch of people interested in buying."

Maya got up to get more wine. She was still in just a shirt up top and underwear below. I watched her walk across the room, my eyes glued to her butt the whole way. She truly was stunning and I still lusted for her. I couldn't believe I stopped us from going further. I felt like an idiot. Who'd care if I was noble if I lost out? Then I thought about nobility. All this, mind you, as I was staring at her butt. Regardless, nobility was alive and well, albeit severely flawed in my case. Part of me wanted to undo everything. Or, better yet, get another chance.

Maya came back and I acted as if nothing was going on in my mind. She handed me a fresh glass of wine and sat down again on the bed opposite me.

She said, "The souvenir idea is actually pretty smart. Don't know why we hadn't thought of it before. But none of us really knows anything about 3D printing or merchandising. Just seems like it complicates things. And would people really buy them? I knew Jared says he has all sorts of people who want to, but the only people he knows are drug buddies."

"There you go."

"There I go where?"

"Drug buddies," I said. "Have you ever been to the library on campus?"

"Duh."

"So you've seen the display they've got? The fossils and petrified rocks?"

"Actually, no," she tilted her head and looked upwards, obviously trying to picture the scene. "Hmmm. I've never really paid all that much attention. I just go there and head upstairs and study."

"Well, they have this cool display of petrified wood and fossils, like I said. But they also have this giant geode. I went there yesterday to work on my video project, and I couldn't stop staring at that geode. It was crazy. It just looked like a big rock on the outside but, on the inside, it was filled with crystals."

"Has anyone ever told you that you're random?"

"Bear with me," I said. "I'm going somewhere with this."

"Sit up against the wall," Maya instructed. I did. Then she said, "Spread your legs." I did. Then she crawled up and sat in front of me with her back resting on my belly. She turned and kissed me on the cheek and said, "No telling how long this might take. I wanted to get comfortable. You're my pillow." I didn't complain.

"So this geode," I said, "I thought about how it was valuable on the inside. That stuck with me. I started thinking about how El Mismo was valuable on the inside of Calavera's. But I was just grasping at something, hoping the universe was giving me a clue. But then your dad told me how Jared claimed that they could mark up those little skulls, sell them for a premium price. That didn't make sense. Little plastic skulls selling for a lot? But then I thought of the geode. I can't say that this is his plan but, if I were in Jared's shoes — and evil, mind you — this is how I'd do it: I'd put the ganchos drug in the little skulls and sell them. Probably make a special line of the skulls, maybe painted differently and selling for more, like a limited edition. But certain people would know what they were. And think about it, Jared wouldn't even have to stuff the skulls until they gave him the code word. So he could sell some of them to unsuspecting people for a high price and then sell others with ganchos in them for those who know the code word or code phrase or whatever."

Maya sat up and turned to me. "That makes total sense," she said. "He uses our whole set up as a front for his dealings. And, if he owns part of the company, he gets to show a legitimate income, which he can build up and build up."

"Right. And if the deal he made with your dad specifies that he gets the lion's share of merchandise, like the little skulls and/or the ticket sales, he would rake it in. And if no one was checking up on him, all the better."

Maya was silent for a moment, soaking it all in. She said, "I think I get it. Jared needed the business—our restaurant—to start failing so he could have some sort of leverage. The whole time he was concocting a way to market things so that it fell in his favor. When things got really bad, he pulled this Witch's Key crap and made it look like he was a hero. And, by then, he was so embedded in the business that Poppy was more inclined to make a deal. And Poppy doesn't know anything about the drugs. Stupid me, I never told him. I didn't want him to find out about the pictures."

"This is why I told you to call the meetings in the morning. We need to tell your dad about this whole thing and then he needs to confront Jared at the restaurant and—"

Just then a loud and sudden *BOOM-CLANK-CLANK-CLANK* shook the whole casita. The wine bottle trembled on the wet bar, and the doors and blinds rattled. Maya and I looked at the window, a bright yellow glow danced from outside somewhere. We both looked at each other, frozen with fear and curiosity. We scrambled and got fully dressed and headed outside.

It was Lalo's tractor. It had blown up. Parts lay scattered all over; some burning, others already charred. A pile of nearby dead branches and debris was aflame. And, in front of the whole scene, scrawled out in burning logs of wood was the M.O. In dancing flames it read "EL MISMO."

33 | Tractor

Maya ran to get her parents but they were already heading out from the house, Lalo slow in his drunken, half-asleep stupor, yet wide-eyed nonetheless. We all huddled together in front of the destruction.

Mrs. Calavera wept. *"¡Ay, Dios mio!"* she whimpered. Maya hugged her silently. Lalo said nothing, just hung his head.

"You have to call the cops," I said. "If you don't, the neighbors will. Then the cops will wonder why you didn't."

Mrs. Calavera said, "The cops, they don't do nothing. Not for El Mismo."

"Maybe not before, but this is different. Before it was only petty crimes. This is too big to ignore. Plus, won't the insurance company need some sort of police report?"

"No insurance on that old tractor," Lalo said. "I cut it a long time ago, cost too much."

"But Poppy, it's your only tractor!" Maya said.

"I know," he said, still hanging his head. "This is all my fault. This is the curse. My curse. Our curse."

I couldn't believe he was just going to pass all this off as some imaginary curse. I put my arm on his shoulder, half wanting to comfort him, half wanting to shake him out of it all. "Lalo," I said, "this is not a curse. I told you, it's a crime. It's manipulation and deception. And we know why. And it's not because of some old family curse."

Lalo looked up at me, his eyes welled-up with tears. "No, it *has* to be a curse," he said. "I didn't believe it was a curse before, but that's all it could be. You said Jared was behind this, but why? I don't have anything. No money, no nothing. Now I don't even have an old beat up tractor."

Maya and her mom hugged Lalo who was now sobbing. I was starting to get all emotional too. It was just so tragic. I thought about how Lalo still had his pecan trees but, without the tractor, even that was in jeopardy.

I asked Maya for her phone and called 911. Before long the authorities arrived and put out the fire, even though, by then, it had died down. The cops questioned everyone but in a half-hearted way. Lalo couldn't really put a price on the old tractor and, when he told the cops it was uninsured, they seemed to downgrade the crime. It didn't help that there was the El Mismo factor. What I thought was a big thing seemed to be just some little event to the police. I asked one of the officers if it would have been more serious if someone had died. He said that the offender obviously meant it as a form of vandalism since it was away from people and at night and a tractor; how no one would be riding around on a tractor at night and, if they were, the vandal wouldn't have been able to pull it off. I told the cop that I had an idea who it was, but he said that would be speculation on my part without any proof. I told him that there was proof and ran back to the casita to get the mask. When I got there, the door was open and the mask was gone. I had to go back to the cop and say that my proof was just stolen. He blew me off.

By the time everything was all said and done, it was well past 2:00 AM. We all agreed to meet in the morning before the staff meeting. Then Maya's parents went inside to bed.

Maya came up to me and hugged me around the waist, pulling herself close to me. She said, "I just want to leave. Leave everything. I don't even want to deal with it."

I comforted her by running my fingers through her hair. I said, "Strange thing is, I *do* get to leave but I don't *want* to."

She looked up at me and gave me a long, soft kiss. Then she went inside.

I stood there outside in the moonlight just looking at the smoldering remains of the tractor and the wood. No one seemed to care if this family crumbled into nothingness. And the guy behind the whole ordeal actually *wanted* it to happen. Someone was going to go down, either Maya and her family, or Jared.

Or maybe even me.

34 | Saturday

I woke up with the sad realization that it was my last full day in Old Mesilla. My last day with Maya. And, worse still, I had all this Sugar Skull Ghost Thief stuff to deal with. Then I thought how Maya was the only server at the restaurant now that Rocky and Esteban had basically walked out. That meant she would have to work the whole day. If I wanted to be near her, I would have to work as well. Working a double on my last day of vacation didn't seem appealing, especially with Jared to contend with. But, if it meant Maya and I could spend some more time together before I had to leave, I guess it wasn't the worst thing in the world.

I laid in bed as the sun crept over the main house and into the window. I figured it was about 8:30 AM or 9:00 AM. It was chilly in the casita and that's the way I liked it. It felt good to be warm under the covers with the chill in the air. The only thing that would have made it better would have been Maya by my side.

Just then, I heard footsteps approaching outside and a quick knock on the door. Maya peeked in the window, shielding the glare from the sun to see inside. "You peeping in on me too?" I asked jokingly not getting up from under the covers. She let herself in and closed the door behind her. She was in pajamas and was hugging herself for warmth. "Hi," she said.

"Hi."

She carelessly kicked off her flip flops and ran to the bed, jumping in right beside me. She dug herself under the covers and nestled up close to me. I adjusted myself to hold her.

"My feet are freezing," she said. "Just a warning." With that she pulled up her legs and tucked her feet under my legs. Under the blankets, I was only wearing a T-shirt and my boxers so my legs were exposed. Sure enough, her feet were freezing. I flinched but didn't move. It felt good to have her warming her feet under me, together our bodies reached perfect temperature equilibrium.

We lay there for a few moments just embracing, listening to each other's breathing mixed with the sounds of the morning. There was a chill in the air and a breeze. Leaves hadn't started falling just yet, so the sound of the wind rustling through the trees was calming.

"I don't want to deal with all this crap," she said. "This whole thing sucks. I just wish I had a good job that paid enough for me to live and take care of my parents so they could just shut down that stupid restaurant and live out their days in peace." She looked up at me. "That's really why I want to go to graduate school. To put an end to all this and not have to count on anyone for anything. And not have to deal with jerks like Jared who take, take, take and give nothing in return. They take advantage of people. They suck. I mean, literally suck. They suck everything out of everything and everyone like a vampire. I just want a good paying job and to be done with it all."

I didn't say anything. What could I say? I didn't have any answers. And, even if I wanted to, I couldn't take care of her, let alone her family. Financially, that is. In fact, I kind of felt like a vampire myself, staying in the casita for free and eating their food. She had a point. Maybe I was a jerk too because I wasn't giving back. But what could I give? So I just held her and listened to her.

"If you could be anywhere in the world at this exact moment in time, where would you love to be?" I asked.

"That's impossible for me to answer."

"Why?"

"Because I want to be far away from here and all this El Mismo stuff. But, at the same time, I'm exactly where I want to be, with you all warm in this bed." She nestled her face against my neck. "Actually, this is one of those times when I just want to die. But not in a bad way, you know? Like I'm so happy and sad and angry and warm all at the same time. And I don't want it to end. I don't want to have to go inside and talk about Jared and Rocky and Estaban and the ghost. I don't want to go to work and serve tables all day and act all happy about El Mismo when people ask. And," she paused, "and I don't want you to go."

"Well, I've gotta go right now," I said. Maya pulled back and glared at me. I added, "Take a piss, that is." I pulled the covers off of myself and went to the bathroom. In the other room I could hear Maya moving around. I heard her crank the emergency flashlight/radio and turn it on. She tuned the radio up and down until she found something she liked and turned it up. It was Van Morrison. I was brushing my teeth to get rid of any morning breath when she knocked twice lightly and let herself into the bathroom. She came up behind me and put her hands around my waist, hugging me tightly.

With a mouth full of toothpaste I jokingly asked, "Are you going to give me the Heimlich?" In response, she made a fist with her right hand, held it with her left, and thrusted it into my solar plexus. It had the effect of pushing every last bit of air out of my lungs and I spit toothpaste all over the mirror. I had never had that done to me before and she was pretty good at it.

Behind me I could hear her giggling. "You asked for it," she said as she went back to hugging me again.

"I asked if you were going to do it. As a joke."

"And I did it as a joke. We're both so funny," she said flatly.

Then she started kissing my back and rubbing my chest. I kept brushing my teeth, trying my best to not let it affect me. She put her hands under my shirt and started stroking my chest and stomach, scratching me slightly. It felt good. I leaned over the sink to rinse my mouth out, and she moved her hands to my back, gently scratching up and down. I didn't move, just let her carry on. Then she moved her hands around to my front again and ran her fingers over my belly. I knew what was coming next and I wanted it to happen yet didn't want it to happen. Didn't want it because I felt weak with her.

I could hear her breathing behind me while Van Morrison finished his song on the radio. Next up was Simon and Garfunkel. "The Boxer." My favorite type of music. And having a pretty girl loving on me made it all the better and all the worse.

She then pressed her hands against my stomach, fingers pointing downward, and slowly inched them lower. Her fingertips slid between the waistband of my boxers and my skin. I shuddered and winced, knowing what I had to do. Before she could go any lower, I held her wrists, stopping her. "Maya," I said, "let's not. We talked about this."

She didn't say anything, just fought me by trying to push her hands down my shorts again. I held her firmly, not letting her advance any farther. I heard her moan ruefully behind me.

"I want this," she said softly. She pulled her hands up and I let go of her wrists. She grabbed my shoulder, leading me around to face her. She looked up at me with burning desire in her eyes. "I want this," she repeated. "With you. I want this with you." She began to unbutton her pajama top. I reluctantly held her wrists again, gently, to halt her progress. She pressed her body against me, our hands sandwiched between us. "And," she said pulling away from me for a moment and looking down, "it's obvious you want it too." She pulled herself back to me and freed her wrists from my grip and wrapped her arms around my waist and started kissing my neck.

"Any man would have to be dead or gay to not want you," I said, my voice quaking. "And, even then, they still might." I bit my lip hard to try to feel something other than her and my lust for her. "But we can't."

"We can do anything we want," she said between small bites on my neck.

"Then we shouldn't," I said. My breathing was getting heavier as I was getting more and more turned on. "You made a vow to yourself and I'm not going to be the one to break it."

"What if I just want to do away with the vow?"

"We would regret it."

This didn't stop her. She grabbed my wrists and led my hands up under her pajama top. She wasn't wearing anything underneath. She placed my hands on her warm breasts and pressed on them. She was panting as she continued to kiss my neck. As much as it hurt for me to do so, I pulled my hands down and held her by the waist and pushed her away from me, or, rather, peeled her off of me.

She looked at me with an angry hunger in her eyes. "Let me make my own decisions," she said fighting to get back close to me.

"Maya, it's not just about you," I said. "It's about me too. I want this just as bad as you do. Probably more. But I can't let myself go any further with you. Not just because of you but because of me. I'll get attached, I know I will. I'll want you all the time. I'll want *this* all the time. It would be torture to not have it, to not have you. I'll be up in Colorado just pining for you like a dog without a bone."

"Or *with* a bone," she said winking at me and trying to pull me close again as I struggled to evade her.

"You say you'd give up your vow for me but then what happens after I leave?"

"I don't know. Maybe we try to do a long distance thing. Maybe we just go our separate ways. Maybe you move to where I'll be." She grabbed the front of my shirt and wrapped one of her legs around mine.

"Maya," I said calmly, mustering up all the strength I could to not take her right then and there. "It won't work out. At least not the way I would want it to. Nor you. I just can't up and move. And I couldn't do the long distance thing. It would drive me crazy, knowing you were out there doing your thing with hundreds of guys hitting on you and flirting with you. Doctor guys and smart university guys, probably professors too as hot as you are. I couldn't take it. I'm not that confident. I know myself. I'd go mad wondering what you were up to. I know that sounds pitiful but it's true. I'm just not at that level yet. And you deserve more. And, as for moving, we're on different paths. You're going to school. I'm just kind of figuring things out. Again, you deserve more."

"And what about just going our separate ways?"

"I wouldn't want to. I'm already so enraptured by you as it is. If we make love, I'll be connected to you even more so. And going our separate ways after that would kill me."

She pouted.

"Let's not do this for both our sakes," I said.

She looked up at me with a scrunched up face, like a child who didn't get what she wanted. "OK," she said and unwrapped her leg from around mine. She put her hands on my chest and raised herself up and kissed me on the lips, soft and slow. Then she pinched both my nipples with vengeance. I hollered in pain and knocked her hands away from me. "That's a double titty twister for making me like you even more than before."

"Thanks, I guess." I rubbed my raw nipples.

"You know what? I've never begged a guy for sex before. You're the first. And, furthermore, I've never had a guy not put out for me."

"I guess that's a good thing."

"It's probably the best and worst thing that has ever happened to me." With that she spun and headed out of the bathroom. I could hear her getting into the bed. "Will you at least lie with me a little longer?" she asked from the other room. I didn't answer, just went in there and got under the covers with her. We resumed our positions as before. "I still don't want you to go," she said.

I had my arm around her and I reached up and ran my hand through her hair, drawing her closer to me at the same time. "This is our last day together, that's the bad news. But here's the good news: everything is going to work out. It has to."

"Everything is a mess!"

"Right now it is, at this very moment. But think about it; we're ninety-nine percent sure that Jared is behind all this stuff, right?"

Maya pulled back and looked up at me. "So what? How does that make everything alright?"

"There's no way that your family is going to give in to him now. When we lay it all out for your mom and dad, they're not going to be OK with giving up any part of their business to Jared. So that leaves only a few options. One: Jared is dealt with and leaves, which takes the whole Sugar Skull Ghost Thief problem with him. That would get business back up and your dad wouldn't be so depressed; he'd go back to work. Two: Jared does something completely crazy and takes the whole business away from your family. Then your family doesn't have to deal with it any more."

"That's horrible! How does option two make everything better?"

"Doesn't make it better, just makes it all right. If your family no longer has the restaurant, your dad won't want you to run it. That means that you could go off to graduate school, get your degree so you can get that good-paying job, then you can take care of them. Both ways you get to go to graduate school and work toward that career in…" I realized at that point that I never actually asked what she was going to school for.

"Neurology," she said, sensing my ignorance.

"Neurology? Well, that makes sense."

"How?"

"Think about it this way: as a neurologist, you'll be dealing with nerves, right? The people coming to you will have problems with their nervous system, a weakness. It will be your job to help them. To heal them and give them strength."

"It's a bit more complicated than that but yeah, sure."

"Everything that is happening to you right now—all this ghost stuff and Jared crap—is making you stronger. Think of it like conditioning. If you can get through this El Mismo stuff, it will give you nerves of steel. And, as a neurologist, you'll need to have strong nerves to help those with weak nerves."

"That's mixing a metaphor with reality." She gently patted my chest.

"I guess so. But it makes sense in a way. As a doctor, you're going to encounter all sorts of crazy stuff, and people are going to be counting on you to keep your head together and do the right thing. And, more importantly, not give up. And you're strong, I can see that. You work hard and do your best for your family and school and yourself. You're going to make it through this, and you're going to go to school and keep going until you come out the other side an awesome doctor. And then you can decide what you want to do with your family and their business and their future. And who knows? Maybe you'll meet a guy along the way who is also a doctor or lawyer or some other profession that makes good cash. Then you could really make sure your parents get taken care of."

"Meet someone? What about us?"

"What we have is great, don't get me wrong. But can you see it going anywhere? You've got so much potential, so much ahead of you. I've got, well, I've got nothing really to offer you. I don't have any money, any college degree let alone a career. Like I said, you deserve more. You deserve a successful guy who will take care of all your needs, who will lead the way and charge ahead. I'm just a guy working in a café, totally confused about who I am and what I'm going to do with my life. I've got nothing to give you."

Maya sat up and looked down at me with furrowed eyebrows. "That's not true, Chulo. You've given me the one thing that no other person has ever given me. And it has nothing to do with money or college or a career or even sex for that matter."

"What did I give you?"

"Hope."

35 | Letter

Maya let me know that her mom would be making breakfast, and both her mom and dad were getting ready for the family meeting. She also mentioned that they decided to close up shop for the entire day due to all the drama with El Mismo and the tractor. A staff meeting (which was basically just a meeting with Jared) was set for noon. I didn't look forward to either of the meetings since I was going to be an outsider giving inside information. Good thing Mrs. Calavera was making breakfast. Good food always calms my nerves.

After I showered, I made my way to Maya's house. Sure enough, Mrs. Calavera was back in action. She was making homemade tortillas and the aroma was heavenly. Piquito was there too, sitting patiently next to Mrs. Calavera's feet, probably waiting for a hand-out.

"Sientate," she said pointing to a chair as I walked in the door. I took it to mean that I should sit down. She poured me a cup of coffee and put a plate in front of me. She then gave me a fresh tortilla right off of the stove. "Put butter on it," she said. *"Muy sabroso."* I lathered the hot tortilla with butter and took a bite. It was probably one of the best things I had ever tasted. For a fleeting moment, nothing else existed in the world except

for that hot tortilla with melted butter dripping off of it. There was no Jared, no El Mismo, no lust for Maya. Just that tortilla. At once I was transported to a land of peace and carbs and fat. I wanted to live there forever.

But reality kicked in. Maya and Lalo made it to the table and sat down. Mrs. Calavera served everyone and we dug in.

There was no use for small talk, so I decided to jump right in. As soon as I opened my mouth, the doorbell rang followed by the sound of a car peeling out and driving away. Mrs. Calavera went to the door. No one was there, but I saw her bend down and pick something up. She brought it to the table and set it in front of Maya. It was an envelope, stuffed fat with Maya's name written upon it.

We all sat and looked at each other in confusion. Lalo said, "Well, open it up." Maya did so. She pulled out a letter and a stack of what looked like one hundred dollar bills.

"What the..." Maya said counting the money. "There's over ten grand here."

"Who's it from?" Lalo asked as Maya handed the stack of money to him. "Read the letter."

Maya opened the letter and scanned it. Then she started reading:

"Dear Maya, Let me start by saying I'm so sorry for everything I did. I'm completely disgusted with myself. I couldn't bear to show my face to you so I left this letter. The money is yours. I have a trust account from my parents. That's how I could keep working at Calavera's and still pay my rent and bills. I didn't need the money; I worked there because of you. I love you and I think you know that. I know you don't feel the same about me. Looking at what I have done, I can't blame you. I don't even like myself. There's no way to repay you and your family for what I have taken from you by acting like the ghost. I don't know what came over me. I wanted you so bad and—" Maya paused, reading ahead silently to herself before continuing. "I wanted you so bad. I would have done anything to have you. Please give some of the money to your friend for what I did to his van. I don't know how much something like that costs so I guess you'll have to figure it out. I want to tell you that I hope everything works out OK with your family. I don't have anything more to do with Jared or the ghost. I don't want to have anything to do with anything. Please use the money for whatever you need. I'm going somewhere, where I don't need money so it's all yours. One last thing, I want you to know that I'm going to do something for you. It will show you how much I love you. Then I will be gone forever." Maya looked up at us all. "It's signed by Rocky," she said.

We sat in stunned silence.

"How much do you think it will cost to get the van painted?" Maya asked me.

"I have no idea," I said. "I'd have to look it up or ask my roommate. He knows that kind of stuff."

"Let me know." She folded the letter and placed it back in the envelope.

No one said anything for a moment. "Where will Rocky go where he doesn't need money?" I asked, breaking the silence.

"I don't know," Maya said. "I hope he's not going to do something drastic."

"He already said he would."

"There's no knowing. He's a weird guy." Maya took a deep breath. "I'm worried he might hurt himself."

"Do you think he'd do something like that?" I asked.

"Don't know. I mean, I never thought he'd do this whole El Mismo thing but he did."

Lalo jumped in. "I'm confused," he said. "What do you mean about Rocky and El Mismo?"

It hit me that we hadn't let Lalo and Mrs. Calavera in on

the whole story. "Rocky is the ghost," I said. They both looked at me with confusion in their eyes. I proceeded to tell them all about Jared and what I presumed was his plan to weasel in at the restaurant and how he employed Rocky and Esteban to help out in his plan. I told them all about the fake video and how I was able to reproduce it and how the camera wasn't even plugged in. I told them about the ganchos drug that Jared was selling on the sly. And I told them about the girl at the liquor store who told me how Jared tried to angle himself into their business too. I left out the part about her dirty pictures.

Lalo sat and frowned. "So he paid Esteban three thousand dollars to set us up with that fake camera?"

"Three thousand dollars and a job as a sommelier in Chicago," I said.

"OK," Lalo said, "then what did he pay Rocky to do what he did? He didn't need money so that doesn't make sense."

I looked at Maya. She looked back at me with pleading in her eyes. "Rocky has an…addiction," I answered. "Jared was going to supply him with a big fix. That's all we know."

"*¿Qué es* fix?" Mrs. Calavera said. Lalo leaned over and whispered something in her ear. She went wide-eyed and nodded. "Ah," she said. "*Ay que Rocky. Pobrecito.*" She had no anger toward him, only pity. A trait I admired.

"Lalo," I said, "this has to stop right now. Today. Jared has to be stopped. Everything hinges on it. You have to cut him out of whatever deal you made."

"But we signed a contract."

"Then tear it up."

"We both have a copy."

"What does the contract give him?"

Lalo hemmed and hawed for a moment. He got up and poured himself more coffee and sat back down. He pursed his lips, stalling. Finally he said, "I gave him half of the restaurant plus eighty percent of any merchandise he sells. Plus eighty percent of ticket sales for El Mismo. He wanted to start charging people to see the skull."

Maya slammed her hand on the table. "What?" she exclaimed angrily. "That's insane!"

"*Mija,*" Lalo said consoling, "I had nothing. *We have* nothing. Jared had ideas and a way to get us back on track. I figured that a small percentage of something is better than one hundred percent of nothing." That seemed to be Lalo's basic philosophy.

Maya sighed heavily and sat back in her chair. "*Ay, Poppy,*" she said. For someone who claimed to not want anything to do with the family business, she was sure angry about her father's decision.

"It doesn't matter," I said. "Even if the contract said that Jared gets everything, it doesn't matter. He's going down. He lied and deceived his way into the contract. I don't know law but I know that he just can't get away with it."

"But he has a contract," Lalo said again.

We all sat in silence.

"He'll be there today?" I asked.

"*Sí,*" Lalo responded.

"You'll have to let him know that you know about it all. Besides, you do know that he's the one behind your tractor blowing up, right?"

"I thought you said that was Rocky."

"Rocky was the ghost. What happened last night was not Rocky. I can't say for sure but I'm pretty sure Jared was behind it. It's too bold for the likes of Rocky. Nothing against him, but that's not his style from what I can tell. Yet, from what that girl told me at the liquor store, it's trademark Jared."

"There's nothing we can do," Lalo said.

"You can't just roll over and let him get his way," I said.

"He's a crook!"

"We're too far into it," Lalo said. "We have a deal."

Part of me couldn't believe that Lalo would just give up. But then again, he had already given up in a way. "I'll go to the meeting with you. I have nothing to lose. If Jared gets pissed at me, so be it. But I can't let him get away with this." I felt Maya squeeze my hand under the table.

"Let's think about this," I said. "We need to go in there with a plan. He's onto us, that's apparent."

"How do you know he's onto us?" Lalo asked.

"Esteban split and Rocky is out of the equation. Jared knows that. He's taking things into his own hands. Look at your tractor. What's he trying to say? What's his message?"

No one said anything.

"For one," I continued, "he's telling us that he knows Rocky's out of the picture for good. Blowing up your tractor was not in the original equation. It was all petty crimes and nuisance. This was an act of resolution, a real danger. It was a big neon sign saying, 'Look what I'm capable of.' Why would he do that? He must think that you're considering backing out of the deal."

Maya chimed in, "But we haven't told him that yet."

"He's thinking ahead," I said. "He may be a maniac but he's not stupid. In fact, he's smart. It's a preemptive strike. He knows something is up and he's solidifying his end of the deal, striking fear into you to weaken you."

"So what's our plan?" Lalo asked.

They all looked at me. I didn't have a plan; that really wasn't my role in all this. But seeing them all looking to me for help made me feel sorry for them. None of them had a plan from this point forward. They each were smart in their own way but were not in Jared's league. Not only was he intelligent, he was manipulative, ruthless, and strategic. I, myself, wasn't in

Jared's league either, but at least I could recognize it. Maya and her family were good people who worked hard. They had their faults but, all in all, they wanted what was right in the world and for their fellow man. Jared would just as soon blow them to bits as he did the tractor if it helped him meet his goal.

"Lalo," I said, "tell Jared to bring the contract with him. For the meeting. Tell him you want to go over it with everyone. That you want to bring everything out in the open and that you're planning for the future."

"Won't he wonder why you're there?" Lalo asked.

That hadn't occurred to me. "That's a good point. Maybe I shouldn't be there."

Maya squeezed my hand again. "You have to be there," she said. "I mean, look at us. Before you came, we couldn't even figure out the camera. We're not built for this sort of thing, brain games and conspiracy and all that."

I didn't know if I should take that as a compliment or not. Did I think like a criminal? "How about I go but not sit at the table. I could go and eavesdrop, like Rocky did when we were talking about the casita." After I said it, I realized that Lalo and Mrs. Calavera didn't know what I was talking about. At this point it didn't matter. I continued, "That way, if things get heated, at least I can do something. I don't know what but something."

Maya said, "You can call the police."

"If I had a phone."

"I'll let you use mine."

"That works. I'll listen in and call the police if I need to."

"You should also record our conversation." Maya suggested. "Just in case Jared says anything that might be useful if there's a trial or something."

"That's not a bad idea. However, at this point, I don't think he'll allow anyone to get him into a courtroom. I hate to say it, but guys like him don't see the inside of a courtroom, let alone prison. The best criminals aren't behind bars. They're too smart or too crazy to get caught. Or, as in Jared's case, both."

Lalo looked deflated. Maybe I shouldn't have said that last part. In essence, I was building Jared up, making him look like an evil giant while, at the same time, telling Lalo and his family that they were just mere mortals with no chance of defeating this incredibly strong enemy. I took a different route. "But here's the thing about a guy like Jared: he's only looking out for himself. That blinds him to other things, right?"

Maya looked at me askance. "What do you mean?" she asked.

"He's too into himself. That must make him have a blind spot somewhere. Plus, he can't be trusted, which means he must not trust other people. That's human nature. Maya, you told me that he doesn't have friends."

"How does that help us?" she asked.

"Basically he's a lone wolf. Luckily, Esteban and Rocky are out of the equation. It doesn't seem like he has anyone else working on his behalf."

"What if he has connections? Like drug world connections?"

"That's a good possibility. But I'm guessing that outside of a few small time dealers, he's working for himself. If he gets help, that comes at a price. And, by getting some thug involved, that would mean he'd have to reveal what he's doing and why he's doing it. That adds a level of danger to his business and his money. And that's what he cares about. Why jeopardize that? Especially when he thinks he's dealing with a bunch of yokels. Myself included. No offense, mind you. But that's been his experience so far. He's been able to outwit you and cast fear into you this long, why would he think you have anything to hurt him with? He thinks you're all pushovers. You can use that to your advantage."

"None of this is a plan," Maya said.

"Maybe you fight fire with fire."

"Like, blow up *his* truck?" She sounded exasperated and confused.

"I don't know," I said. "Maybe. Or at least make him think you will. Look, I'm not saying you should stoop to his level, but you need to speak to him in his language."

"So we're not as smart as him and we're not as crazy as him," Maya noted. "Yet we're supposed to deal with him as if we are? He'll see right through us." She had a point.

"What's the one big huge thing that you have that Jared doesn't have?" I asked Lalo.

He looked to the side, thinking. "The farm?" He said without confidence.

"No. A family. You have your wife and daughter. Jared may not think you're smart or crazy but he can't deny the love you have for your family. And that love gives you strength and resolve. I'm sure you would do anything to protect your family. Am I right?"

"Of course. They're the only thing that matters to me."

"Jared is putting your family in danger. How does that make you feel?"

"Makes me mad."

"Good. Use that. Use it against him. Make him know that you'll do whatever is needed to protect your family. His motivation is money. Your motivation is your family. I believe your motivation is as strong, if not stronger than his. That means your resolution is stronger. That's your power."

"That's good," Maya said. "But I hate to nag, it's still not a plan."

"This is not my fight," I said. I turned to look at Lalo. "It's yours," I stated directly to him. "This is not my family, it's yours. The restaurant is not mine, it's yours. This is your fight.

It should be your plan."

Lalo sat back in his chair, eyebrows furrowed. After a moment of contemplation, he stood up straight. "You're right," he said firmly. "This is my fight. So my plan is to get the contract from Jared, tear it up, and get him out of our lives in any way possible."

It was a simple plan. I can't say it was the most ingenious plan in the world but, for lack of a better plan involving complex machines and slight of hand or anything else they use in the movies, it was a plan that might work.

Lalo's whole demeanor had changed. Gone was the pushover that cowered to Jared and his silly schemes, replaced with the resolve of an angry husband and father who would fight to the death for his family. Sure, his plan lacked sophistication but he made up for it with the absolute insane dedication of a father whose family was put in danger. I could see it in his eyes. He was now willing to tear Jared to pieces to protect his family. Of all the plans in the world, this one, at this moment in time, as simplistic as it seemed, was the best plan I had ever heard.

Would it work? There was only one way to find out.

36 | Confrontation

I drove myself to Calavera's for the meeting at noon. I didn't know what I would be doing afterward nor could I predict what exactly would transpire. And while I didn't want to drive the bus around, I thought it might be good for me to have my own transportation in the event of craziness.

I got there and waited out of sight, around the side of the building. Maya showed up in her car, her parents in another. She probably had the same idea. I made eye contact with her from afar, and she gave me a slight nod. Before going in, she made her way to me and told me to wait outside and she would come get me when the coast was clear. She went in and I waited. After a couple of minutes, she came back out.

"I told them I forgot my phone in the car," she said. "When I go back in, I'll make sure no one sees you go in behind me, OK?" She handed me her phone. "Here, I'm sure you know how to use it. I opened the voice recorder app so all you have to do is start it. I've silenced everything so it won't go off. We're sitting next to the wall near the hallway to El Mismo. It's pretty thin and we won't turn the music on so you should be able to hear. If, for some reason, Jared gets up to go to the bar, you'll need to duck into that other little room with the dining table.

I'll ask him where he's going so that you'll know if you have to hide."

I nodded.

We made it inside easy enough. I could hear Lalo and Jared talking about football. Small talk to stall. Jared had his back to the door so he didn't see me sneak in behind Maya. Even though there was no real danger to the situation, my heart was pounding. I knew something was going to happen. Had to. I also knew that if Jared found me snooping, he might lay into me like he did to Rocky. Probably worse since I was trying to wreck his entire plan.

I walked softly down the hall and stood near the entryway to the small room with the big table. That way I could just duck in there fast. Maya was right, I could pretty much hear everything. Without the music or customers, their voices echoed in the emptiness of the dining room. I started the audio recorder app on the phone. A red dot appeared and a timer started. I held the phone up at the same level as my ear so that it would record what I was hearing.

I heard Maya apologize and take her seat. Lalo cleared his throat. "Are we all ready to start?" he asked. Sounds of affirmation followed. "We need to talk about our agreement," Lalo announced. "Me and you, Jared. We need to bring everything out into the open. I haven't shared much with my family; I've been half ashamed but mostly just afraid. I've been putting it off, not wanting them to know. But now we need to get everything out there. Everything."

No audible response. I wished I could see Jared's face, but something told me he was putting on his best expression of innocence.

"As you know," Lalo continued. "the ghost of El Mismo has had a profound effect on all of us and the business as a whole. Recently, the ghost has been held in check. Jared and

I believed that it was the key—*La Llave de la Bruja*—that he wears around his neck that did that. We figured out that when Jared wore the key, the ghost stayed put. Jared and I talked about him selling me the key but he counter-offered with a stake in our business. He has shared with me his ideas for monetizing our El Mismo attraction and, at the time of the signing of the agreement, it seemed like a good idea." Lalo paused. "However, I have received some disturbing news and have had some unfortunate incidents as of late that lead me to believe that I have been deceived." Someone grunted, sounded like Maya. Lalo went on, "Jared, it has come to my attention that you are the person behind the hauntings of the El Mismo ghost, or the Sugar Skull Ghost Thief as the papers call him. We know that you employed Esteban to fake the videos and that you also employed Rocky to commit the crimes dressed as the ghost. We know that you have been selling drugs, even here in our restaurant."

There was a moment of silence. I could feel the tension in the room.

"Do you deny any of this, Jared?" Lalo asked.

I heard shifting in seats. There was a sigh, as one might make out of frustrated. I took it that it was Jared since he spoke right after. "Those are harsh allegations," he said, his tone serious. "You would be wise to consider not only who is giving you your information but also what you risk by accusing me. All I know is we have a deal. Signed by both of us. And that deal is for the future of this operation, of Calavera's. The deal gives me a stake in the business. Why, may I ask, would I want to ruin the business that I have a vested interest in?"

"You didn't answer the question," Maya said. "Do you deny anything that my father has accused you of?"

"Let me guess, Rocky was the one who told you I hired him. Am I right?"

"Yeah."

"Did he tell you what exactly I hired him for?"

"Yeah. He said you hired him to run around as the ghost thief and make trouble."

"Well isn't that convenient of him. He runs around making trouble and blames it on me. Like I'm some idiot who gets off on him stealing girls' panties."

"What?"

"Yeah, that's what he stole. Girls' panties. A bunch of them. Sure, he took other stuff but it was mostly girls' panties. He'd go out being a peeping tom and catch them undressing. If anyone saw him, he would just run away as if he was the ghost. Then he would go back and steal their underwear. Sometimes their dirty underwear. I bet he didn't tell you that, did he."

No one spoke.

"Don't believe me? Go look in his locker. It's full of girls panties and bras and all that. There are some other things too, like weird toys and figurines and some cooking utensils, but mostly it's all girls' underwear.

"What I actually hired him to do was paint the mask and make a costume. I printed the mask out with my 3D printer and I needed him to work out the costume. I didn't have time. You all know I've been working here every day, doubles."

There was a brief silence. I could almost hear the gears turning in the heads of Maya and Lalo. Not so much Mrs. Calavera. She wasn't into trying to figure all this out.

I wanted to go in there and ask some questions myself. For instance, why did Jared wear the key if he knew it was Rocky? That didn't make sense. And what about Esteban? Why would he fake the video. I was mentally trying to pass my thoughts to Maya.

Jared spoke again, "I didn't find out about all this until the other day when, apparently, Rocky tagged the Microbus. Oh, man was I pissed! I actually thought the whole ghost thing was real. I mean Rocky? Who would have ever thought he'd do such a thing? Before I found out about that, I was so convinced that the ghost was real that I broke out the key. I even showed it to Rocky, told him that a witch said it would help. And for about a week it did. I thought I was onto something. Something that could help not just me but the whole restaurant, all you guys. But the witch told me that I couldn't sell the key. That, if I did, I would get a curse worse than the one I was trying to alleviate. So I worked out a deal to partner up. And you guys know how into this place I am. I just thought that I could work hard to get it back up to snuff.

"I was pissed at Rocky for tagging the VW. I mean, you have to understand, that was my pride and joy for so long. I put a lot of work into that thing. And to have it tagged by some idiot peeping tom because he was all jealous of you and Perk? Well, you can't blame a guy for laying into him. I told him the deal was off. I didn't pay him. I don't care how much he likes that goofy show 'Firefly,' I kept those autographed pics. He did tell you about the autographed pictures, right? My cousin has a boner for that show too and he collects memorabilia. He had some extra signed pics and I found out that Rocky liked that show so I thought it would be a good trade—he gets the pics and I get the costume."

Everyone was silent.

"The costume was to promote the restaurant," Jared continued. "It was supposed to be a surprise. I was going to show it to you all once the deal went into effect. Lalo told you that it starts January first, right?"

"I didn't tell them any details," Lalo responded.

"Well, I didn't expect business to drop like it did. I didn't expect this whole stupid ghost thing. It's a shame all this happened."

I had to hold myself back from going in there and just laying into him. He was lying, I knew it. But, from the absence of questioning from Maya and her dad, they may have been buying the whole thing; hook, line, and sinker. The hauntings started long before the deal was made. Why would Jared say the costume was for the deal? Or did he say that. No, he just said it was to promote the restaurant and that he was going to surprise them when the deal went into effect. I started wondering if I had assumed too much.

"So what exactly did Rocky tell you? I bet he made up some stupid thing about his payment. The guy's sick. Half of the underwear he got was from high school girls. Did he tell you that? After he tagged the bus, I got suspicious. Now, I'm not proud of this but I broke into his locker and found all sorts of stuff. He had framed pictures of these girls and he kept their underwear in ziplock bags taped to the framed pictures so he knew who wore what. I recognized a few of the girls, little sisters of friends I knew. I haven't told them about it yet. That's kind of a weird thing to bring up. 'Hey, guess what. This guy I work with dressed up like a ghost and watched your little sister undress then broke into your house and stole her dirty underwear.' Can you imagine? Eventually I'll have to tell them, but I wanted to confront Rocky face to face. Actually, I wanted to beat his face in. What a pervert! Although it should come as no surprise that he would do something like this. I mean look at what he does to you, Maya. It's not like everyone doesn't notice him trying to be all sly and take pictures of you."

"But we asked him," Maya said, "and he didn't deny the fact that you were paying him in" she paused. "In dirty pictures."

"What? Did he specifically tell you that?"

I ran back over that night with Rocky. I remembered that I was the one who brought up the pictures. Rocky didn't bring them up. What if he didn't even know about them before I said anything? Stupid me! The more I thought about it, the more Jared was making sense. Maybe this whole thing was about Rocky getting his jollies from peeking in on girls and stealing their stuff. I started to doubt myself. But then I thought about Esteban's fake video and the ganchos drug.

"We asked him about them," Maya said, "and he said he was running around as the ghost in exchange for them."

"Do your parents know about," Jared paused, "about, you know?"

"No," Maya said. I couldn't see her but I could tell she had said it through gritted teeth.

"About what?" Lalo asked.

"Nothing, Poppy," Maya said dejected.

"You know me, Maya," Jared said softly. "You know I would never…"

"What about Esteban," Maya said resolutely. She wasn't convinced. Good. "Why would he fake the video? Rocky said you paid him three thousand dollars and gave him a contact in Chicago in exchange."

"I gave him a contact in Chicago, that part is true. But just one guy giving a lead to another. We all knew it was his dream. But give him three grand? That's ridiculous. But, come to think of it, Rocky might have. I don't know if he shared this with you, but he's got some big trust fund. I bet you anything Rocky paid Esteban to fake the videos. Fooled you all. Fooled me too. I was wondering about that. I was even going to go in there and check the cameras myself, but I'm not hip to all that techno crap."

"What about the ganchos?" Maya said. She sounded desperate, like she really wanted to pin Jared down, but he was poking holes in everything I had told her.

"They're a bunch of weirdos on the wall," he said. "What about them?"

"Not the paintings. The drug."

"What drug?"

"The drug you call ganchos," Maya snapped, accompanied by what sounded like a slap on the table for emphasis. "You're selling it here at the restaurant."

"Who told you that?"

"I, uh, I heard it and," Maya paused. "And, I wish I didn't have to say this in front of my mom and dad, but you gave some to me."

"What I gave you was ecstasy. And you're such a lightweight it was no use telling you what it was. I just let you have your fun. I mean, come on. Who doesn't know what ecstasy feels like?"

"Well," Maya said in a broken voice. "I guess me, before then."

"*Que es* ecstasy?" Mrs. Calavera asked.

"*Una droga,*" Jared replied flatly.

"*Aye, mija,*" Mrs. Calavera moaned.

"I'm sorry, Mamita," Maya said. "I made a mistake. It won't happen again, I promise."

"I'm no angel," Jared said. "I've done things I'm not proud of. But I want to put all that behind me. Be a true businessman. Like you, Lalo."

There was silence. "It's so absurd, really," Jared continued. "So I'm selling a drug named after a bunch of freaks in the paintings on the wall. Let me guess, some druggie told you that. Probably someone who's pissed at me for something or other. Maya, you know I got mixed up with some pretty sketchy people. But selling some drug under your noses? Did you hear this first hand? Who was it?"

"Perk heard it," Maya replied. "He told me about it."

"And you trust him?" Jared asked. He was speaking with a sense of authority. "How well do you know him? How well *could* you know him? Did it ever occur to you that he may be lying? Or, even worse, that he is so disillusioned that he believes everything people tell him? I don't know him. I mean, he seems like a nice guy and all but, no offense, he's soft. And guys like that are gullible. I bet some pretty girl saw him and heard of me—probably one of my exes—and used him to get back at me. I've dated some crazy chicks. Maya, you know that. I've told you some of my horror stories. At least I know it wasn't Zoey. I've spared you the details of that ordeal, for her sake. She's gone completely insane. Seriously. I had to take her to a mental institution. She was jealous of the fact that you and I went out together. She never really knew but, when I told her, she went ballistic. She started blubbering and shaking and saying all types of weird stuff. In the end, she didn't even realize where she was. I'm still waiting to see what the doctors say. I swear, between Rocky and Zoey, I'm surrounded by lunatics!"

No one said anything. And I knew that, if I were at the table, I would be speechless as well. Was I so gullible that a girl could pull one over on me? Was I so intent on pegging all this on Jared that I concocted the whole thing in my mind?

"Look, I'm still here," Jared said. "Rocky got found out and he split. I haven't seen him since I laid into him about the van. Good thing I haven't. I'd have crushed his face in. And Esteban? That punk. It's safe to assume he was feeling the heat so he split as well. Both of them left you high and dry. And who stuck around? Me. And now I'm your scapegoat? Trying to take away the deal we have? I've worked hard for you. I still work hard. I want Calavera's to thrive. But this? You guys accusing me of sabotaging the whole thing and letting Rocky get away with his stupid shenanigans? I mean, we should string the guy up. Esteban too. Look at what he's done to all of us!" Silence followed.

At about that time I started to feel like Grade A, all natural dog crap. The feeling of stupidity and regret was inundating me. Who did I think I was? Sherlock Holmes? I was just some guy without any formal education who worked in a café and didn't even have a car. Maya and her family put their trust in me and I had misled them down some rabbit trail, putting them all in danger by letting Rocky go. If Rocky was able to fool me and Maya and her whole family, Jared included, and if he was as sick as Jared was claiming, maybe it wasn't beyond him to blow up the tractor.

But why?

Maybe it was to frame Jared. Maybe Rocky thought that, if he could pin everything on Jared, that he could get away scot-free. Or maybe to create a diversion so he could steal the mask back, eliminate evidence. After all, it was stolen from the casita when we were all distracted with the tractor after it blew up.

I felt small, embarrassed, and useless. I was glad I was on the other side of the wall. I didn't want anyone to see my face and I didn't want to see anyone. I thought about just sneaking out, packing up my stuff, and heading back home. How stupid could I have been?

But that wouldn't have been right. As uncomfortable as it was going to be, I had to confront them all, especially Jared. Let them know how sorry I was about the whole thing.

"I know what we need to do," Jared said. "We need to find Rocky and make him face the music. We need to hold him accountable for all he's done. Justice needs to be served, dammit!"

I heard Lalo grunt in agreement. I could picture him nodding.

"He can't just go around watching teenage girls undress and stealing their personal stuff," Jared said, raising his voice like an orator. "He's violating them! He needs to pay to get that

VW bus repainted. He needs to give back everything he stole and pay for all the damage."

"Yeah," Maya exclaimed. "We need to get that bastard!" She was obviously convinced. That made facing her even harder.

"Yes, we need to get that bastard once and for all," Jared said emphatically. "For the sake of all of us. For the sake of Calavera's as a whole!"

Sounds of affirmation.

"He'll lie through his teeth though," Jared continued. "You'll have to be prepared for that. He's already got this whole thing figured out. He's smarter than he lets on. But that can't stop us. He's hurt you guys too much. I mean, come on. You said it yourself, he blew up your tractor. That's your livelihood! He just blew it up! Could have even killed someone. He's slime, that's for sure. But we can take him, right?"

"Right!" Sounded like all three of them were in agreement.

"I'll show the cops his locker with all the stolen stuff. And I'll show them the mask. I mean that's proof enough to get him put away just for the crimes that he's already committed! It's even got his hair in it. They can test it for DNA."

I looked down at Maya's phone in my shaking hand. I was just about to stop recording when something hit me, something Jared just said. I thought about it for a second. Jared continued talking in the other room. He was making some sort of plan with the Calaveras as to how they were going to triangulate the city and find Rocky.

I froze, not knowing how to proceed. Jared was rallying his troops while I was unable to move, unsure if I should go in there and point out what he said. Or maybe I didn't hear exactly what he had said. I doubted myself left and right. I looked down at Maya's phone again. It was still recording. I didn't have time to listen to the whole recording to see if I heard right. Basically, I was already screwed. If I was wrong about this last little tidbit, how much more screwed could I have been? I'd have to walk away with my tail between my legs as it was. What did I have to lose? With my resolve strengthened (or weakened to the breaking point) I made my way to the dining room to confront Jared.

As I walked in, Maya caught my eye. "Perk," she said. "I, um, I didn't hear you come in." They were at a table for four, Jared was standing, his arms leaning on the table and looking like an angry boss. Lalo had a manilla file folder in front of him, Jared had a letter-sized clasp envelope in front of him, his right fist pinned it down on the table top.

They all stopped planning and looked at me. Lalo had a sense of disgust on his face.

Maya said, "We know why all this is happening. Jared figured it out."

"No, he didn't," I said resolutely.

Jared straightened up slowly and approached me. He put his hand on my shoulder. I was trembling and I knew he must have felt it. "It's OK, Traveling Man. We're going to get it all taken care of. It's our fight and we need to fight it. Don't worry, we'll let you know how things turn out."

I brushed Jared's hand off of my shoulder. "Don't touch me," I said.

"What's your problem, dude?"

"You're a liar and a cheat!"

"Hey," he said shrugging in disbelief, "I'm just a guy trying to help out Lalo and his family."

"You're only trying to help yourself," I said.

Maya came to me and held my arm. "You obviously didn't hear what Jared had to say. Rocky is behind this whole thing."

"Like hell he is," I said, still glaring at Jared with no response on his part.

"What, do you have some brilliant observation to add?"

Jared asked. "I'd love to hear it." He sat down and leaned back in his chair. He no longer looked charming but cocky.

"Just let it rest," Lalo said with a sigh. "You were wrong, Perk. Jared has a better understanding of it all. Now, we're wasting time. We need to go get Rocky."

"Lalo," I said, "I was not wrong. Jared actually got me to thinking I was but I'm not. He's smart and a great liar but he's not perfect. He made a mistake."

Everyone went silent. Jared just looked at me as if I was some stupid kid that didn't know anything. "Please," he said, "enlighten us."

"You're good, I'll give you that." I took a step back before continuing. If I was right, Jared might make some type of move at me. I didn't want that. "You've got a brain on you, that's for sure. Always a step ahead. But you went two steps ahead. You anticipated something, but it didn't happen. And you said something about it."

At that, Jared discarded his cocky attitude and sat up, drilling me with his eyes.

"First you said that Lalo told you about the tractor," I said. "He didn't. And there was no way you would have known. Only the cops were there and they pretty much blew us off when they heard the tractor was old and uninsured. Second, you said you had the mask and that you could use it against Rocky. But *we* had the mask. How did you get it if we had it?"

Jared looked at Maya, then her dad, then her mom, then back to me. "Rocky gave it to me this morning," he said. "He told me about the tractor and gave me the mask."

"No, he didn't. You said it yourself, you haven't seen him since you beat up on him after he tagged the bus."

"I forgot that I saw him today," Jared shrugged. "Must have slipped my mind."

"It slipped your mind that you talked to this big mastermind behind the whole plan? Especially when you said that, if you saw him again, you'd bust his face in?"

"Were you eavesdropping in on our conversation?" He stood up angrily.

"I was. And recording it." I waved Maya's phone in the air, still recording. I handed it to her and she poked at it, turned the volume up a notch, taking it off silent mode. It buzzed and she slid it into her back pocket.

"I think you must have your facts mixed up," Jared said. "I mean you have up until now, right?" He looked to Maya and her parents for agreement but they looked at him puzzled.

"Oh," I said, "and it must have slipped your mind that this same guy whom you claim is framing you for everything just came up and handed you the mask for no reason? You want us to believe that? How stupid do you think we are?"

Jared didn't say anything. For the first time since I met him, he looked somewhat unsure of himself. But that didn't last long. "You don't know what you're talking about," he said dismissively. "I've got all the proof to put him away. We need to go get him. Come on guys." He made a come-with-me gesture to the Calaveras but none of them moved.

"Come to think of it," Maya said, "Perk's right. We didn't tell you about the tractor. And how did you get the mask?"

"I've got all the proof!" he said, voice raised. "It's Rocky. I've got the proof."

"You may have your so-called proof," I said, "but you also have your own guilt. This is on you. Always has been."

No one said anything. It was a stalemate.

Just then Jared's phone buzzed on the table. He looked down at it and frowned then picked it up and said, "I'm in the middle of something. Can I call you back?" Then he listened for a few seconds. "What?" he exclaimed. "Are you joking? Really? Right now? I'm on my way."

He hung up his phone and dropped it into his pocket, simultaneously taking out his keys. "I've got a problem. Bigger than this. I've got to go right now." He turned on his heel and reached for the clasp envelope. Lalo, with surprising speed, snatched it up before Jared could get to it.

"We're not done here, Jared," he said curtly. I could tell that he was no longer convinced of Jared's story.

Jared reached for the envelope but Lalo evaded him. Jared was getting frustrated. "Give it back, old man. I don't have time for this. I really gotta go."

"You're lying to us, aren't you, Jared?" Lalo said bitterly. "The deal is off. I'm tearing this to shreds!" He held the envelope up in his hand and shook it.

Jared held up his hands as a sign of resignation. "Have it your way. But you might want to look inside before ripping it up. The contract's not in there." He started walking backwards toward the door.

"What's in here then?" Lalo asked.

"A bargaining chip. I thought you might find some way to back out." He kept backing up, heading toward the door. I could sense Maya getting up out of her chair. Jared smiled and said, "The deal is still intact or those go viral. Everywhere."

Lalo, Mrs. Calavera, Maya, and I all looked at the envelope in Lalo's hand. By the time we looked back at Jared, he was gone, the open door slowly shutting.

Lalo lowered his hand with the envelope and looked at it askew. Mrs. Calavera drew close to him, hugging his arm and looking curiously as he slowly opened the clasp. He pulled out a stack of letter-sized sheets. His face tensed as he flipped through them. Mrs. Calavera looked on in sad disbelief then covered her eyes and said, *"Aye, mija."*

I looked at Maya and she was as white as a ghost. "Those" she began to say in a stunted and shaky voice, "those are the pictures of me."

37 | Chase

Lalo shoved the pictures back into the envelope and walked up to Maya and handed them to her. He didn't say anything, just looked at her in anger and disappointment, shaking his head. He turned his back on her and slowly walked out the front door. Mrs. Calavera had retreated to the kitchen. She was crying loudly. Maya threw the envelope down on the table and looked up at me, her face wet with tears already. I gave her a hug and just held her.

"I screwed up," she sobbed. "And now Poppy has seen… he's seen something no father should ever see. I've ruined everything." She buried her face in my chest.

I tipped her chin so that she could see me. "You didn't ruin anything. You did something that you're not proud of. But Jared is blackmailing you and your family with it. This just proves that he's truly the one behind all this. He's the crook, Maya. He's the bad guy."

"We can't do anything now. Poppy won't let it. I know he's ashamed of me, more than anything now. But he won't allow Jared to release those pictures. We're done for. I'm pretty much done for. I mean, what must I look like in their eyes? Their daughter acting like that. And I only have myself to blame."

"Don't you see, Maya? He didn't give you ecstasy. He *does* sell that ganchos drug. And it did have an effect on you. You were not in your right mind. And, even if you did mean to do what you did, it doesn't give him the right to shame you like that in front of your parents. You trusted him with your body and he betrayed that trust. Worse yet, he's using it to get what he wants. We can't let that happen!"

"It's over, Perk," she said, shaking her head. "We should just let him get what he wants. I'm sick of the whole thing. And now? With my mom and dad seeing those pictures? I just want to leave." She held my face in her hands. "Take me with you. Back to Colorado."

"Maya, this is far from over. We can figure something—"

Just then Maya's phone buzzed. She pulled it out. It was a text. She read it with a look of confusion, then turned the phone to me. It was from Rocky. It read: "I told you I would do something for you."

We looked at each other confused. A few moments later, her phone buzzed again. Another text. This one was a video. Maya pressed play and we watched as the screen displayed Rocky setting the phone down to take a video of himself. He walked backwards into the frame. He was in a room with a desk and a desktop computer sitting on top of it with all the components: monitor, keyboard, printer, mouse. There was also a big box with glass sides. I recognized it as a 3D printer. There was a file cabinet and bookshelves in the background. There were posters on the wall of pop icons like Bruce Lee, Bob Marley, Che Guevara.

"That's Jared's house," Maya said.

Rocky raised up a large sledgehammer and spoke, "I'm going to destroy it all. He keeps the files on his computer. No backup. He's not that computer savvy. I saw his set up when he," Rocky paused. "When he gave me a sample of…of the pics. I'm sorry, Maya. I'm going to make this right." He took a few steps back and raised the sledgehammer over his head and swung it down with force. The hammer crashed down hard on the computer tower, busting it open and exposing the guts inside. Rocky reached in and pulled out the hard drive. He set it on top of the keyboard and smashed it over and over again. The desk started to crack and whine. He didn't stop. He continued to smash every piece of the computer and its components, his wild, long, wavy blond hair flailing about him like a madman, which he was.

The video stopped and we stood there speechless. Then her phone buzzed again. It was another video. Rocky was talking into the camera. He was breathing hard from exertion. "And... now...I..." He strained, speaking between gasps of air. He looked directly into the camera, through the fallen locks in his face. His eyes were dark and demented. "I...burn...it... down!" He flicked open a Zippo lighter and struck it. A flame danced in front of him. Then the video stopped.

"We've got to show this to my dad," Maya said.

"No time," I said, leading her to the door. "We need to get over there."

"Over where? To Jared's? What are we going to do? Try to put out the fire?"

"No. We have to see what's going on. We need to see what's going to happen to Rocky. The call, the one that Jared got? I bet it was about his house. Someone must have spotted Rocky. But if Jared does something to him, we won't have anything."

"We don't have anything now."

"We have Rocky. But who knows what Jared might do to him. We gotta get over there. Now!"

Maya didn't fight me on it. We headed out of the front door and started running to the bus. "No," she said. "Let's take my car."

I didn't know how far Jared lived or what exactly he drove but he had a head start on us. But, true to form, Maya stepped on the gas. And hard. She told me when we first met that her car was modified. I thought it just meant she got nice rims and a new paint job. I found out pretty quick that most of the modification was under the hood. I held on for my life as she raced through the rugged, narrow streets of Old Mesilla. As we sped, the scenery grew less populated with houses and more with farms. She ran a stop sign at a T intersection, turned right, and embarked on a straight, open road. I had thought she was going fast before but she kicked that little red car into another level altogether. Farms and open space were on both sides of the road. The open land passed by, giving the illusion that we were going slower than we actually were. It wasn't until I looked over at her speedometer that I realized we were moving along at around ninety miles per hour—almost twice the speed limit on that road. I said a prayer to myself that no one would pull out in front of us. Would she be able to react in time?

"He lives down this road," Maya said. "About twelve miles. He may have the jump on us but I'm pretty sure I'll close the gap." She seemed to know exactly what she was doing. When she came upon traffic, she slowed and weaved through them, then picked up speed in no time. She had done this before.

"Can we catch up to him?" I asked.

"I don't know. Maybe."

"What does he drive?"

"An old beat up truck. It's what he drives when he's not restoring some other car or bus, like yours."

"How fast is it?"

"Not fast. But might be fast enough to beat us." She slalomed around a slow-moving tractor with precision, not missing a beat. Up ahead were, from what I could see, pecan trees lining both sides of the road. We blew by them so fast that they were a blur. I held onto the door handle tightly. Maya was tense, biting her lip and peering ahead with intense focus.

Ahead of us, in the distance, I saw a vehicle on the side of the road. A man was standing beside it. As we got closer, I could see that it was a truck. "Be careful with that dude," I said.

"That's…" Maya squinted. "That's Jared!"

"What's he doing?"

"That old truck of his must have broken down. Piece of crap."

Even though we were pretty far off still, Jared must have recognized us as well. He strolled out into the middle of the street directly in front of us and waved his hands over his head, as if he was signaling for help. Maya was speeding fast toward him, not wavering.

In the opposite lane, a large truck was heading our direction. Maya didn't slow. Jared didn't move. The truck kept coming.

"Don't hit him," I said, pleading. "You'll kill him!"

"If he doesn't move, it's his own fault. Besides, maybe he doesn't deserve to live."

"Maybe not, but that doesn't give you the right to murder him."

She kept up her speed. Jared lowered his hands to his side and stood firm. The truck continued its approach. In this game of chicken, something had to give. If Jared didn't move, Maya couldn't swerve around him to her right or she might hit his truck. If she chanced it to her left, she would be directly in the path of the oncoming truck.

"You have to slow down!" I said. "We're going to hit something! Slow down! It's not worth it!"

She kept going. Jared didn't move. The truck was just ahead of us. It was going to pass Jared about the same time that we were going to reach him.

"Oh my God!" I said, feeling my heart pound in my ears, even over the roar of the car and the wind through the windows.

"Watch this," Maya said. Then, under her breath I heard her say to herself, "I hope this works."

She accelerated even faster and, at the same time, flipped up a cover on the dash next to the steering column, revealing a small metal switch. "Nitrous oxide," she said and flipped the switch. She floored it and the car thrusted forward, pressing us against the seats. Jared was still dead ahead. The truck was still heading in our direction, not slowing down, horn blazing. I braced myself for the shock of impact as I imagined Jared's guts flying up against the windshield. Maya locked her elbows, grabbing the wheel tightly. At the last possible moment, Maya turned slightly into the middle of the road, riding the dividing lines. Jared was ahead of us, slightly to our right, waving his arms. The truck just yards directly in front, still honking, swerving slightly. There was no shoulder on the road so he didn't have much room. As we passed Jared, Maya snapped the wheel to the right and threaded the needle between Jared and the oncoming truck. For a fraction of a second, I could hear Jared yelling one thing, the truck driver yelling another, and the horn blaring between the two. I believe I uttered an appropriate word or two myself but I can't remember. The whole thing felt like it lasted five minutes but, in reality, must have only been a matter of seconds.

I sat in shock as Maya leveled out straight into her lane. The effect of the nitrous oxide over and done with, the car slowed to its previous speed. "Whoo!" Maya exclaimed, a full smile across her face.

"Are you insane?" I asked, still holding on for dear life.

"I told you. Modified!"

"You could have killed him. Or us. What if the nitrous oxide didn't work?"

"We had enough room. The truck was swerving."

I looked behind us. Jared was hollering and flailing his arms. The truck was wobbling as it tried to regain it's balance on the road.

"His truck broke down, Maya."

"I know. Isn't it great?" She was smiling broadly.

"No, I mean it doesn't matter how fast we go. He can't really catch up. You didn't have to speed past him. You could have just slowed to twenty-five and he still couldn't have caught up."

Maya, still looking ahead, gave an upside-down smirk. "But I wouldn't have been able to use the Nos," she said. Then she looked at me and smiled. "Let me have my fun. It's the only thing I have in this whole crapfest."

"The only thing?"

She reached over and held my hand. "And you, Chulo. I've got you."

With the realization that she didn't have to speed, she slowed down. Still above the speed limit but not dangerously so.

"Do you think Rocky will still be there?" she asked.

"Probably. I bet he'll be waiting for you. He seems dramatic like that, don't you think?"

"Yeah. But what are we going to do? What are we supposed to say? How do we keep Jared from getting to him?"

"Rocky said he's turning himself in. Maybe the cops noticed something and have reached him already."

"I doubt it. The cops don't really patrol out here. Maybe whoever called Jared called the cops too, but I doubt that as well. Jared and the police are not quite BFF's. I guess Rocky might have called them."

"Not if he wants you to see him in action," I said. "He wouldn't have sent you those texts if he didn't. Basically, he invited you to his show." We drove in silence for a moment. "Do you think he's already started a fire?"

"I guess we'll see," she answered. She pulled out her phone from her back pocket and handed it to me. "Maybe he sent another text."

I looked. "Nope," I said and handed the phone back to her. She slid it back into her pocket. "How far now?"

"Not quite sure. Three, maybe four miles."

I was starting to feel confident about the situation. Sure, Jared was a tool and a crook, but now things seemed to be out in the open. And sure, Rocky was teetering on insanity himself, but he may have just succeeded in getting Jared off of our backs. Who knows? Maybe Jared had the contract in the house and it was burning down at that very moment.

"Here's what I think we should do," I said. "We should call the cops and report Rocky. If someone hasn't already. Someone might have, especially if there's a fire and smoke. A neighbor."

"Jared's place is secluded. You can't see it from the street or the sides. Lots of trees. His neighbors aren't close and they all keep to themselves. Jared especially. He doesn't want anyone in on his business. I know he kept some stuff at his house. Remember I told you people would come around? Dealers. Probably a dealer who called him. Like I said before, Jared doesn't have friends."

"So should I call the cops or not?"

"I think we should get there first and see exactly what's going on. Maybe he didn't burn the place down, only busted stuff up. Maybe."

We passed a mile marker that read "9." Maya pointed at it. "About three miles from here," she said and sped up slightly.

Then the car sputtered.

Maya looked at her dash, punched the wheel with the butt of her fist and cursed. "We're out of gas," she said grimacing.

The car died and Maya navigated it off of the road and we rolled to a stop on what could be considered a shoulder, although it wasn't paved, just dirt and rocks.

We got out of the car and looked down the road. "At least we're further ahead than Jared," I said. Maya didn't seem to appreciate that fact. "If we walk and Jared walks, we'll get there long before he does.

"Even if we run, it would take us thirty minutes," Maya said exasperated.

"Yeah, but it would take Jared longer."

Maya didn't buy into my silver lining. She simply kicked the tires of her car and called it names in Spanish. After a few good kicks and cursing, she leaned against the car's front end and crossed her arms.

"We can hitch a ride," I said. "It's only a couple of miles."

She didn't respond so I took that as a sign of agreement. I stuck out my thumb as a car approached. I had never hitched a ride before but the practice seemed easy; stick out your thumb and someone stops. You get in the car and tell them where you're going and they go.

Only no one stopped. I kept at it. It seemed like a better idea than walking.

"Come put your thumb out too, Maya," I said to her. "You're a lot better looking than I am. Maybe they'll stop for your sake." She didn't argue that either, just resigned and came up next to me and put out her thumb unenthusiastically.

"I'm calling my mom," she said, pulling her phone out of her back pocket.

"It would take her forever to come pick us up."

"Not for that. I just want to tell her what's going on so she can tell my dad. I need to let her know where we are, just in case...you know. Just in case something weird happens."

"Why don't you just call your dad?"

Maya gave me a dirty look. I took it to mean that her dad was probably hitting the sauce pretty hard right about now. "Ah," I said. "No need to explain."

She called her mom and told her about Rocky's texts and how we were heading to Jared's. I could hear Mrs. Calavera pleading with her daughter to not go, but Maya was stubborn about it. She conveniently left out the fact that we were hitchhiking.

Two more cars passed. Two more rejections. Then a car came along, this one with Jared in the passenger's seat. He must have hitched a ride too. As it passed, Jared simply stared us down and flipped us off. The car sped off. Maya cursed again.

"I guess that puts him ahead of us," I said. Maya didn't respond.

We kept our thumbs out. A small pickup truck approached and came to a stop in front of us. Inside was a big brown-skinned man with a long grey goatee, dressed in a tattered white V-neck shirt. He had huge arms. Not fat but not lean. Muscular but not defined. The steering wheel barely able to rotate above his rotund belly. I couldn't see how he could get in and out of the small truck but he was in there so obviously it had happened.

"You kids look like you need a ride," he said. He had a stunted way of speaking, accentuating each word with the same gruff inflection.

"We do," I said as we opened the door to get in. Maya made to go in first but the guy put his hand in front of us in a stop gesture.

"You first," he said pointing to me. "In the middle."

I didn't fight him on it, just jumped in. Maya scrunched up against me and pushed me into the big man. We were packed in like sardines. The man reached down and shifted the gear into first. As he did, he couldn't help but brush his arm up and down the side of my body and leg. I realized why he wanted me in first. Probably didn't want the confusion or discomfort of doing the same to Maya.

"Where to?" he asked as his goatee danced in the wind entering in from the open windows.

"Only a few miles ahead," Maya said. "We have an emergency."

"Ah," he said flatly.

"Thanks for picking us up," I said.

"Don't thank me," he said and pointed to the ceiling of the truck. "My boss told me to pick you up. I would just as soon as leave you there but I have to do what my boss wants me to do."

"Who's his boss?" Maya asked me in a whisper.

"I think he means God," I whispered back.

"Oh."

We didn't say anything more for a couple of minutes. "Up there," Maya said as she pointed up ahead to the right, beyond the pecan trees that lined the road on each side. In the general direction Maya was pointing, above and beyond a row of thick fir trees, smoke was rising. It was pluming black and grey.

"That's it!" Maya exclaimed. "He's doing it! He's burning down Jared's house!"

38 | Burn

The big man sped up and turned off the road at Maya's direction. Jared's house was not visible from the street. The front was lined with fir trees and the drive to his house snaked behind them. The driveway was also lined with the same thick fir trees. We could only see a few yards in front of us at any time, the drive curved back and forth so much. But we could smell smoke and hear crackling. We could also hear yelling.

We emerged from the trees to find a long, paved driveway, roughly the length of a football field, leading to Jared's burning house. Jared and Rocky were in front of it. Jared was clinching his fists and yelling at Rocky. Rocky was yelling back at Jared. It looked like Jared was ready to pounce. I figured he had only just arrived there himself. There was no sign of the car that Jared was in. They probably dropped him off at the street and he ran to his house. It was only Rocky, Jared, Maya, me, and the big man.

The big man stopped the truck well short of the house. Smart, since the house was burning. The three of us got out of the truck and walked toward them tentatively. The house was not completely ablaze, but it was burning inside. We saw flames licking through the windows. The man asked Maya what was going on. Maya gave him a condensed version of the story. Jared was trying to take over her family's business and pin it on Rocky. Rocky was unstable and had just busted up Jared's house and set it on fire.

"Did you call the police?" the big man asked?

"Not yet," I answered. "But I think this would be a good time." Maya, listening to us, pulled out her phone and made the call. Then we approached even closer so we could hear exactly what Jared and Rocky were yelling about.

Jared was inching toward Rocky. Rocky was backing away at an equal pace. "You're going to pay for this, you idiot!" Jared yelled.

"I've already paid my dues," Rocky spat back. "It's time you finally pay for what *you've* done!"

"You're crazy!" Jared countered.

"Maybe, but you're crazy too!" Rocky yelled back. "At least I'm not evil!"

Jared looked at his house. It seemed as if he was debating whether to go in or not.

He looked back at Rocky. "You don't know what you've done!" he yelled.

"I know exactly what I've done! I've stopped you once and for all!"

There was about fifteen feet between Jared and Rocky. "Run, Rocky!" Maya yelled. Rocky heard her and looked our way. As soon as he turned his head, Jared made his move. He closed the gap between him and Rocky in a flash. He was quick and Rocky was slow to react. Jared grabbed Rocky in a reverse headlock. He curled his arm around Rocky's neck with Rocky facing him, bent at the waist, looking toward the ground. Jared hiked Rocky upward and Rocky did what he could to fight it, but he was no match for Jared.

Jared pulled Rocky to the front of the burning house. The

flames were higher. Rocky fought in vain. Then Jared reached over with his right hand and grabbed the back of Rocky's pants at the waist and situated him in front of him. He got square and reared back his right leg and swung his knee into Rocky's ribs. It was a vicious blow. We could hear Rocky's ribs break with muffled pops beneath his fleshy side. Rocky didn't make a sound. Most likely there was no air in his lungs. Jared did it again, this time to Rocky's stomach. Jared released his grip and Rocket dropped to the ground like a sack of potatoes.

I looked at Maya and she looked at me. We both made a start to run in their direction. Maybe between the both of us, we could contain Jared. Then two odd things happened: 1) a flame shot over twenty feet straight up into the air behind Jared's house, and 2) Maya and I were frozen, unable to move in spite of our running legs.

We looked behind us and the big man had a handful of the back of Maya's and my shirt. He was stopping us from advancing. His eyes were wide and he bit his lip looking at both of us. Then he grabbed each of us around the waist and picked us up and started trotting away from the house.

He was quick and strong. His arms were like those of a gorilla, or how I imagined a gorilla's arms would be.

"What are you doing?" Maya screamed at him. "He's going to kill Rocky!"

The big man didn't let up. He just held onto us tighter and kept trotting. He was holding us, each on a hip with our heads to the front as he ran in the opposite direction of the house. I lowered my head to see what was happening with Jared and Rocky. Everything bounced upside down but I could see Rocky lying in the fetal position on the ground and Jared standing above him looking at his house. Another flame burst upward from behind the house.

Jared noticed the flame then turned and looked our way.

Then he started running after us like an Olympic sprinter. Was he coming to try to take us out too? He was gaining on the big man. Rocky still lay like a lump on the ground. From my perspective, the whole scene bounced upside down as the big man carried us. Another shot of flame flew into the air from behind Jared's house. Jared was quickly closing the gap between us. I could see fear in his eyes, not hate. What was going on?

From the other side of the big man I heard Maya screaming for Rocky, her voice halted with each step the man took. He was breathing heavily but he kept trotting. We passed his little pick-up truck. I wasn't fighting him but Maya was kicking and screaming.

I could see Jared just a few yards behind us running wildly. I braced myself, thinking he was going to take down the big man and us in the process. But he didn't. He just ran right past us into the tree-lined drive. The man followed in his direction.

In the distance, still near Jared's house, Rocky struggled to get to his feet, arm holding his side. I pushed against the beefy arms wrapped around my middle. "We have to go back for Rocky!" I said emphatically. The big man still trotted, breathing heavy, not uttering a word.

We entered the mouth of the drive. I looked ahead of us. Jared was nowhere in sight. He must have been far ahead by now. I looked behind but couldn't see anything any longer; the trees were obstructing my view of the house. The big man threaded down the driveway and stopped after the second turn. He put us down on the ground and knelt on one knee, pressing us to the ground with the palms of his huge hands.

"Let us up!" Maya yelled.

"No," the big man said without emotion. "There's a propane tank behind the house. It can blow at any second." His voice was amazingly calm and steady.

"But Rocky!" Maya cried.

The big man let up on us a bit. "Don't get up," he said and then he got to his feet and trotted toward his truck, faster now that he wasn't carrying two people. Maya tried to get up but I pulled her back down.

I scooted close to her and held her tight. "If that thing blows," I said, "there might be metal flying all over. That big guy's crazy for going back. But it's Rocky's best chance. You and I can't do anything. If we get up, we could get killed."

Maya stopped moving and sank into me and started whimpering. We heard the big man's truck door close, and he started up the motor and peeled out, heading toward the house. Then all we could hear was the crackling of the house burning and the start of a high-pitched whine. The whine grew louder and shriller, louder and shriller. I pulled Maya close to me and covered her with my body as best as I could. The whine grew louder and shriller still. Then, for a brief moment, it stopped. All noise seemed to halt for a fraction of a second.

Then *BOOM!*

The ground rumbled beneath us like an earthquake. I kept my head down and covered Maya with my whole body. Waves of intensely hot air shot through the trees and blew over us. I could sense the tall thick trees leaning, eclipsing the sun. Pieces of hot metal and wood and a number of other materials rained down on us. Nothing big, though. And dirt. Lots of dirt and dust. I instinctively pulled my shirt over my mouth, Maya did the same.

I held Maya closer still. I could hear her crying and saying, "Rocky, Rocky…" I didn't know what to tell her. I couldn't say for sure if Rocky was alive or dead, much less the big man.

Maya pushed away from me. "I need to go see," she said.

"Wait," I said. "There's nothing we can do now. Plus, we don't know if there's another propane tank."

We just lay there for a moment. Then I said, "But…but

we can't let Jared get away." With that, I got up and started running down the drive toward the street.

"Perk!" Maya cried out from behind me. "Wait!"

I didn't wait, just ran down the drive. We hadn't seen Rocky or the big man pass by us. We didn't know if they were even alive. And Jared knew about the tank. He knew and he just left Rocky there on the ground. That was as good as killing him. By nature, I'm not violent. But I can't stand to see selfish, evil people getting away with things. I didn't know what I was going to do when I caught up with Jared. *If* I caught up with him. But I was angry and that's all I had to go on at that moment.

I made it to the end of the drive and past the row of trees that lined the street, shrouding the property. I didn't see Jared. I ran to the street and stood in the middle. I looked to my right. Nothing. I looked to my left, the direction back to the city. There he was, about a quarter of a mile down the road, walking briskly and, from what I could tell, talking on his cell phone. Probably calling one of his dealer friends to come pick him up.

I started running in his direction. He must have sensed me because he turned to look behind him and saw me running toward him. He just shifted his body and started walking backward, staring at me. I kept running.

The fact that he didn't run away from me gave me pause. Why? It would have been easier if he had, would have simplified the equation. I could just go tackle him or push him like I had done to Rocky.

But he didn't run.

He slowed his pace and stood still, allowing me to catch up to him. What should I do? Keep running toward him and try to knock him down? No, he was too smart to allow that to happen. And too quick. He would just dodge me. Should I go toe-to-toe with him and try to bring him down? Something told me he had been through a few brawls and would have had an advantage on me since I, myself, had been through exactly zero scuffles. So I just stopped once I arrived within fifteen yards of him.

"What are you gonna do?" He asked, jutting his chin. "I've got someone on the way and you can't stop me. No way your scrawny ass could do anything to me."

I was out of breath which didn't matter, really, since I didn't have anything good to say in response. I stood there glaring at him.

"You gonna stare me into submission?" he scoffed.

"You're not getting away with this, Jared," I said.

"Getting away with what? Rocky's the one who was going to get away with it all. And it seems like he's out of the equation. You can thank me for that. Now run along and go play with your little friend Maya. Leave the business to the big boys like me and Lalo."

"You're such a prick!" I said through my teeth. "Do you really think I'm stupid enough to fall for your lies? I see through them. And so does everyone else now."

"OK. You got me on one minor detail. Nice work, Sherlock. But it doesn't change the fact that I have Lalo over a barrel with those pics." He smiled for an instant then it broke into a look of concern. But then he tried to recover and smirk. The pics. He had printed them up for Lalo but where were the digital files? Rocky said he didn't back stuff up to the cloud. And Maya said he was a private type of guy, especially about his house and possessions.

"A-ha!" I said. "I can read you like a book. The pics were at your house, digital files on your computer. And now your house and everything in it is up in flames."

In the distance, sirens blared. The authorities were heading our way. Jared's face tensed at the sound. Then he peered over my shoulder. Whatever he saw made his face tense even more, eyebrows furrowed over his dark eyes. I turned my head around and saw the big man's little truck pulling out of the drive from between the trees. I couldn't see the details but it looked a bit more beat up than before. There were two people in the front with something big in the back, a lump.

I was relieved to see the truck heading our way. Four against one was better odds than one-on-one, especially when one was me and the other Jared. A sense of satisfaction waved over me. This whole thing was almost over. If they could get to us before Jared's ride could, we might have a chance to contain him for the authorities.

I turned around to tell Jared that the game was over but, when I did, he was right in front of me. Startled I flinched and stepped back a step. Jared wasted no time and punched me solidly in the gut. He had long bony arms and gnarly fists and his swing was accurate and powerful. The fist hit me like a sledgehammer and lifted me off of the ground slightly. All the air immediately escaped my lungs and, at the same time, I felt like throwing up. I fell over onto my side and involuntarily dry hacked while trying to breathe. It felt like I was drowning in air.

Jared must have known I was down for the count because he started jogging away, in the direction of town. I looked back and saw the truck heading my way. I slowly caught my breath and raised myself up off of the ground. The truck skidded to a stop in front of me. I was surprised to see Maya behind the wheel. In the passenger's seat was Rocky, worn and ragged and shirtless. I made my way to the driver's side door and looked in the back. The big man was in the truck's bed, lying down. He was on his right side, holding his left arm. It was bandaged with a what was obviously Rocky's T-shirt. There was blood seeping through the bandage.

"He got hit with some metal from the propane tank," Maya said. "We need to get him to a hospital."

"OK," I said. "But what about Jared?"

"Jump in the back."

I did. Maya peeled out, her wheels spat gravel from the shoulder like buckshot in our wake. She sped toward Jared who was still jogging down the road. He was on his phone.

"Look!" Maya yelled and pointed ahead of her, her arm extended outside the window. In the distance was a car heading our way.

"Who's that?" I asked.

"It's Mamita!"

The car was heading our way at a fast pace. Trailing them, in the distance, were the authorities, sirens blaring.

Jared, seeing what we saw, halted his progress. Maya pulled up behind him and I jumped out of the truck. "Give it up," I told him, surprised at the authoritarian sound of my own voice. He turned and gave me a sneer. He was trapped and he knew it.

Mrs. Calavera had brought Lalo with her. They pulled up on the side of Jared opposite us, hemming him in. They both got out of their car and stood at a safe distance. They might not be able to fight him but they could keep him from going anywhere.

Maya got out of the truck and stood beside me. "We need to figure something out quick," she said. "I can't leave...I don't even know his name. The big guy. I can't leave him long. He's hurt bad. He needs to see a doctor." Rocky stayed in the truck.

"OK," I said. "Call an ambulance. They'll probably need to see Rocky too. But don't leave. I don't know what's going to happen."

Maya obliged and I focused my attention on Jared. It was in that moment that I started to see how small Jared really was. By that, I mean in character. The big man, even though we didn't know his name, meant more to us than Jared. Simply because of his character. In fact, I was thinking we should just let Jared go. Let him wander into nothingness, or some other stupid scheme. And we could focus on the good people of the world.

That thought lasted only a moment, until Jared looked at us and spit. "Alright," he said, "so you got me. What are you going to do? Drag me into the authorities? I'd like to see you try."

Just then the same authorities he was speaking about raced by us, lights flashing and sirens blaring; obviously headed to Jared's house. We stood as the air from their passing vehicles struck us in a breeze.

I addressed Lalo, beyond Jared. "He doesn't have the contract, Lalo. It was in his house. And now it's burned to the ground."

"You're wrong," Jared seethed. "I've still got it. Safe and sound."

Maya tugged at my arm, pulling my neck to her as she raised her head to whisper in my ear. "I don't think he's lying. *Safe and sound?* He's got this big safe—as big as a fridge—and he keeps all his important stuff in it. Drugs, money, all that. It's fireproof."

Jared smirked. I figured he knew what Maya told me.

"So you have a safe," I said with a shrug. "Good for you. But what do you think the police are going to say when they open it and find all your drugs?"

"And pictures of Maya," he retorted, stabbing his finger in the air toward her.

"You're cracking, Jared," I said. "I read it in your face earlier. The pics were digital. And would the police really care about some pictures of girls?"

Jared went pale as his face shed it's smile. He was in a state of panic. He started to walk away from us, away from the road and into the empty farm field. In the distance was a mountain range. Maya looked at me oddly then we both looked at him walking away like a zombie.

"What is it, Jared?" I yelled to him. He didn't respond, just stumbled backward. He turned and walked away.

"Don't let him get away," Maya said as she gave me a shove in Jared's direction.

I started jogging after him. He turned around to see me. He was still pale but was slowly recovering his composure. He took off into the field toward the mountain range. I ran after him. He wasn't as quick of a runner as I thought. He was built for short, powerful actions. Not jogging. He lumbered over the dirt. I gained on him. I could hear Maya and her parents following behind us.

The whole scene seemed anticlimactic. Was I going to simply catch up to him, tackle him and sit on him until the police came? Could it be that easy?

The next moment answered my question as Jared came to a stop in the middle of the field. There were no plants, just corrugated furrows of dirt. I slowed down to a stop as well. He had not only regained his composure, he was filled with rage; where his face was pale and white, it was now red and burning with hate.

"This ends now," he said in a low, guttural voice. I felt shivers up my spine. I looked back and saw Maya and her parents far off behind. Rocky had joined them, limping along. By the time they caught up with us, Jared would have the time to snap my neck.

I turned back to Jared. "Not until you back out of the deal," I said. "Agree to tear up the contract and maybe Lalo and his family will take it easy on you."

"The deal? Forget it. It's over. It's all over."

I was confused. "Is that a yes?"

"It's an *'I don't care.'* I'm through with them. And you. And the restaurant. I'm going to walk away and you're going to let me." He turned to resume his path toward the mountains. Was that his plan? To hide out in the hills like a bandit?

I ran after him and grabbed his shirt. "You're not going anywhere," I said. Instantly he turned around, ripping his shirt out of my hand. He reared back with his right fist. I knew what was coming, another vicious blow. Instinctively, I folded my hands over my stomach and started to bend over, hoping to guard against his powerful fist.

I quickly found out that he wasn't aiming for my stomach, but for my face. Yet, in the nanosecond between him advancing his fist in my direction, and me doubling over, he was unable to alter the trajectory of his punch. I just happened to lower my head and caught the full brunt of the blow on my forehead. I heard the thick thud of the blow resonating in my head as well as muffled cracks. I fell backward, dizzy. *Great,* I thought, *he's gone and fractured my skull. Probably given me brain damage. As if life wasn't hard enough before...*

I had fallen on my back. My ears were ringing as the stars in my eyes whirled around the empty blue vastness of sky. As the ringing in my ears subsided, I heard Jared cursing. I raised myself on my elbows to see what was going on. He was stomping around cradling his right hand with his left.

I shook my head and got to my feet. I was a bit dizzy but able to stand. I looked back to see Maya, her parents, and Rocky stop near us. They stood there like an audience. I had thought that perhaps they would pick up rocks or sticks and fight Jared with me but they just stood there looking at us. Jared continued his stomping.

I felt my forehead gingerly. It hurt and I was getting a headache but it didn't seem like my skull was broken. I remembered the skull of El Mismo. The forehead was big and thick. Maybe my own skull was the same. Maybe all our skulls are that tough in the forehead region.

Jared stood up straight, still holding his hand. "Damn you!" he yelled my way. "You broke my hand!"

"Serves you right," I said. "Now just give up and come with us. You need to answer to the cops."

"Never," he said insolently.

Rocky advanced in our direction and stopped a few yards away from us. Maya bridged the gap as well and arched away from Rocky so that the two of them were equal distance from us but separated from each other by a short distance.

"Give it up, Jared," Rocky said. "It's over. And you know what they're going to find in that safe of yours."

Jared focused on Rocky. "That's my personal property," he said, "my business. No one has a right to that safe but me."

"If the police have good reason, they do." Rocky pulled some folded papers out of his pocket. "I called the police. Before you even got there. I told them what you have in the safe. Sent them an email with the sample pics you gave me."

"You trying to frame me, Rocky?" Jared, still nursing his broken hand, walked up to Rocky and peered down at him.

I made my way to where Maya was standing. I leaned toward Maya and, under my breath, told her to call 911 again and tell them that we had a drug dealer assaulting people, and to tell them where we were.

Maya slinked away from the situation to make the call. I shifted my focus to Jared and Rocky. I was prepared to jump in if needed. Although I didn't know what I would do exactly. I thought that, if nothing else, I might be able to hold Jared with the help of Rocky and Lalo.

Rocky was holding his ribs yet didn't back down from Jared. "I'm turning myself in, Jared," Rocky said. "And I'm going to tell them all about you. What you've done. Not just to Maya and her parents but to those girls. I'm going to tell everyone!"

Jared took a swing at Rocky with his left hand but Rocky was able to duck it. Jared was off kilter with a hurt hand. Rocky took a few steps back and looked our way. "I admit it," he said. "I was running around as the ghost in exchange for pictures of girls. Pictures that Jared took. Porno stuff."

Jared made another attempt at Rocky but it seemed half-hearted. Rocky eluded him again. "They were all sex pics," Rocky said. "And a lot of them were...they were high school girls. Underage."

Jared looked in our direction. "He's lying," he said emphatically.

"No I'm not," Rocky countered. "It's true. He would have parties with those high school girls and give them that ganchos drug of his. Then he would get them to do, you know, raunchy stuff. And I," Rocky paused. He started getting emotional, "I wanted to see them. It's sick, I know. I'm sick. I can't help it. That's why I'm turning myself in. It's not just the stupid ghost stuff, it's this...this addiction. This...I don't know...fettish? No, it's not that. It's worse. I've seen things I shouldn't have seen." Jared kept trying to grab at Rocky but it was useless. Rocky was able to get out of reach. It seemed like Jared was giving up.

Rocky pointed at Jared, "The pics, those pics of the underage girls? Those he kept in the safe because he was paranoid about someone getting into his computer."

"Lies," Jared yelled.

"It's the truth!" Rocky looked at Lalo. "You need to know. This is the guy you're getting into a deal with. He's just as bad as I am. Worse, maybe. And the cops are going to find out the truth when they search the safe. I told them all about the ganchos and the pics." Then he turned to Jared. "Good luck hiding that big ol' safe of yours. The cops are going to confiscate it and you'll have no choice but to open it up for them."

Jared froze. Then he straightened out again and stood tall, letting his arms fall to his side. He inhaled deeply then exhaled. A moment passed. The sound of sirens started to rise in the distance. Maya had returned and was standing by my side. Rocky and Jared stood a few yards apart from each other.

Jared looked at each of us. He stopped at me and sneered. "You," he said with complete distain. "This is all because of you! You just had to come around and stick your nose in everyone's business."

I didn't say anything. My heart was pounding so hard that I could feel it in my ears.

Jared started walking toward me. "If the cops are going to get me on anything, they're going to get me on beating the hell out of you!" He started running at me. For a fraction of a second I thought about using the Boss Boot defense. It worked on Rocky, right? But I doubted it would work on Jared. Instead, I stood my ground. Quickly, I put my arm across Maya's torso and pushed her back behind me, then jogged away from her. Jared adjusted his course.

Once I was far enough away from Maya to keep her from the interaction, I stood my ground. Jared was not one hundred percent. He was wild in his advance. My plan was to dodge him and trip him. But then he bounded toward me at the last moment, opening his arms wide like some bird of prey. I tried to dodge to my left but he wrapped his right arm around my neck and pulled me to the ground. We rolled around a bit, my back to him. Then he tightened his grip and started choking me. His right arm was perfectly positioned around my neck to cut off air and blood and anything else that the body needed to supply my brain to sustain my life. I tried to yell but nothing came out. I just kicked and tore at his arms with my hands. I was weaker than him and he had leverage. No contest.

I heard Maya screaming for him to stop but it was no use. He just held on as tight, if not tighter. I was helpless. *Here I come, God. This is it. He's going to kill me. I'm sorry for all the stupid crap…I mean stuff I've done. I'm sorry for watching those porno videos online. I'm sorry for ignoring those phone calls from my mom when I was busy. I'm sorry for not going to church as much as I should. I'm sorry for…*

The sound of sirens intensified. They were headed our way. I looked downward, in the direction of Maya and her parents and Rocky. They weren't coming to help. Rocky stood there holding his side and, strangely, I could see Maya holding Lalo back. Why? Did she want me to die at the hands of this lunatic?

Hands!

Jared's left arm was holding the wrist on his right arm, making the vice around my neck. Instead of trying to pull his arm off, I reached up with my right hand across my body and grabbed a limp, broken finger on his right hand and pulled it forward. It moved easily and felt sickly weird, like bony sausages. Jared screamed in pain, right in my ear. The sound stung my eardrums but my grasp was having an effect on him as he loosened his grip ever so slightly.

The sound of sirens continued to grow. I could now hear the low roar of the motors from the speeding automobiles. Jared's grip was loose enough to allow me to to catch my breath for a moment. "A little help here!" I pleaded. Still, no one came to my rescue.

Jared let go of his right wrist, freeing his left arm. He punched me in the side. It hurt but it was not a hard hit. He didn't have the right position to deliver anything powerful. And I was squirming so his fist couldn't connect squarely. I kept pulling his broken finger. He yelped again, cursing loudly at me. I could tell that I was manhandling his middle finger.

The same one he used to flip us off earlier. That gave me a tiny dose of satisfaction. I yanked on his finger again. More cursing.

Then he reached up with his left hand and tried to find my eyes with his fingers. He was going to gouge out my eyeballs! *"Gah!"* I cried and turned my head from side to side, still grabbing onto his finger. I torqued it in my fist side to side and that made his whole body tremble. For a second he went limp and I tried to slip out of his grasp. But he held on, wrapping his legs around my legs like some mixed martial arts grappler.

The sirens blared loud. The police were finally here. It felt as if they had taken an hour to arrive. I heard cars driving up onto the dirt field, their tires grinding to a halt, the muffled organic sound of rubber skidding on dirt and gravel was music to my ears.

The sirens stopped and I heard the shuffling of people getting out of the car. I tried to look down and in their direction but Jared was arching me backward so all I saw was sky. I yanked on his finger again, pulling backward and both our bodies followed the direction of my pull. We were now lying on our sides and we wrestled a bit. Unfortunately, this left us facing the opposite direction of the police. Jared tightened his grip even stronger than before. I felt like my neck was going to snap. He laid slightly on me, pressing his weight on me so that it cut off any life-giving blood or air to my brain.

"Police," said an authoritative voice loudly. "Let him go!"

I could feel Jared craning his head back over his shoulder to look at the cops. He tried to roll us over but I yanked on his finger again. I heard him grunting in pain behind me.

He grabbed my hair with his left hand and twisted my head forcefully. He yelled, "Come any closer and I'll snap his neck!"

"Release him right now!" the police officer yelled. Jared held on. I was starting to see stars in my eyes for the second time in the same day. We were facing the mountain range off in the distance, and the stars in my eyes whirled around it. I tried to gulp air but it was in vain. He was choking out any possibility of breath.

"He's killing him!" I heard Maya yell. "Do something!" I thought that it was odd that she was asking the cops to do something when she had been the one keeping Lalo from lending me a hand. But I was thankful for any help at that moment.

I started seeing double. Was this what it felt like to die? I closed my eyes and sent up a prayer. *God, I'm sorry for wasting my time watching zombie movies when I should have been feeding poor people or something. I'm sorry for not praying or even reading the Bible like my mom told me to. I'm sorry for not living up to my potential. I'm sorry for…*

"Let him go and we'll work this out," one of the cops said. Jared didn't let up. I could hear him breathing hard behind me. The whole thing felt surreal and strangely comforting. I was choking and that was really uncomfortable, but I started to feel weightless and serene, a surrender. I stopped fighting. I really couldn't. My arms didn't want to move anymore, didn't care to crank his broken finger. I just relaxed and let whatever was going to happen happen.

"Do something!" Maya screamed. "Do something!"

Then I heard a strange pop followed by a zap and crackling. Jared began to shake. His arm went stiff but was no longer strangling me. It took me a second to realize what was happening. He was being tased.

I rolled forward, face down in the dirt, and Jared rolled away from me the other way. I gasped for air and breathed in some dirt in the process. Coughing and wheezing, I grabbed at my throat. Now that the blood was back to my brain, I could feel and sense everything around me.

I rolled around to see the cops heading toward us. Jared was on his back struggling and wailing. The cops were able to wrestle Jared and get him cuffed. They got him to his feet and one cop pulled him away while the other came and told me to hold tight and someone would come check me out. I could hear more sirens heading our way, more authorities.

I sat up and leaned back on my arms. Maya ran to me and fell beside me. "Are you OK?" she asked, fear and excitement in her voice.

"You almost let him kill me," I said. "Why did you hold your dad back?"

"I'm sorry. You're not dead though, right?"

"I'm not quite sure." Something occurred to me. "Why didn't I feel the electricity of the taser?"

"It's an arc thing, between the two barbs," Maya explained. "Don't worry about it."

Medical student, I thought.

"I knew the cops were right here," Maya said, as she put her hand to my cheek. "I wanted them to catch Jared in the act of trying to kill you. If I let my dad in on it, there would be confusion. This way there was no question about it."

"That's…that's actually smart. Still, I could have died. I was about to, you know? I started making amends and everything."

"Well, Chulo," she said, "you're not dead yet." She bent over and kissed my neck. "There. All better."

"I'll live to pimp out hoes another day," I said. She slapped me gently then threw her arms around me and kissed my dirt covered face. She made a big show of spitting out the dirt afterward. "Ha-ha," I said facetiously.

The back-up cops, firemen, and an ambulance arrived and they were huddled around, getting the scoop. Jared was being hauled off into the back of a cop car. He was being read his Miranda rights. "This ain't over!" he yelled in our general direction. "I'll have your neck for this!" For all his smarts, I thought that yelling a threat while being read his Miranda rights was a foolish move. *Anything you say can and will be used against you in a court of law.* Not the best time to be telling me that he'll have my neck, especially after already trying to choke me.

Lalo and Mrs. Calavera arrived by my side and knelt down. *"La cabeza es como el adobe, mijo!"* Mrs. Calavera said stroking my forehead.

"What did she say?" I asked Maya.

"She said you're a good fighter."

I doubted the translation but didn't press it. I took it as a compliment.

39 | Clean Up

A medic checked my vitals and cleared me. No big deal, just a bump on my head. Luckily, I had caught Jared's fist in such a way that it didn't cause too much harm. They cleaned me up a bit and gave me an ice pack. We talked with a cop after the dust cleared. He said the big man was taken to the hospital. Apparently, he had gone back to save Rocky but, while driving away, the propane tank exploded and blew up most of Jared's house with it. Some shrapnel from the explosion struck the big man, severely lacerating his left arm, right above the farmer's tan line. Maya had tended to it the best she could, bandaging it with Rocky's shirt, which kept him from bleeding to death.

Rocky sustained a few broken ribs and some minor scrapes and bruises. The big hurt to him was the legal stuff. He told the cops that he was turning himself in and they drove him away. The cops did say that the safe was at the location just as Rocky said it would be. It was pretty much the only thing left intact of Jared's house. Everything was either blown to bits or burnt. The cops said that, now that they had probable cause, they could find a way to open the safe and search its contents. Lalo told them about the contract and they said they would get back to him on that.

The police took a statement from each of us then released us. They said they would take care of the big man's truck. Lalo brought some gas and they got Maya's car up and running. I rode with her back into town.

"Well, that sucked," I said as we edged back onto the road, "But I guess it's good too. Jared's out of the picture and everything."

"Yes and yes." Maya drove conservatively and I could see gears turning in her head.

"What are you thinking about?"

"The future. Still. What this means for us, for our business."

"Wouldn't it mean that everything is OK?"

"Stuff like this gets around," she said. "If Rocky was right about the underage girls—and there's no reason to not believe him—that might reflect bad on us. I mean, we hired a guy who was into that. Two guys. Obviously those girls are daughters of people in the community. What does that say about us?"

"But you didn't know."

"Yeah. But people are weird, you know? Especially parents. And there's also the drug dealing too. That was done at the restaurant." Maya sighed. "Do you think we'd get in trouble for that?"

"You didn't know about that either," I said. "But it's not like you didn't do anything about it. And neither Jared nor Rocky are going to be working there. Or anywhere else anytime soon for that matter."

"I guess you're right."

Maya turned on the radio and just left it on whatever station it was on. A pop tune played. I didn't recognize it. Not that it mattered. We drove in relative silence all the way back to Maya's place.

When we arrived at Maya's I was surprised to find out that it was already past four in the afternoon. Everything seemed to go so quickly.

I went into the casita and ran a bubble bath. Why not? I needed to relax. I also poured myself a glass of wine from what we had left over. Why not that too? My head hurt but only in front, not like a headache. I had developed a bruise on my forehead but it wasn't horrible, only swollen a bit. Jared didn't catch me with a knuckle, more like the flat of his fist so the impact was spread over a larger area. My neck hurt but, in comparison to being dead, it felt alright.

I lay in that bathtub for a long time. I had the wine bottle near so I poured myself another glass and even refilled the tub with more hot water and bubbles when it cooled. A knock came from the front door and the door opened. "Perk," Maya called out as she made her way inside.

"I'm taking a bubble bath," I answered. "And trying to get drunk."

"Oh," she replied. "Can I come in?"

I looked down, the whole tub was filled with thick mountains of bubbles. Nothing exposed. "Sure," I said.

She came in with a cup of her own, one from the other night. She poured herself a glass of wine, lowered the lid on the toilet and sat down. "My mom started a fire in our fireplace and we burned the pictures."

"Sounds like a good place for them."

"It was embarrassing but cleansing."

I just nodded. "And how is your dad?"

"He's OK. He's not mad at me now. He said he understands that I'm my own person and will make my own choices. And he said that I shouldn't do drugs. Which I shouldn't. Probably a no-brainer for someone wanting to become a doctor."

"He's a good dad."

"He is." She sipped her wine. "That bath looks inviting. I'd hop in with you but I know you won't let me."

"No, I won't."

She scooped up a handful of suds and blew them in my direction. They landed on my face. She giggled. "You're cute, you know that?"

"I do. You've been saying that since day one."

"I have, haven't I?" She smiled and stood up, sipping her wine. "We're going to have something of a party tonight. Since we're all home at the same time for once and this whole ghost-slash-Jared-slash-Rocky thing is over, and..." she paused. "And it's your last night and all. We just wanted to celebrate. When you're done with your manly-man bubble bath, come over and we'll get started. Mamita's cooking. Chile rellenos. Your favorite." She leaned over and kissed me on the cheek. "Thank you," she said in my ear.

I didn't say anything. She left and I just lay there, steeped in bathwater. Thank me? I thought about everything that I had been through the last week. And how she and I spent so much time together. Part of me wanted to thank *her* for the adventure. Granted, I almost got killed, but it was still worth it.

We had a great time together that evening. We each shared our individual experiences. Maya and I told her parents more about what we saw and did. I went into detail about how I figured out some stuff and who I talked to, where I went. By the end of it, we were imbued in optimism, and the bad stuff seemed but a memory. Even Piquito seemed to share in the joy. It was as if a demon had been exorcised, which, in a way, it had been. Lalo was bright and upbeat. He talked about getting back in the game and what they should do about business. He mentioned hiring cooks again and advertising and even utilizing some of Jared's ideas. Best of all, he talked about how Maya should go to school. This brought Maya to tears, which brought Mrs. Calavera to tears, which brought Lalo to tears and, even though I was not really part of the equation, watching them cry made my eyes water too. Weird how that happens.

Maya and I didn't spend any time alone that night except for a brief moment saying goodnight. I gave her a kiss and held her for a long time. I told her that I needed to get an early start in the morning. She said, "I know." We didn't say anything more. Then she went to her house and I went to the casita and fell soundly asleep.

40 | Sunday

I woke with a start. The bus! I had completely forgotten that it was at the restaurant. I hoped it was alright. Last thing I needed was for it to sustain any more damage. Or, worse yet, get stolen. I got up and took a shower and hastily gathered all my stuff together. But I couldn't find my keys. Great. Did I lose those in the scuffle? I couldn't remember. So much for my early start.

I made my way to Maya's house for one final breakfast with the Calaveras. The aroma of Mexican food hovered in the air and intensified as I drew closer to the source. It had a calming effect. I walked in and everyone was already sitting at the table. Lalo got up and poured me a cup of coffee and set it down at an empty spot. Mrs. Calavera gave me a fresh hot tortilla. I was going to miss this.

"I have to go pick up the bus," I said to Maya. "I left it at the restaurant. But I can't find my keys."

Lalo dug into his pocket and pulled out my keys and placed them on the table near me. "No you don't," he said. Then he gestured with his chin to the front door. "Go look."

I picked up the keys and went to go see what he was talking about. Outside, in front of his house, was Chuck's VW bus. The family followed me outside.

"You picked it up for me? Thanks."

"No," Lalo said, "go look." He pointed to the bus. I walked over to it and found that the "EL MISMO" tag was no longer there.

"Whoa!" I exclaimed. "When did *that* happen?"

"I have a friend who does this type of work. He owed me a favor. I called him yesterday, after we got back. Told him you were leaving and he got on top of it. Good man."

"Wow! Thanks!"

Lalo came up and put his arm around me. "You're a good man too, Perk," he said.

No one had ever really called me a man before. It felt nice. And to be called a *good* man felt even better.

I packed everything up into the Microbus and said my good-byes. I saved Maya for last. Her parents gave us some alone time. Mrs. Calavera even picked up Piquito and took him inside with her.

I hugged Maya tightly. "This whole thing has been crazy and wonderful and scary and awesome," I said.

"Mm-hm," was her response.

"It feels like some insane dream."

"Mm-hm." She clung to me tightly.

I pulled back and lifted her chin. She was crying.

"Don't cry," I said. "Things are going to be alright with you."

"I know that. I'm crying because I'm going to miss you."

"I'm going to miss you too."

"I told you that you were brought here to help us," she said. "And I believe that. I know I'll go my way and you'll go yours. But for this time, this past week, you had to be here with us. Maybe God brought you here."

"I thought you didn't believe in God," I said.

"Well, I believe *something* brought you here. And whoever or whatever it was, I'm thankful. I don't think you realize how much of an impact you've had on us. On the whole business. Everything."

I didn't say anything, just looked at her. She was so beautiful. For a fleeting moment I thought that I should just stay. I could stay and we could get married and have babies and live happily ever after. But that was just a delusion. I wasn't going to stay and she wasn't going to stay either; she was going to go to medical school and become a doctor.

She wiped her eyes and took a deep breath. "Albuquerque's not that far from where you live," she said.

"Five hours. About."

"Maybe you can come visit."

"Yeah. That would be nice."

Maya kissed me on the lips. Her arms were wrapped around my middle and she squeezed me. "Thanks for dancing with me," she said softly.

"It was one crazy waltz." I kissed her and whispered "Good-bye." She released me and I got into the bus and headed out of town.

41 | Souvenir

When I got back, I wanted to tell everyone about what happened, but I thought twice about it. All I said was that I had an adventure. The story was too crazy, and I didn't think people would believe me. And, if they did, I didn't want to have to repeat it over and over again for anyone who wanted to hear it. Mostly I wanted it to be something that I had all to myself. Myself and Maya and her family. It was our adventure, not anyone else's.

I realized, after I was on the road, that I never got Maya's phone number. I guess that's one of those things that we just assume—that, if we're spending so much time with someone, we automatically have their phone number. But I never even used my phone to call her so I never had it.

I was back home for a good two weeks before calling Calavera's. She answered and I told her I made it back safe. I asked her what had happened with Jared and Rocky. She said that they both pleaded guilty during the initial hearing. Rocky had done so because of his guilt. She said Jared did because he made a plea bargain to give up some names of people whom he did business with. They were going to give him a shorter sentence because of it. She said the lawyers asked them if her family would go along with it. They agreed as long as he was to never set foot within a hundred miles of Calavera's or anywhere where either she or her family lived. After his prison sentence, that is. And, from what I understood, he was going to be in there for quite some time, even with a reduced sentence.

I asked about this mysterious Zoey girl. Maya said that part of Jared's story checked out, in a way. He did commit her to a mental institution but only after an overdose. The specifics of the overdose were cloudy and it's suspected that Jared played a part in that as well.

She also said that it was a good thing I called because Jared's lawyer was going to get a hold of me about the plea, that I needed to agree with it as well since I was a part of all this too. After all, one of Jared's charges was against me, for assault and attempted murder. I gave her my information to pass along to the lawyer and told her I would be awaiting his call. I also said I'd add something about him staying far away from me too.

We didn't talk long after that. It was clear that we weren't going to do a long distance thing so there was no reason to draw things out. I hung up and felt like we had reached some sad yet happy end to it all.

Chuck got his bus. I didn't tell him about the vandalism and fixing it. Why? It didn't matter. It wasn't wrecked, only painted. Mr. Argyle got his commercial and was happy as a clam. It was the best deal I had ever made. And the people in the video seemed to enjoy it as well. Not bad for a week's work.

Since returning home, I have wondered if the whole thing was the Law of Attraction at work. I said I wanted a vacation but, instead, I got an absurdly odd adventure that exhausted me. But maybe that is a vacation, just a different type of vacation.

I will say this though: I'll be more specific about what I put out there to the universe to deliver. Next time I say I need a vacation, I'm going to make sure that it doesn't involve crazed drug dealers or ghosts. That said, I'm more than OK if it includes a hot, fiery girl. Latina or otherwise.

Outside of the memories, I did bring back one souvenir: the scorpion in the glass. I keep it on my bookshelf. Every time I look at it, I am reminded of Maya and her family and Calavera's and Old Mesilla. And, of course, the cursed and blessed skull of El Mismo.

The End

The End

If you enjoyed this book,
please give it a **review.**

Check out *"The Story of the Story"* on my website.
It's a fun behind-the-scenes look at
"The Sugar Skull Ghost Thief."

Go to:

jason-salas.com/ghoststory

And enter the password: **elmismo**
Shh… I don't share this sort of stuff with just anyone. :)

Sign up for my email and get an **ebook**
copy of my short story *"Party of Two"*
as well as the **audiobook** version read by **me!**

Go to:

http://jason-salas.com/email/

Enter your email. It's that easy!

Acknowledgments

This book is my first novel (hopefully of many) and, as such, is the longest of any of my previous writings. Along the way, I encountered two things: 1) unforeseen obstacles (which should be expected), and 2) amazing support. Sometimes the support came in relation to the obstacles, other times the support was just there because people cared about me. In any case, I'm blessed.

First, I must thank my Mom, Glenda Ogas, and Dad, Al Salas. They each helped me in their own way. My Mom was my first beta reader—reading small sections at a time as I finished them. She is a gentle and fun soul who appreciates the value of a good yarn. She saw the extreme rough drafts and encouraged me along the way, pointing out where I may have stumbled while cheering me on the whole way.

My Dad helped out in a completely different way. Basically he gave me sturdy support by allowing me to be me. My Dad is a hulking figure who can pretty much do anything he wants to. He's smart and handy, efficient when it comes to anything that is mechanical. He can mentally pull things apart and assemble them back together. His support was in helping me see the direction I needed to go.

I would be remiss if I didn't acknowledge the folks who helped me out on Patreon as I was making a go with my comic strip *Perk at Work*. While that strip is on indefinite hiatus, the characters live on in my writings. Those kind and generous folks—the Patreon Patrons—helped me understand that people do believe in me, more than I could have ever imagined.

I give credit to my editor Ron Donaghe. He and I write very different material yet we agree on what writing should do and how it should sound. Ron guided me through the process and pointed out where I slipped up. I underestimated the value of hiring a professional editor. Ron was worth every penny I spent on his services. A bit more about Ron's influence on Old Mesilla is in *The Story of the Story* (found online).

My beta readers need to be acknowledged as well. My aunt Alma Singleton and I are kindred spirits; both writers, both lovers of culture and fun. Auntie Alma, as I call her, helped me with the cultural nuances of the characters and their interactions as well as contributing seemingly subtle yet glorious suggestions. My good friend Trevor Hodgkins gave me some stern yet welcome feedback which I chewed on for many hours before hitting the next draft. Trevor is an insanely funny guy and talented writer and performer. I had no choice but to take his critiques seriously. He was honest and I appreciated that and needed it. He is also a supporter of my work and, at times, a partner in crime. Maria Del Villar is a constant supporter who also gave me amazing support and insight into the story. My sister Carrie Cecava gave me perspective as I was moving along. She helped me understand my characters from a woman's point of view. All my beta readers are invaluable and I appreciate each and every one of them.

There was one person whom I must acknowledge in helping me bridge an unforeseen gap. Antonio Bustamante is a good friend and brother in Christ. I was stuck trying to write about a pecan farm without any experience. On a whim, I went over to his home. He and his family have always welcomed me regardless of time or circumstance. Antonio, a former pecan farmer, was kind enough to sit and answer my questions about how a pecan farm is tended to. In addition, he added some incredible insight. The details regarding pecan farming that Lalo shares with Perk were, in real life, details Antonio shared with me. My prior research paled in comparison with the first-hand accounts in Antonio's experience. The pecan farm may seem like a matter-of-fact secondary element of the story, a mere setting, yet it holds significance in regards to time, finances, and lifestyle as well as providing a platform for Perk's growth, not to mention his romantic endeavors.

In an ironic twist, the last (but certainly not least) acknowledgement is in regards to the first thing people see when encountering this book: its cover. The cover was beautifully designed and illustrated by my longtime good friend J. Lopez. I have always loved his work. I asked him if he would be interested in designing the cover, just threw the idea out there knowing that he was busy but hoping he might give it some consideration. He came back at me with the bones (no pun intended) of the cover design, replete with illustration and color. We worked out the textual elements and *voila!* A cover was born. More on the cover in *The Story of the Story.*

More *"Perk at Work"* books by Jason Salas
Available at jason-salas.com/books

Open for Business
The first volume of
"Perk at Work" comics.

Another Day, Another Dollar
The second volume of
"Perk at Work" comics.

Back To Work
The third volume of
"Perk at Work" comics.

Coffee Break Stories
Four short stories featuring
the characters from
"Perk at Work."

www.ingramcontent.com/pod-product-compliance
Lightning Source LLC
Chambersburg PA
CBHW020226260626
47156CB00002B/559